Anthony Gilbert and The Murder Room

>>> This title is part of The Murder Room, our series dedicated to making available out-of-print or hard-to-find titles by classic crime writers.

Crime fiction has always held up a mirror to society. The Victorians were fascinated by sensational murder and the emerging science of detection; now we are obsessed with the forensic detail of violent death. And no other genre has so captivated and enthralled readers.

Vast troves of classic crime writing have for a long time been unavailable to all but the most dedicated frequenters of second-hand bookshops. The advent of digital publishing means that we are now able to bring you the backlists of a huge range of titles by classic and contemporary crime writers, some of which have been out of print for decades.

From the genteel amateur private eyes of the Golden Age and the femmes fatales of pulp fiction, to the morally ambiguous hard-boiled detectives of mid twentieth-century America and their descendants who walk our twenty-first century streets, The Murder Room has it all. >>>

The Murder Room
Where Criminal Minds Meet

themurderroom.com

Anthony Gilbert (1899–1973)

Anthony Gilbert was the pen name of Lucy Beatrice Malleson. Born in London, she spent all her life there, and her affection for the city is clear from the strong sense of character and place in evidence in her work. She published 69 crime novels, 51 of which featured her best known character, Arthur Crook, a vulgar London lawyer totally (and deliberately) unlike the aristocratic detectives, such as Lord Peter Wimsey, who dominated the mystery field at the time. She also wrote more than 25 radio plays, which were broadcast in Great Britain and overseas. Her thriller *The Woman in Red* (1941) was broadcast in the United States by CBS and made into a film in 1945 under the title *My Name is Julia Ross*. She was an early member of the British Detection Club, which, along with Dorothy L. Sayers, she prevented from disintegrating during World War II. Malleson published her autobiography, *Three-a-Penny*, in 1940, and wrote numerous short stories, which were published in several anthologies and in such periodicals as *Ellery Queen's Mystery Magazine* and *The Saint*. The short story 'You Can't Hang Twice' received a Queens award in 1946. She never married, and evidence of her feminism is elegantly expressed in much of her work.

By Anthony Gilbert

Scott Egerton series
Tragedy at Freyne (1927)
The Murder of Mrs
   Davenport (1928)
Death at Four Corners (1929)
The Mystery of the Open
   Window (1929)
The Night of the Fog (1930)
The Body on the Beam (1932)
The Long Shadow (1932)
The Musical Comedy
   Crime (1933)
An Old Lady Dies (1934)
The Man Who Was Too
   Clever (1935)

Mr Crook Murder
   Mystery series
Murder by Experts (1936)
The Man Who Wasn't
   There (1937)
Murder Has No Tongue (1937)
Treason in My Breast (1938)
The Bell of Death (1939)
Dear Dead Woman (1940)
   aka *Death Takes a Redhead*
The Vanishing Corpse (1941)
   aka *She Vanished in the Dawn*
The Woman in Red (1941)
   aka *The Mystery of the
   Woman in Red*

Death in the Blackout (1942)
   aka *The Case of the Tea-
   Cosy's Aunt*
Something Nasty in the
   Woodshed (1942)
   aka *Mystery in the Woodshed*
The Mouse Who Wouldn't
   Play Ball (1943)
   aka *30 Days to Live*
He Came by Night (1944)
   aka *Death at the Door*
The Scarlet Button (1944)
   aka *Murder Is Cheap*
A Spy for Mr Crook (1944)
The Black Stage (1945)
   aka *Murder Cheats the Bride*
Don't Open the Door (1945)
   aka *Death Lifts the Latch*
Lift Up the Lid (1945)
   aka *The Innocent Bottle*
The Spinster's Secret (1946)
   aka *By Hook or by Crook*
Death in the Wrong Room
   (1947)
Die in the Dark (1947)
   aka *The Missing Widow*
Death Knocks Three Times
   (1949)
Murder Comes Home (1950)
A Nice Cup of Tea (1950)
   aka *The Wrong Body*

Lady-Killer (1951)

Miss Pinnegar Disappears (1952)
  aka *A Case for Mr Crook*

Footsteps Behind Me (1953)
  aka *Black Death*

Snake in the Grass (1954)
  aka *Death Won't Wait*

Is She Dead Too? (1955)
  aka *A Question of Murder*

And Death Came Too (1956)

Riddle of a Lady (1956)

Give Death a Name (1957)

Death Against the Clock (1958)

Death Takes a Wife (1959)
  aka *Death Casts a Long Shadow*

Third Crime Lucky (1959)
  aka *Prelude to Murder*

Out for the Kill (1960)

She Shall Die (1961)
  aka *After the Verdict*

Uncertain Death (1961)

No Dust in the Attic (1962)

Ring for a Noose (1963)

The Fingerprint (1964)

The Voice (1964)
  aka *Knock, Knock! Who's There?*

Passenger to Nowhere (1965)

The Looking Glass Murder (1966)

The Visitor (1967)

Night Encounter (1968)
  aka *Murder Anonymous*

Missing from Her Home (1969)

Death Wears a Mask (1970)
  aka *Mr Crook Lifts the Mask*

Murder is a Waiting Game (1972)

Tenant for the Tomb (1971)

A Nice Little Killing (1974)

Standalone Novels

The Case Against Andrew Fane (1931)

Death in Fancy Dress (1933)

The Man in the Button Boots (1934)

Courtier to Death (1936)
  aka *The Dover Train Mystery*

The Clock in the Hatbox (1939)

Snake in the Grass

Anthony Gilbert

An Orion book

Copyright © Lucy Beatrice Malleson 1954

The right of Lucy Beatrice Malleson to be identified as the author of this work has been asserted in accordance with the Copyright, Designs and Patents Act 1988.

This edition published by
The Orion Publishing Group Ltd
Orion House
5 Upper St Martin's Lane
London WC2H 9EA

An Hachette UK company
A CIP catalogue record for this book is available from the British Library

ISBN 978 1 4719 1002 9

www.orionbooks.co.uk

To
Eileen
who shares my admiration for
the indomitable spinster

CHAPTER ONE

1

It was the first day of spring, not only by the calendar hanging on Con Gardiner's wall, but also by Nature's calendar which was usually less reliable. Everywhere twigs and boughs were tipped with green, the scillas in a neighbour's window-box showed bravely blue and there was scarcely a window that didn't show a plant in a pot, a daffodil or hyacinth. As Con came out of his flat and turned towards the Live and Let Live where he dined six nights out of seven he saw there were gulls sitting along the chimney-stacks, reminding him of the storks he had seen in Austria—oh years and years ago in a different world. The world to-night seemed to be touched with a kind of magic; even the old woman from the house opposite who was walking the animal known as Dog, seemed to realise some change in the air, and Con for the first time understood that once she had been a young girl, and the dog, who walked as if on four grey pokers, had once gambolled and chased a ball and crept out at night on his own secret business.

A promise of coming rain made the air deliciously soft, and he could smell spring in the burgeoning plane trees all along the pavement. Burgeoning, he repeated to himself—a rich extravagant word indicative of a reckless hope. On such an evening it seemed as though for him, too, life must suddenly fling open the doors and invite him in. He was only thirty and it was absurd to imagine that everything of importance that was to happen to him had happened already, that the rest of existence would be like sitting in a cinema, watching the same film go round and round, gradually getting fainter until presently the lights would go out and the show would be over for good.

At the Live and Let Live they all knew him—Lucie, the girl behind the bar that was already filling up, Belotti the little dark manager, all the girls in the dining-room, Nora and May, the Irish sisters, Mrs. Waters, who had come down in life through an unfortunate marriage, Alice who looked consumptive and Shirley, who made eyes at all the men to give them pleasure, they all smiled at Con.

'Evening, Mr. Gardiner. Quite like spring, isn't it?'

Belotti came to pull out his chair and Nora whispered quickly, 'Pass up the duck, Mr. Gardiner. Mixed grill's the best thing on the menu to-night.'

He felt at home here, the only place really where he did feel at home. His flat—one large room with bath, service and breakfast provided—was no more than a perching-place. And the office where he spent all his days in dreary legal business, the sort that deals with property and wills, was no more than a way of earning his bread. His private life seemed to have stopped five years ago; he had stopped living as dwarfs stop growing.

He ordered soused herring and for the first time in years recalled the past without a sense of despair. It wasn't fair to Meriel to hold her responsible for what had happened to him; she'd been very young when they became engaged and he supposed the war and his own unforgettable experiences in it had changed him into a stranger. And yet—it was his belief in her and their love that had kept him sane during those three years in a prison camp, the humiliation, the anguish and the fear. He saw now how absurd it had been to try and make her understand. It had been useless, of course.

'Con darling,' she'd said, looking as shining and untouched as a girl on a Christmas card, 'the thing for you to do is to try and put all that out of your mind. Don't brood on it. I quite see it was dreadful, but it's over.'

He couldn't make her see it wasn't so simple as that. Things don't happen once in time, and that's the end of them. What has happened once goes on happening for ever, the past's as real as the present; look back and the road hasn't rolled up behind you, the prison camp was still there, his fear and pain; and his stark disbelief when Meriel told him she couldn't marry him, after all.

'We've both changed, Con. We aren't the people we were four years ago. Life's progress, not standing still, and certainly not walking backwards.'

The following year she'd married Bertram Forster, done very well for herself people said. And since then Con had fought shy of girls, couldn't believe the next one wouldn't be the same as Meriel.

The soused herring came and was as good as Nora had promised and after the mixed grill he had blue cheese, and Belotti came and talked to him for a few minutes. The room was nearly full now; he recognised some of the regulars, waved or nodded to them. They were a solid crowd, business men with their secretaries, elderly residents whose wives couldn't cope with dinner six nights a week, a few women dining in pairs, one or two singles like himself. A few looked as though they'd taken root there and the Day of Judgment would find them plying a vigorous knife and fork and discussing business deals as if the Kingdom of Heaven depended on it. As he made his way out through the bar his heart suddenly burnt in his breast, because there, among the sedate couples, the chaps with their heads together, the young fellows setting the world in order as he'd done a dozen years ago, he beheld the miracle that happened every now and again, the miracle that was as sudden as the spring to revive hope even in his shrivelled heart, two youngsters—nineteen? twenty?—the girl with her hair tied up in a horse-tail, the boy dark and glowing, sitting at a small table, hands touching, drinks forgotten, dumb, entranced—love unblemished and without fear. He felt something rend in his heart. Surely it couldn't all be over for him, the singing and the gold. He pushed the door open violently and emerged into the cool, exquisite air.

An old man was standing by the door offering mimosa. 'Take some back to the wife,' he suggested. 'Only two bob.'

Con hadn't a wife, but he bought it just the same; as a young man, no older than that boy in the bar, he'd hitch-hiked through countries where mimosa was as common as laburnum, say, in Earl's Court. Memory came flooding back. Is this all? he was crying as, carrying the mimosa with a scrap of tissue paper round the grey-green leaves and the scent almost lifting him off his feet, he turned towards his flat. He'd forgotten his original intention to defeat loneliness at the cinema—it was Lana Turner to-night. Some tide was rising in him that had lain sluggish for years.

It was the sort of night, he thought, excitement flooding his whole being, when you waited for things to happen.

What things?

Your guess was as good as his.

2

The girl was standing under the second lamp-post, and she moved forward as he approached. He saw with a sense of surprise that she was going to speak to him. Surely she didn't imagine—it wasn't that sort of a neighbourhood. She must be very new to the job to suppose she'd even make a living in these streets. A moment later he realised she was as new to this sort of thing as he to hope. All the pros. had a certain walk, you couldn't mistake it, it seemed to come naturally to them, an invitation—a word came into his mind—seductive—though they'd never seduced him. And then think of the trouble they took over their appearance, though you might yourself find it depressing to a degree, all that eye-shadow and lipstick and artificial lashes; still, it showed they took their profession seriously. This girl wore a carelessly belted green mackintosh with a scarf over her hair, and looked as if she'd hardly stopped to powder her nose. And she moved like someone accustomed to walking in sensible shoes, not a stranger to daylight as those others were. The light from the lamp fell on her resolute face and he saw that she was quite young, twenty-two perhaps, but there was a hint of desperation there, and he felt his heart quiver. Already, without a word spoken, he was aware

5

of a link, two people in desperate straits but not defeated—that was it, not defeated.

She moved with a boyish slouch that contrived somehow to be graceful, had an olive skin and grey eyes with long silky black lashes, and she hadn't plucked her eyebrows.

Her voice gave him a fresh sense of surprise—of pleasure, too. It was a deep husky drawl, no whine, no harsh confidence, nothing arrogant or cajoling; and she didn't waste her words.

'I say,' she said, planting herself in front of him. 'Will you lend me a pound?'

The request was so startling that he gasped out, 'Why on earth should I?' before he could stop himself.

'Because I need it, of course. Do you suppose I'm doing this for fun?' There was a note of scorn in the attractive voice. 'A woman I asked told me my best bet was to hang about near the Live and Let Live and catch some man alone who'd just dined. She said they were always more generous then.'

'Why a pound?' he asked curiously. What on earth could you do with a pound these days? He was pretty sure she wasn't asking simply because she wanted something to eat. She looked harassed but not starving.

'If I have a pound I know where I can get a bed for the night,' she told him eagerly. 'It may be the first day of spring, but it's still jolly cold for sleeping out.'

'But why should you? I mean, haven't you got a home.' How mean he sounded, and yet all he wanted was to keep her there; once she moved off he'd be immured again in the prison of his loneliness. He remembered the young couple in the bar, and his heart was racing.

'Not any more. Oh, come on, I don't suppose a pound means a lot to you. It's not that I'm really a beggar, but I left all my money in the flat—and I can't go back.'

She had a red leather bag slung from her shoulder, and she opened it, frank as a child, to show him an empty wallet.

'I was in such a hurry I forgot. But it doesn't matter really, if only I can tide myself over till to-morrow.'

'What happens to-morrow?'

'Oh, I can get a job.'

'You sound very sure.'

'Anybody can get work who really wants it,' she told him, triumphant in her confident youth. 'And I'm not particular what I do. I mean, I can cook after a fashion, well no, perhaps that wouldn't be a very good idea, but I could look after children, or wheel out some old body who's no more than ninepence in the shilling. There's not much competition for that sort of thing.'

'But you'd need a reference,' he pointed out, forgetting his own troubles in the warmth of her companionship.

'Should I? Well, I suppose I could write myself one.'

'That wouldn't be legal.'

'Why not? I shouldn't be getting the job in my own name, of course, so if I recommended myself as having been employed by Mrs. Graves no one would be any the wiser. Anyway, I daresay lots of people don't fuss, they're too keen to get anyone.'

He had begun to walk slowly up Redman Street,

his hand on her elbow. He couldn't remember when he touched her, but somehow it seemed natural enough, and she didn't appear to think it odd, either.

'Where is—was—your home?'

'What a lot of questions you ask. Morris House, Morris Street, though I don't see what it is to do with you. I'm free, white and twenty-one, and have a perfect right to leave home if I want to.'

It seemed to him a remarkably inefficient flight, no money and apparently no luggage. The situation was as fishy as the soused herring.

'Haven't you got a husband?' he asked abruptly.

'That's just my trouble.'

'Oh! Well, as you've just reminded me, you're a free agent, but—I'm older than you—and young married women living apart don't have a very easy time.'

'Young married women living with their husbands have hell.'

He couldn't find anything to say to that and began to feel for his wallet. When she saw this the girl said, and for the first time there was a note of strain in her voice, 'I did make it clear, I hope, that this is only a loan. I mean, there's no question of payment for value received. I shall send it back the first minute I can.'

'Look here,' said Con, surrendering completely to the situation, 'a pound won't see you far. Why don't you let me make it a fiver?'

'Because, as I told you just now, I intend to pay it back, and it's five times as difficult to repay five pounds as one. Anyway, I don't need more than one. I know of a place in Knowles Square, on the corner, where I can get a room for fourteen-and-six, with breakfast. That'll tide me over till the morning and in the morning I shall look for a job.'

'You sound very sure, but you mightn't get one right away . . .'

'You sound as prissy as a maiden aunt,' she retorted, frankly. 'In fact, far more prissy than my aunt ever was. And don't suggest I might go to her, because I couldn't, short of committing suicide, and not even to please Toby do I intend to do that.'

'I take it Toby is your husband?'

'Let me try and guess your name,' she gibed gently. 'Sherlock Holmes?'

He felt himself colour, and anger stirred in him. 'Why I should worry about you I can't imagine,' he began, and she exclaimed, in surprise, 'Why, you're not, are you?'

'Yes, I am. Absurd, isn't it? You so obviously can look after yourself. All the same—you're certain this place in Knowles Square is all right?'

Her hand slipped through his arm.

'Sorry I laughed at you. Goodness knows I haven't much to laugh about. Yes, it's all right. I used to stay there with Aunt Laura before I married. Mrs. Ryrie will remember Aunt Laura even if she doesn't remember me. For her sake, she'd probably have given me a bed for nothing, but I couldn't ask her, really, I couldn't. I know I've come down in the world a lot since I married Toby, but even so I draw the line somewhere. It's her bread-and-butter and I don't suppose things are any easier for her these days than for anyone else. I asked you for the pound,' she added innocently, 'because I thought you didn't have a married look. Are you married?'

He shook his head. 'No.'

'I thought not. You can generally tell. I didn't

want to make trouble for you, and wives . . .' She paused. 'Not that life's all sack and sugar for wives. I should know. As a matter of fact, I did think of a station waiting-room, but they lock them up about midnight, I believe, and I don't want to be picked up by the police for loitering with intent, whatever that may mean. I know they say people with clear consciences aren't afraid of the police, but all I can suppose is there can't be many clear consciences in the country.'

He took out three or four pound notes and tried to push them into her hand.

'I told you,' she began to sound angry, 'I only want one. By the way, what's your name? Is it all right if I post the money back?'

He told her—Con Gardiner—'I live here,' he added, as they reached the bombed site on the corner of Devon Street.

'What—in a tree?'

'Of course not. No. 16. That's my flat on the first floor. Mrs. Fairfax is always reminding me it's the best flat in the house.'

She laughed. 'You sound like someone in charge of an Ideal Homes stall. Personally I can't see it matters much where you live, only who you live with.'

'I live alone.'

'Then I hope you like yourself. Anyway, it has its points.'

He made a last desperate effort. 'If you change your mind in the morning—things look so different in the morning—don't be too proud to—to go back,' he urged her.

She stared. 'Who are you really? The Moral Welfare Officer or P.C. 49 in plain clothes? Listen. I married a heel. I don't blame myself for that. I was nineteen at the time and I thought he was wonderful. About five hundred other girls also thought he was wonderful. Where I was different from the others was that I stood out for marriage. Toby roared when I suggested it. "What's *wrong* with marriage?" he repeated. "Try it and see." That ought to have warned me, but it didn't. The Archangel Gabriel couldn't have persuaded me Toby was no good. I was over the moon with love. Aunt Laura had died a few months earlier, I was independent.'

'Wasn't there anyone else to pull the wool from over your eyes?'

'I wouldn't have thanked them,' she said, simply. 'You don't know Toby. He's the world's charmer. Even you, who are so buttoned-up and—and precise, would find him irresistible at first. He only has to go into a room for everyone to want to do something for him—lend him a house or act as banker or have him as a permanent unpaying guest. And the answer's simple—charm. Lots of people have it, but in Toby's case it's a profession. It keeps working hours; when there's nothing to be gained by it he switches it off, as you switch off a light when you leave a room. And then there's nothing but darkness. It's like that with him. When the light's out—and for me it went out a long time ago—there's only darkness there.'

'But'—he hesitated—'I mean, I don't want to seem curious, but what happened to-night, particularly, to screw you up to this?'

'If it hadn't been to-night it would have been next week or next month. Anyway, it's not the first time I've left him, though I promise you it'll be the last. I'll never go back to that flat—never, never. The other time I was stupid enough to let him know where I was working and he came round and made the most artistic scene, swore I was his one hope, played up his war experiences—no, don't ask me what they were because I long ago gave up believing a word he says—and old Lady Thingmajigg was horrified—not at Toby but at me.' Suddenly her young warm voice changed, became brittle and thin. 'It passes my comprehension how you could abandon a man who has been through the furnace. We must all be prepared to pay our share of the tragedy of war, those of us who were fortunate enough only to see it from afar . . . !' She broke off, her voice changing again. 'She saw it from a place on the West Coast where they never even heard a bomb. Anyway, that was the end of that job. Back I went with Toby like a lamb to the slaughter (though he'd tell you there's nothing particularly lamb-like about me); that was six months ago. Granted I made a fool of myself when I married, it doesn't seem fair I should have to pay for the rest of my life, does it? Since then I've had odd jobs that keep us going and I've a tiny income from Aunt Laura—you've forgotten your note-book, haven't you?'

'My note-book?'

'Oughtn't you to be taking all this down? Suppose you're asked questions later?'

'Who's likely to ask me?'

'Toby might.'

'Do you seriously imagine I'm likely . . .'

She half-stamped her foot in exasperation. 'You don't know Toby. If you did, you wouldn't waste time asking all these silly questions. As for why I left him to-night—he said, as if I were his slave or his pet dog or something, "Go round to the Hat and Feather at six-thirty and let Gerry know I shan't be coming along till a bit later. Remember, this may mean a lot to us and forget all about your Lady Clara Vere de Vere act. Be nice to him. Understand?" I understood all right, and if you knew Toby as I know Toby you'd understand too. I told him when I'd sunk that low I'd prefer to choose my own men, and what did he think I was? He began to tell me and I paid him back twenty shillings in the pound—I should think we could have been heard at Piccadilly Circus. It's wonderful what good memories people have when the occasion demands it. Then he said perhaps I wouldn't mind seeing him in gaol, and I said, short of a coffin, there was no place where I'd sooner see him. And then I came away in such a hurry I forgot my purse. Quite a sordid little story, isn't it?'

They were so close he could feel the shudder that ran through her; he was shaking, too, partly with fury at the unknown Toby but mainly with a sense of excitement because for the first time for five years he felt himself part of a pattern, though he had not the faintest notion then what that pattern would prove to be.

'Speaking as a lawyer,'—he began, but she clearly wasn't listening to his advice.

He pushed the pound note towards her and she took it with trembling fingers and folded it small and pushed it into her bag.

'Is that what you are? I should have guessed. All that good advice.' She laughed, a pretty good imitation of the real thing. 'Thank Heaven I met you when I did. Some of the others I met first seemed to think this was Bargain Night. All this lot twenty shillings. I even thought I might go back, but of course I can't, I can't.'

'You won't need to,' Con pointed out steadily.

13

'Remember, my original offer stands. If you want any other help—just a little friendly companionship, say, to remind yourself that all men aren't cut to Toby's pattern—well, you know where I live.'

'I may take you up on that,' she said unexpectedly, and his heart began banging about again in the most idiotic fashion.

'You haven't told me your name,' he remembered suddenly. 'At least, you said Mrs. Graves . . .'

'I was christened Charlotte. Aunt Laura always called me Caro.' She smiled. 'Sounds like a dog, doesn't it?'

'I'd like to call you Caro, if I may.'

'Oh!' She laughed outright then, a sound so deep and innocent, so joyous in spite of her wretched situation, that he felt his own heart lift again. He'd forgotten anyone could laugh like that. 'Then you think this is only a beginning.'

'I felt when I came out as though the whole evening were a beginning, and this time I'd like to see the play through.'

The gods, they say, sitting aloft, hear our most foolish boasts and aspirations, and sometimes they take us at our word. Sometimes, probably, they don't even hear. But this was Con's evening. They were listening and they took him at his word, chuckling maliciously, perhaps, thinking, Cocksure young fellow biting off more than he can hope to chew. Well, he's asked for it.

But as Con remained rooted to the spot, watching the girl move away, he felt a fresh uprush of tenderness; she moved so easily, and at such a good pace, whatever she had suffered that night; her step was purposeful.

'She won't accept the future if it's not to her

liking,' he reflected. 'She's not like me. She intends to mould hers herself.' The gods might have whispered, 'And how!'

His heart swelling as though a whole new vista had been revealed as a fog rolled back, he turned sharply. As he did so, the curtains of the ground floor at No. 16 fell softly together. He felt shaken with fury. Prying, speculating old eyes—was there no privacy anywhere? And hadn't he the right to lend a girl a pound? Common-sense said, 'Be your age. You'll never see that pound again.' But he gave common-sense the brush-off. This was the first day of spring, on the calendar, in Nature and now in his own heart.

3

Up in his own room he couldn't settle to anything. He put on the television, but it made no sense, just a lot of capering, gesticulating figures, as meaningless as marionettes; he sat staring at them, but all he could see was Caro, Caro walking away from him with her head high, Caro with no luggage, no future and no money except the pound he'd loaned her. Ah, but she had herself, and that was a fortune. How he envied her having herself. The wireless was no better; it was the mixture as before, the politicians bickering, cost of living rising, trouble in the Far East, uncertainty at home, and (of course) more rain on the way. He twirled the knob. A crooner mourned:

Maybe I'm wrong again,

Trusting in you.

Trusting? Was that what it was? Had he, after five years, begun trusting another human being, and that someone of whom he knew nothing at all really, a strange half-savage girl suddenly appearing as if from the pavement, asking for a pound to go to a house in Knowles Square? A house in Knowles Square. He knew the part well, went by the corner every day on his way to the Underground. It was a cul-de-sac with a block of flats on the other corner, and a typical London garden opposite. The first almond tree of his experience blossomed in Knowles Square every spring; he saw it, delicate and dauntless, raising its frail inimitable blossom to the grey skies of the last month of winter. And to-night she, Caro, would be in the house on the corner.

He started up, switching off the dismal singer, as a new thought struck him. She had said a Mrs. Ryrie had it. Well, she might have done once, but it belonged to a Dr. Goddard now. He saw the plate every day, registering the name in the idle manner one does. Dr. Goddard and Dr. Hugh Goddard. Brothers, he'd wondered? Father and son? At all events you could be sure of one thing, there'd be no asylum there for a young woman who was escaping from her husband and had nothing—not even a toothbrush—between herself and virtual destitution, except the pound he'd loaned her. He looked round, glad of the chance for action. She'd have discovered her mistake by now, be wondering what on earth she could do. Snatching up his hat, he hurried down the stairs.

There was a party on in Dr. Goddard's house. Lights blazed in all the windows and cars of every type from a lordly Jaguar to an Austin of such ancient vintage you wondered how it stayed on the road at all, running-board gone, signals missing, roof patched, were parked all round the Square. He hesitated. It seemed so obvious she wouldn't have called here.

She never meant to, jeered a voice in his brain. She bought you for a sucker. Try him for a pound, she decided, don't ask for more, he might get suspicious, call the police. Englishmen hate a fuss, hate to look fools. It's worth a pound to them to keep their ridiculous dignity. Now fever possessed him; he had to know, had to know—if there ever had been a Mrs. Ryrie here, he meant. He found himself on the doorstep, pressing the bell. A girl came running out, so pretty, so young—as young as Caro, but untouched, unscarred, as Meriel had been, as once, presumably, Caro had been.

She smiled. 'Come in.'

'I—I beg your pardon.'

'Hugh's somewhere about.'

'I'm afraid—there's some mistake. I thought—a Mrs. Ryrie used to live here.'

'Ryrie?' The pretty forehead wrinkled. 'I never heard the name. Are you sure this was the number?'

He muttered, 'The corner house,' but she shook her bright head.

'We've been here for two years. I don't know who had it before that.'

She smiled again, and then someone shouted 'Sally' and she called back, 'Coming,' and then, on an impulse, 'Well, come in and have a drink anyhow. Daddy might know. He'll be back presently.'

But he couldn't stay. Some incomprehensible

sense of urgency drove him onwards. He began some laboured explanation, but she wasn't listening. He came away, passion beating up in his blood like a rising wind.

There was one other way he could prove the truth of her story. We live in Morris House, she'd said, Morris Street. He knew Morris Street; it was the other side of the park. If he hadn't been so—dazzled—wouldn't it have occurred to him earlier that there was something a bit—odd—about her coming so far to look for help? But he could dispose of that one, at least. Naturally, she wouldn't want to beg in some place where she might be recognised. Besides, if she was honest and truly believed this Mrs. Ryrie still lived in Knowles Square . . . He forgot about looking a fool, forgot he'd had a long day and his leg ached if he walked too much on pavements; he clung like mad to the hope that her story *was* true. And it would be easy to prove; he'd only got to find out if there was a man called Graves living in Morris House. Hope still laboured in him like life in a new-born child, an agony and a desire.

Not many people were about; the sky was thick with stars against a black velvet background, as though some celestial jeweller had suddenly tossed out all his stock, letting it fall where it pleased, with no sense of order, the whole mass twinkling and glittering, taking your breath away with its beauty. In spite of his limp, he made a good pace, marching up Cornibeare Road, past the closed shops and the coffee-stall at the corner, past the Underground Station and the wine shop that seemed to stay open to all hours. Everyone Served, it said, and Whisky For All At Cut Prices, it offered. He was followed for some distance by a black and white cat stalking him as though he were some enormous bird it was confident of snaring, but presently he left her behind and there was nobody except the man at the all-night garage and the infrequent half-empty buses going up and down from the cinema to the river.

Morris Street was an off-shoot of a wide handsome terrace, and Morris House was a jerry-built structure with walls so thin you could hear the people in the next flat eating celery. A board in the hall said No. 8. Mr. T. Graves. So that part at all events was true. But—how far did that get him, in fact? He had a sudden nightmare vision of her and Toby chuckling and saying, 'Well, see how many mugs are out to-night.' He might be simply one of them. What, after all, did he know about her? She said Toby was a crook, but what proof was there that she wasn't as bad? Just his hunch and he hadn't made such a success of things that that was anything to go on.

These flats had an unsavoury reputation that matched their shoddy appearance, though in fact they hadn't been put up so very long ago; even the doorway looked furtive and Con thought the policeman on duty gave him an odd glance. There was no night porter and the front door was never locked, which was very convenient for tenants whose professions often took them out at unconventional hours. He found himself hurrying up the stairs, like the mechanical man that, once wound up, couldn't stop, not even when his feet carried him over the edge of the cliff. There was a light under the door of No. 8 and he rang the bell violently. If Toby opened the door, what was he going to say? He'd look a bit silly, wouldn't he? But then, who cared?

He could think of something, ask for a spurious Mrs. Chapman, pretend it was the wrong flat. But in point of fact he didn't have to do anything of the kind. Because it wasn't Toby who opened the door but a man in a blue uniform. However the row had ended it must have been serious, because the police had moved in.

4

The shock was so great that for a minute he stood, staring, incapable of speech. The police officer was the first to recover.

'Mr. Graves?' he suggested.

Con shook his head. 'No.' Then, in an uncontrollable burst of fear, he added, 'What's going on here? I mean, what are the police doing on the premises?'

'Just our job,' replied Detective-Sergeant Mason. 'Well, if you're not Mr. Graves, were you expecting to see him?'

'I was passing,' adlibbed Con, 'and I wondered if Mrs. Graves was in.'

The other man shook his head. 'I'm afraid not.'

The relief was so great that for an instant Con thought he'd fall down. Because when he first saw the policeman the preposterous thought flashed through his mind that in desperation Caro had returned and, finding things too much for her, had taken the easy way out. An instant later he was wondering how he could ever have thought of such a thing. She wasn't the sort that throws up the sponge, gives Life best. No, she'd fight back with teeth, nails, anything.

He thought the officer was eying him oddly.

'You know the household, sir, perhaps?'

'I've met Mrs. Graves. I don't know her husband at all.'

'Ah! That's a pity.' The fellow might have been made of granite for all the emotion he displayed.

'Why?' Con tried to emulate his companion's cool air.

'We could do with some help.' He drew the door wider open. 'Come in, sir.'

'I've told you, I can't . . .' But even while he protested he found himself walking over the threshold.

'Do you mean you've never actually met him?' the sergeant continued, closing the door.

'Never.'

'So, of course, you wouldn't know what he looks like.'

'Obviously not. What on earth's all this leading up to? Has the chap got himself murdered or something?'

The policeman seemed to freeze and swell at the same time.

'Why did you say that, sir?'

'You're being so infernally mysterious . . .'

'You said murder.'

'Yes. Well . . .' He tried to laugh it off, then was suddenly as rigid as his companion. 'Oh no,' he said speaking more to himself than to the man beside him. 'No, it can't be that.'

He looked about him vaguely. It was a horrible little flat, a narrow passage containing a telephone and a trumpery little table, a couple of rooms opening one left and one right—sitting-room and bedroom, he supposed—with doors beyond leading to the inevitable bathroom and kitchenette. The policeman was opening the bedroom door.

'This way, sir.'

'But . . .' Once again he was like the mechanical man; he followed where the sergeant led. The bedroom was very much what you might expect, a cheap pretentious set in pale wood, a low bed, contorted dressing-table with a great bare mirror in which he saw his own stricken face. He looked away and found he was staring at the bed. Someone was lying there, but it wasn't Caro, because the policeman had said Caro wasn't in the flat. So it had to be Toby, hadn't it? The officer went past him and turned down the sheet, and still feeling hypnotised Con moved nearer. So this, he thought, was Toby, the social pirate, the natural gangster, the man who could charm people as St. Francis had charmed wolves. Only there was something wrong with that simile. St. Francis had been a saint and tamed wild beasts. Toby had been a wild beast preying on people who, if not precisely saints, were presumably decent citizens who'd have been a lot better off if they'd never met him. Worst of all, he'd preyed on Caro. It didn't occur to him at this stage that all he knew about Toby was what Caro had told him.

He heard his own voice say, 'So that's Toby?' and the policeman jumped in with a sharp interjection.

'Toby?'

'Mr. Graves.'

'I thought you didn't know him.'

'I didn't. But his wife referred to him like that.'

'You know Mrs. Graves well?'

Did he? Two hours ago he hadn't even heard her

name; yet already it seemed incredible there had ever been a time when he hadn't known her.

'Have you seen her recently?' the officer pursued. 'By the way, I don't think you told me your name.'

'I don't think you asked,' returned Con, pleasantly. But he supplied it—and the address. No reason why he shouldn't, was there? The officer repeated his question.

'As a matter of fact, I saw her to-night.'

'Really, sir? Where was that?'

'In Redman Street. I was coming back from dinner . . .'

'The lady hadn't been dining with you?'

'No. I never . . .'

'Yes, sir? You never . . .'

'I was going to say that Mrs. Graves had never dined with me.'

'I see, sir. Did she happen to mention her husband?'

'She said she'd left him in the flat.'

'And—did she give any explanation of her presence on the other side of the Park at—what time would this be?'

'Oh, between eight-thirty and nine. I was in my flat in time to hear the nine o'clock news, and I suppose we may have talked for ten or fifteen minutes.'

'And—I think you said you weren't expecting to see her?'

'Of course I wasn't.'

'Just a chance meeting?'

'Just a chance meeting.'

'Did she happen to say why she was there or mention any plans?'

'She said she was going to see an old friend—well,

not a friend exactly, someone she and her aunt had known before she married.'

'A lady? Or—perhaps she didn't say.'

'She even told me her name, since you're so interested. A Mrs. Ryrie of Knowles Square.'

All the time he couldn't take his eyes off the dead man. Toby Graves, in life, had been handsome in a rather vulpine fashion, with a big hawklike nose, brown eyes, a bit protuberant, fine dark lashes and eyebrows, a pencil of moustache on the taut upper lip, high cheek-bones—a brigand's face, thought Con, wondering how it must have appeared when the flame of life burned behind the features that were now so meaningless. Nothing changed a man so completely as sudden death. Novelists might say, 'He looked as though he had fallen asleep'; and clergymen, wishing to comfort the bereaved, spoke of the perfect peace of death. It was all untrue—unless by peace you meant the utter negation of living. Why, the first thing that struck you about a dead face was a feeling that this was only a mask, something that had never been alive. Like looking at a wax image. Not only no future, but no past. Suddenly for the first time the whole truth smote him. This was Toby Graves (he had no doubt of that), Caro's husband who a few hours ago had been living and was now dead!

'Dead!' He spoke the word aloud, as if to convince himself. Of course, he'd seen dead bodies before; any man of his generation in uniform or out of it could say as much; and often in circumstances that made this tawdry flat seem like Buckingham Palace. But there was something about this particular body that filled him with a sense of—dereliction. Corruption! Yes, that was the word Caro had said;

darkness; they meant the same thing. Even in life there must have been that stamp of decay on Toby; it would have been useless for Caro to make any appeal here, and she had known it. He shivered to think what her short married life—two years had she said?—three?—must have embraced.

The police sergeant was eyeing him oddly. 'Mrs. Ryrie!' he repeated. 'Well, it shouldn't be difficult to trace the lady there.'

'Harder than you think,' returned Con, but his voice sounded quite absent. 'She's left—Mrs. Ryrie, I mean.'

'Oh? Then—you saw Mrs. Graves again? Or . . . ?'

'No. But after she'd left me I remembered that a Dr. Goddard has the house, so I knew, of course, she wouldn't get in.'

'And you don't know where else she might have gone?'

'I thought she might come back here.'

'It's where she lives,' the officer conceded. 'Still, perhaps this Dr. Goddard knew where Mrs. Ryrie had moved to.'

Con shook his head. 'They didn't know the name at the house.'

'You mean, you went with her? But you said . . . ?'

'No, no. But I walked round to Knowles Square . . .'

'And Mrs. Graves had called there?'

'I don't know. Yes, I suppose so.'

'Didn't anyone mention her coming?'

'There was a party on,' said Con, shortly. 'She could see at once Mrs. Ryrie had moved.'

'So she didn't ask?'

'I don't know. I haven't seen her since.'

'But you came up here in the hope of seeing her?'

He said sullenly, 'I thought she might have come back.'

'But—had she given you any hint she might not be coming back? And if this lady had left Knowles Square some time ago . . .'

'Obviously Mrs. Graves didn't know that.'

'Which implies that she hadn't been in touch for some time.'

'Well,' said Con rashly, 'she wouldn't need to be.'

He could see suspicion in the sergeant's mind rising like milk boiling in a pan.

'Who is Mrs. Ryrie, sir?'

'I've told you, I never met her.'

'Had you ever heard her name before to-night?'

'Never.'

'Mrs. Graves hadn't mentioned her?'

'No.'

'And Mr. Graves . . . ?'

'You've got a weak memory, sergeant. You keep forgetting I'd never met Toby Graves.'

'Of course, sir. So you told me. But he'd know about you, that you were a friend of his wife's?'

'I doubt if he'd ever heard my name.'

'You mean, you used to meet her without his knowledge?'

Con felt like Laocoon, struggling with the deathly serpents.

'No.' He drew a deep breath. 'All right, sergeant, you can have it. You won't like it, though.'

Common-sense warned him that in the face of murder—and already he was convinced that's what Toby's death was going to turn out to be—it was absurd to expect to conceal the facts. The sergeant listened attentively.

'Well, sir, why couldn't you say so right away? That alters things considerably. I got the idea that Mrs. Graves was a friend of yours, but if she was just a person who stopped you in the street to borrow money, well, you wouldn't have any motive for wanting to conceal the facts, would you?'

'Who's talking of concealment?'

'Well, we've been quite a long time getting to this point. Mrs. Graves asked you, a complete stranger, to lend her a pound to go to the house of a Mrs. Ryrie, who let lodgings. It turns out that Mrs. Ryrie hasn't been there for more than two years; there isn't actually any proof that she was ever there.'

'Except that Mrs. Graves . . .' He felt the colour mounting in his thin cheek.

'I said proof, sir. Still, it'll be easy enough to discover that. It looks as though the lady didn't intend to return to her husband. Is that the impression you got?'

'Well, I didn't think she'd be coming back to-night.'

'Quite so. Was she carrying any luggage?'

Con thought. Was she? He couldn't recollect . . . He told the truth.

'I don't remember.'

'If she had most likely you would recall it.'

'I don't see why.'

'Did you just stand still during your conversation? Or did you walk along a few steps? Or . . . ?'

'We walked along.'

'So if she'd been carrying a bag you might have offered to take it from her?'

'Yes—if I'd noticed it.'

The officer turned towards the dressing-table. 'There's a bunch of keys here,' he said. 'Latch-keys and some belonging to a lady's dressing-case and hat-box. The case and the box are on the premises. Of course, she could have had others, only—all her things are on the dressing-table—quite nice silver, too—and her toilet articles are in the bathroom. She didn't even pack a dressing-gown—unless, of course, she had two of everything.'

'Then,' said Con desperately, 'it looks as though she didn't take any luggage. Came away in a hurry, I suppose.'

'This purse, too.' With maddening deliberation the officer lifted it from the mantelpiece. 'That 'ud belong to a lady.'

'If she hadn't forgotten it she wouldn't have needed to borrow from me. I should say she intended to come back in the morning and pick up her things . . .'

'You could be right, sir,' acknowledged Detective-Sergeant Mason, but not as though he believed a word of it. 'She didn't say anything about why she should suddenly decide to—er—light out?'

'He wanted her to go round to the Hat and Feather and entertain some friend of his, and when she objected, well, there was a bit of a breeze, and she marched out. Probably,' he added weakly, 'she just wanted to show him he couldn't ride roughshod over her.'

The policeman's glance at the body was eloquent. Con cried out suddenly, 'For pity's sake, cover him up again. What was it, anyway?'

'That was a nasty place he had on his head,' remarked the officer, smoothly. 'He didn't get that falling on a soft carpet—and the gas-fire in the lounge is built in, as you'd know . . .'

'I've never been inside this building before, let alone this flat,' Con pointed out. Momentarily he was being reminded of those days in the jungle when you lay hidden, hearing the feet come closer and closer and knew that, barring a miracle, it's all U.P. And the miracle doesn't happen. It didn't happen here.

'Of course not, sir. Well, it is built into the wall, and there's no kerb, nothing at all he could have fallen against, if he'd stumbled, say, and of course in a flat you can't fall downstairs.'

'Well, then,' suggested Con, 'perhaps he was coshed.'

The policeman's head began to turn, as if someone were working it with a wire. It turned right round until it seemed to Con their two faces were almost touching.

'We thought of that, too,' he agreed. 'Only—it doesn't seem to make sense. The cosh-boys do their stuff for gain, fill their pockets with anything they can lay hands on before they scarper.'

'And nothing's missing?'

'I wouldn't say that, sir, seeing we don't know just what was in the flat, but there's a lot left behind any cosh-boy would have made off with. That purse, for instance, there's money in that, and there's upward of twenty pounds in Mr. Graves's pocket—supposing it is Mr. Graves, that is. And nothing missing from the jewel-case so far as we know, and though the stuff in it isn't worth much you'd expect a cosher to have given it the once-over. And then the safe . . .'

'The safe?' Con exclaimed, looking round.

29

'It's in the other room, only a little thing, but when a man imports a safe, and I've yet to see the block of flats where a safe's part of the furniture provided by the landlord, it's usually because he's got something worth locking up.'

'And—are you telling me you found the safe packed with valuables?' Con sounded dazed.

'Well, not packed, sir, but a chap who knew his way about would have helped himself.'

'God lord!' exclaimed Con. 'D'you mean—they're generally described as incriminating documents, I believe?'

'What are, sir?'

Con shook himself. 'I thought perhaps you'd found papers in the safe, that might be worth money to an unscrupulous chap.'

'Well, of course, if we'd found those we might understand why the money and those silver articles on the dressing-table—a bit old-fashioned but nice quality—hadn't been touched. But we didn't. And another thing,' he went on reflectively, 'cosh-boys don't generally leave their weapon behind them.'

Con felt as if a grenade had exploded in his brain. 'You mean, you found a cosh on the premises?'

'That's right, sir. Close beside the body. One of these kids' things they made such a fuss about in Parliament about a year ago. It's true they're not dangerous when they come out of the toy-shop, but if they're filled with shot, as this one was . . . they can be quite a proposition.'

'But—are you suggesting that Graves—or Mrs. Graves—kept a cosh on the premises?'

'I wouldn't know, sir. I'm like you—I've never been in this flat before. Only—I have had quite a bit of experience with cosh-boys and it's the first time I've ever found one left behind. And another thing—we've had the flat tested for finger-prints—naturally. And though there are plenty one way and another there are none on the cosh and none on the door-handle and though there are some prints on the jewel-case they tie up with others we've found in the kitchen, and it doesn't seem very likely a cosh-boy would go in there. You don't generally find anything worth pinching in a kitchen.'

'I suppose anyone experienced in housebreaking would have enough sense to wear gloves,' said Con consideringly. 'Everyone knows about gloves, even kids.'

'That's true, of course. Only—if it was a cosh-boy or anyone from outside how did he get as far as the lounge? The usual procedure is to hit your victim over the head as soon as the door's opened, and then you'd return your cosh to your pocket and strip the flat and go out. But it didn't happen that way. The body was found in the lounge. So it looks, doesn't it, as though Mr. Graves knew whoever it was attacked him, and they were standing together in the lounge when he was struck down.'

There was a long silence, then Con said, 'The safe? That was open?'

'The key was in the lock. It was a simple enough combination; and no one had been monkeying about with that.'

Con pulled himself together with an effort. 'I'm afraid I can't help you. As I've told you already, I knew nothing about Mr. Graves . . .'

'Except what Mrs. Graves had told you, of course.'

'Which wasn't much.'

'Simply that they didn't get on . . .'

'I didn't say that. I said . . .'

'That she'd borrowed a pound off you, a complete stranger, because she couldn't come back here this evening.'

Con was silent; through that silence he heard Caro's voice. 'I can't go back, I can't. I can't.' Why not? Because she knew what she'd find if she did? It was easy to see what the detective-sergeant made of the situation. Con wasn't sure the total didn't tally with his own.

'Of course, the person we want to get hold of now is Mrs. Graves. I suppose she didn't mention where she might go if she couldn't get in at Mrs. Ryrie's?'

'It never went through her mind that she wouldn't.'

'You don't think perhaps she might come back to where you live—had she got the address?'

'She was going to pay back the loan as soon as possible, in the course of a day or two,' said Con, hastily. 'No, I'm sure she wouldn't go there. And even if she did no one could let her in.'

'The porter . . .' began Mason but Con said, 'It's not that sort of flat. It's simply one of these old Victorian houses split up into service suites.'

'Still there'd be someone—a landlady or . . .'

'There's Mrs. Fairfax, she has a flat on the ground floor.'

'So if someone rang the bell and asked for you, she might know.'

'She might,' Con agreed, 'but I'm quite sure Mrs. Graves wouldn't go back there.'

'No harm making sure,' said the policeman smoothly. 'She's on the telephone?'

'Of course. You can ring up if you like.'

'We'll have to use the public call-box in the hall. This one's out of action,' said Mason.

They went down—no one was stirring—the house seemed empty except for themselves—and Con dialled his own flat—in case your landlady put your friend to wait, said Mason. Con knew he didn't believe anything of the sort; he suspected that Caro was lying hidden up there, and would naturally assume it was him, Con, telephoning. But the bell rang on and on with the desolate note of all unanswered telephones, and after a minute he hung up the receiver, and dialled Mrs. Fairfax. Mason's hand came out and took the receiver as the sound of the bell was cut off.

'Mr. Gardiner?' said Mrs. Fairfax in reply to his question. 'No, I didn't know he was out. Well, of course if he doesn't answer his telephone it does look . . . I'm sure I heard him come in some time ago and he's such a regular gentleman, never goes out once he's back from his dinner. No, no one's come for him . . .'

Mason hung up. 'Nothing that end, Mr. Gardiner, I'm afraid. Thank you for your co-operation. We'll keep in touch. By the way, did you happen to notice if the lady was wearing ear-rings?'

Con looked startled. 'Mrs. Graves? I—I don't know—is it important?' But of course it was important or the fellow wouldn't have asked him.

'It could be. Of course, some ladies' hats make it difficult . . .'

'Ah!' Con's head came up with a jerk. 'I remember now—she was wearing a scarf, so of course I couldn't see.'

'That explains it, then.'

Con looked at him curiously. 'Why do you ask?

33

I should have thought if you'd looked in the jewel-box . . .'

'That's just it, sir. There weren't any there. And yet we found an ear-ring close by the body. We were wondering if you could help us about the pair. I believe ladies don't always notice when a ring slips off, catch gets loose or something . . .'

So if Caro was wearing one ear-ring now and it tallied with the one found by the body, that meant—that meant . . . He said sharply, 'It must be in the jewel-box. You didn't notice . . .'

'Well, sir, we turned it out, had a thorough look. A nice article it was, pearl with a diamond surround. Still, the other one could be at the jeweller's being repaired.'

Yes, reflected Con, and Toby Graves's middle name could have been Galahad. The one was about as likely as the other. His heart sickened for that defiant figure who'd stopped him by the lamp-post. If she was only wearing one ear-ring—if she hadn't discovered her loss. He found he was shaking again. And trust Mason to notice that and put his own construction on it.

'We mustn't keep you any longer, Mr. Gardiner,' he said pleasantly. 'I'm afraid we've delayed you a good deal, as it is. There's only one more thing.'

Con stiffened. 'Yes?'

'Do you happen to remember the colour of the scarf Mrs. Graves was wearing?'

He didn't, of course. It had just been a scarf; and the light was fading, and he didn't notice much; he tried to explain.

'That's where our female witnesses score,' said Mason, looking as if he'd known what the answer was going to be. 'They always notice a thing like that, probably even notice the pattern. Do you remember what else she was wearing?'

'A coat,' said Con. 'Green, with a belt. A sort of mackintosh affair, I think. But surely you're not thinking of putting out a description? Can't you realise that as soon as Mrs. Graves hears about her husband's death she'll get in touch with you without delay?'

He said it with a conviction that surprised himself.

'Just routine, sir. Happen to notice anything else? Bag? Gloves? Jewellery?'

'She had a bag, red that was, one of these shoulder affairs. I don't remember anything else.'

'Quite so, sir. What you have told us has been very helpful. And if we should want any more assistance from you we shall know where to find you, shan't we? You're not thinking of leaving town during the next few days?'

'I have to work for a living,' Con assured him grimly, and that was a mistake, too, because the officer immediately asked for his employer's name and address—'in case we needed to get in touch with you in a hurry.'

Con gave it, reflecting that Mr. Tucker would like the situation very little better than the police. Mr. Tucker's firm didn't handle anything sensational, wouldn't even touch divorce. As for murder, you never heard that ungentlemanly word in his refined office.

'I think that's everything,' said Mason, snapping the elastic round his notebook like a policeman in a film. 'Come in a car? No? Ah well, the buses'll still be running. Oh, and Mr. Gardiner, if Mrs. Graves should—er—surface before we've managed to get in touch with her, you'll be sure and let us know, won't you?'

5

He didn't even try to conceal his suspicion that Caro was guilty of her husband's murder. Con found he was trembling like a man with the palsy. What the devil d'you know about it? he wanted to shout. You've never even met her. Line of least resistance, of course. Whenever a man was found murdered the wife was the first suspect. Common-sense told him that if Caro was innocent her obvious course was to come into the open and refute the charge, but experience warned him that common-sense isn't always a trump card. Come to that, common-sense hadn't been his strong suit this evening either. He remembered hearing Mr. Tucker say once that honest men on the whole made the worst witnesses; they were so conscious of their own innocence they became aggressive when it was doubted, whereas rogues had a smoothness of manner that juries were inclined to find far more reassuring. In his imagination Con could hear him now when the Graves murder became public property and his own part in it became known.

'Really, my dear Gardiner, for a man of our profession you have behaved with singular naîveté. You of all men should realise the imprudence of becoming involved in an affair of this kind.'

As though, reflected Con angrily, a member of a legal firm was immune against the storm of sudden passion, armed against falling in love most unsuitably—Con granted him that—was, in short, a robot whose whole existence was governed by somebody or other's Jurisprudence.

His indignation (on his own account) and his alarm (for Caro) sent him back at a fine pace, so that his feet had swallowed the distance between Morris House and Devon Street almost before he was aware of his surroundings. There was a policeman on the corner, and Con regarded him with instant suspicion. But the man didn't seem to pay him any particular attention as he brushed past and opened the door of No. 16. As he took his latch-key out of the door Mrs. Fairfax came out of her ground-floor flat. She was a large fair woman as shapeless as a seal, with a gift for the obvious.

'Oh, you're back, Mr. Gardiner. Someone telephoned.'

'Really? Leave a message?' He closed the front door.

'No. It was a man.'

'Well, if it's important I daresay he'll ring again.'

'He asked if anyone had come for you to-night. Were you expecting anyone?'

'No,' said Con sincerely. 'I suppose it was the right Gardiner.'

'There isn't anyone else of that name living here. Still, it may be someone who looked up in the telephone book and got the wrong number.'

She was a comfortable woman; that sort of explanation satisfied her entirely. Con gave her a vague smile and went upstairs. As he switched on the light in his own flat he glanced through the uncurtained windows. The policeman was walking up and down on the opposite pavement. Con wondered if he'd been told to note any unusual happening and report back to Detective-Sergeant Mason, but if the officer glanced up at him *he* wasn't looking; all his attention was focused on the little gold moon that could be seen through the darkening glass.

It was to be a night of incidents. Con had only just had time to switch on the electric fire when there was a shriek of brakes, a crash and a cry. The officer went past at the double; Con leaned out of his window. About a dozen other people were doing the same thing. A motor-cycle had come into collision with a van at the turning, and the lorry driver was explaining vociferously that it was the cyclist's fault; he gestured widely and the officer was making notes. The cyclist said nothing in his own defence. He wouldn't ever be able to say anything again. Like Toby Graves (if the body was Toby and Con hadn't much doubt about that) he'd done with argument for ever. A small crowd collected at once, despite the hour; one or two voices were uplifted. One, particularly shrill, accused the driver of murder.

'Now then, now then,' remonstrated the officer, 'no one's talking about murder.'

'That's all you know,' reflected Con. By this time to-morrow they wouldn't be talking of anything else. He'd forgotten, in the way people do, that Toby Graves was only a grain in an immense beach of sand, and not interesting to anyone outside his own circle.

As he stood watching the macabre scene, seeing the policeman send a chap to telephone for an ambulance, Con realised that the little owl who had once lived on the bomb-site had come back.

'Hoo-oo!' he called. 'Hoo-oo!'

The mournful note found an echo in Con's

troubled heart. Who-oo? Who-oo? Who had killed Toby Graves? It seemed in real distress, too, for instead of stopping after a few cries it went on and on. Hoo-oo! Hoo-oo! Con opened his side window. One of the reasons he'd taken this particular flat had been because it had windows in two walls; from this one he could see over the bombed site where a house had once stood and where the two trees in the little urban garden still flourished despite all Hitler's efforts. Each spring they put out leaves in defiance of their sordid surroundings; for the place had become a rubbish tip and a playground for the unselective young who found half-bricks, bits of ancient stoves and battered frying-pans an excellent substitute for the weapons beloved of their screen heroes. As he glanced towards the trees to-night he felt his blood chill; for a third tree was added to their number, a little tree, no more than a sapling, dark and rigid as its companions. And it was from this little tree that the plaintive cries continued to come. As he watched it moved, not as trees move in a wind, but forward, a few cautious feet. Con pulled out his cigarette lighter and snapped it on, let it burn for a moment and put it out. He repeated this twice. The owl cried once more and was silent; the sapling retreated and was immobile as the two trees in whose shadow it now stood.

At the street corner the crowd had thickened; the ambulance was on its way, and the constable was trying to disperse the ghouls who had apparently sprung up out of the pavement at the first signs of distress. The voice of the lorry-driver, harsh and, like Jaques's soldier, full of strange oaths, was still in the ascendant. Con slipped down the stairs. In the hall Mrs. Fairfax stood at the doorway of her flat.

'What's all this noise in the street?' she enquired.

'An accident. I'm just going to see.'

He went out quite openly. A tiny new moon swung in the trees, looking like a slice from a fairy melon. Instinctively he bowed three times and turned the money in his pockets. A chuckle reached him from the shadow of the tree-trunks. Everyone was busy with the tragedy up the road, and nobody noticed him slip over the dilapidated wire that was supposed to keep the kids out, and vanish into the hollow left by the bomb.

'Caro!' he whispered. 'Are you crazy?'

'I thought you were never coming back,' she exclaimed crossly. 'It won't help you if I die of pneumonia on your doorstep. I've been watching your flat for ages to see the light go on. You didn't tell me you were going out.'

'I didn't know I was.' The petulance of her tone was a blessed relief. That, he reflected, was how wives talked to husbands, or sisters to brothers, not criminals to men they've only just met. 'How long have you been there?'

'It seemed absolutely hours. I couldn't go to Mrs. Ryrie after all; she isn't there any more. I tried one or two other places, but they all gave me one look and said Full Up. So I thought—you did say if I wanted any more help I could come to you.'

'And I meant it.'

'That's a good thing, because there isn't anyone else. You're all I have. I'm in a jam.'

Con thought, 'How can she be so calm? But of course she doesn't know the police are in the flat.'

'You see,' she went on, 'I've decided it's not much good staying in London, because Toby could get at me too easily, and no one's going to employ you if you've got a half-crazed husband raging round the house, probably waving a revolver.'

'Has he got one?'

'Toby? Oh, Toby has everything. Yes, he's threatened me with it more than once. The trouble with Toby is you can never be sure if he's in earnest or not. Half the time I don't believe he knows himself.'

'Caro!' His hand tightened on her arm. 'Did he threaten you with it to-night?'

'I don't know what you mean by threaten. He was waving it about, and he said, "One of these days we're going to see headlines in the papers: Mystery on the Third Floor." He always said he kept it for self-protection.'

'Against gangsters?'

'Don't be ridiculous. Toby 'ud be on the side of the gangsters. No, against me, of course.'

He felt his heart thump again; she felt it, too.

'Con, what on earth's that for? Have I terrified you? Do you think I'm going to cosh you?'

He cried sharply, 'Why did you say cosh? Go on, tell me. Why?'

'Con, have you gone crazy?'

'Answer my question.'

'Well, it's the weapon of the moment, isn't it?'

'Is it? Have you ever had one? Have you?'

'You'll break my arm if you hang on to it like that. As a matter of fact, I have—at least Toby had.'

He let her arm go, with a sort of groan. 'It only needed this.'

'I haven't got it with me. Don't be alarmed. It's in the flat.'

'I know it's in the flat. Or rather, it probably isn't. Most likely the police have impounded it by now.'

'The police?'

'Yes. They're in your flat. Didn't you know?'

'Of course not. How do you—know, I mean?'

'Because I've just come from there.'

'From Morris House?'

'Yes.'

'But why? What were you doing there?'

'Looking for you. I realised soon after you'd gone that you wouldn't get in at Knowles Square—I remembered a doctor has the house . . .'

'So you came along to see if you'd been led up the garden? If perhaps you'd squandered a pound . . . ?'

'Caro, be quiet. There's a policeman on the corner and you're in enough trouble as it is. Anyway, no one could blame me if I did have doubts. What do I know about you?' His voice intensified. 'That you were ready to ask a stranger for money, that you'd had a row with your husband, that you were going to see someone who doesn't live in the district any more.'

'Yes,' she agreed, 'all very suspicious. Well, now you've been to Morris House—by the way, did you see Toby?'

'I don't know.'

'You—don't—know?'

'You forget, I never met him. I saw someone . . .'

'In the flat?'

'Yes.'

'Oh, that would be Toby. Didn't he say . . . ?'

'He didn't speak. He couldn't. He'll never speak again. He's dead.'

To his amazement she didn't turn a hair. 'What nonsense you talk,' she exclaimed, and the petulant note was back in her voice. 'People like Toby don't die so conveniently. He's a terrific practical joker.'

'Well, this isn't a practical joke. Ask the police, if you don't believe me.'

He felt her go very stiff and still in the curve of his arm.

'The police! Are they in on this?'

'It was a policeman who opened the door. He thought it was you.'

'What on earth were they doing there? Well, thank goodness I didn't go back. I didn't mean to anyway.'

'You'll have to go back now.'

'Of course I shan't. I shall go down to the country, as I'd planned, and get a job. I thought if you'd lend me a kitbag and the rest of the five pounds you offered earlier in the evening . . .'

'Caro, please pull yourself together. Your husband has been murdered . . .'

'What? You didn't say that before.'

'The police think he was hit on the head with a cosh. They found a cosh beside the body. You say you had one . . .'

'One of these kids' things they made such a fuss about in the papers some time ago.'

'Loaded.' The word was a statement, not a question.

'Toby filled it up with shot, just for a sort of lark. We never used it, of course.'

'Well, someone's used it now, and a man's dead. Did you keep it locked up or anything?'

'Of course not. It lay about in the sitting-room. It was there to-night when I left.'

'You're quite sure?'

'Of course I'm sure. Listen. When I told Toby I

wasn't going to stall his precious friend, and they could both go jump in the lake for me, Toby said, "Perhaps you'd like me to bring him round here for a change." I said, "Well, this isn't much of a place, but it's the only home I've got, and I don't want your friends here." He never had come round; and then I picked up the cosh and waggled it and said, "If you do—bring him, I mean—I'll entertain him with this." So if you're thinking of finger-prints you'll find mine all over it.'

'That's one of the odd things,' said Con. 'There don't seem to be any prints on it. And another thing. Tell me, do you wear ear-rings?'

'Yes. With a face my shape they're as necessary as—as lipstick.'

'Are you wearing them now?'

She put up her hands instinctively and touched her ears. 'Now you come to mention it, I'm not. I was making up my face when Toby made his stupendous announcement and I broke off to join in the fun and I forgot all about them.'

'You're quite sure you're not even wearing one?'

'Quite sure. Anyway, the craze for wearing a single ear-ring is out of date even in the provinces. Why do you ask?'

'Have you got a pair of pearls surrounded by brilliants?'

'Yes. Con, what is all this?'

'They found an ear-ring like that by Toby's body.'

She uttered a cry that he tried to choke off an instant too late. Someone had heard. In the wall of the house above them a light flashed on, curtains were drawn back, a window was raised. Caro turned, blinking, in the direction of the light.

Con snatched at her, forcing her face down on his shoulder.

'Don't let yourself be seen,' he muttered. 'Aren't you in enough trouble as it is?' His arms went round her. 'That'll be old Miss Elliott. She has the flat next to mine. She lives at her window, and what she sees from there would stagger you. If she thinks we're just a pair of lovers . . .'

'Lovers!' snorted Caro, straining to get her breath. 'I feel as though I'd been tossed into a burning fiery furnace.' And indeed the heat of his mood and his galloping heart made the comparison less absurd than it sounded.

'Disgusting!' shrilled an old voice. 'As if the cats weren't bad enough.'

Caro snorted again, but with suppressed laughter this time. Con thought uneasily that hysterics would probably be the next stage.

'The police ought to do something,' the indignant old voice went on. And then the window was slammed down and the curtains rattled back into place. Even after the light had gone out again Con didn't move; nor did Caro attempt to free herself. They stood so close, so still, they threw only one shadow. Slowly Con's heart-beats became more normal; he was flooded with a sense of amazement that for an instant overwhelmed his apprehension. Because it had happened at last, the miracle for which he'd ceased to hope; death, as the hymn said, had burst its bonds, and he'd come alive again. That for an instant was all he could apprehend.

Then Caro moved and slowly they drew apart. 'Con,' she whispered. 'You did say murder?'

'Yes.' His voice was as low as hers. 'Caro, about that ear-ring? What really happened to-night? Think carefully before you answer, because presently you'll be telling the story to the police.'

'The truth,' she began and he said, 'Ah yes, but let's make sure we both tell the same truth.'

She said slowly, 'I can't explain about the ear-ring. I hadn't been wearing them for some time, about a month, I think. One of them wanted a new clip and I kept putting off taking it to the jeweller, partly because Procrastination is my middle name, and partly because we never seemed to have a spare pound.'

'Dear Toby seemed to have plenty of money in his pocket this evening,' commented Con injudiciously.

'Toby? Well, he's collected it since breakfast then. He asked me to buy a bottle of gin and when I asked what I used for money he said surely I could rustle up a couple of pounds. It so happened he was cleaned out . . .'

'According to the police, he had over twenty pounds on him when they found him.'

Caro seemed less surprised than he had anticipated. 'That's always the way with him.' He noticed she still spoke of him in the present tense, as if she hadn't as yet accepted the fact of his death. 'One day he hasn't got half-a-crown and the next he goes everywhere by taxi and talks of getting a decent flat.'

'Haven't you any idea where his money comes from?' asked Con.

She shook her head. 'For some time it's seemed to me just as well not to know. Anyhow, I began to get suspicious when he let them cut off the telephone for non-payment and never settled the account even when he had the money.'

'I should have expected him to find that pretty inconvenient.'

'Oh, it cuts both ways,' returned Caro. 'He might have thought it worth the inconvenience to know that if he was out I couldn't take any messages for him. I've told you I don't know what his business was, but I should drop dead with heart failure to learn that it was straight dealing.'

'When you're answering the questions of the police, lay off these comments on your husband's character,' said Con uneasily.

'I'm not going to see the police,' retorted Caro.

He could have shaken her. 'Don't be absurd. Of course you must. It was all right before to plan going away without a word, but now you know he's dead you haven't any choice.'

It was Caro's turn to groan. 'Oh Con, what on earth made you choose the law? You can't even add two and two. How do I know Toby's dead? There are only two answers. One—because he was dead when I left the flat. And Two—because you've come haring back to tell me. But he wasn't dead, which wipes out (1). And you've told the police you've no idea where I am.'

'I wasn't to guess you'd be waiting here when I got back,' Con expostulated.

'Oh darling, don't be too innocent. Even a week-old police constable wouldn't believe that one. Of course they'll think you knew all about it—could you even prove we never met before to-night?—and went up to Morris House to find out the lie of the land—in other words, to find out if the police had moved in yet.'

'Yes,' agreed Con, in a voice of enormous surprise. 'Of course you're right. All the same . . .'

47

'So you see,' Caro went on as if he hadn't spoken, 'it would be perfectly idiotic for me to go dashing back. No, no. I shall stick to my original plan. I shall go to the Station Hotel at Paddington—no, don't say I shan't get a room at short notice, I don't want one—but they let you sit up there all night, Aunt Laura and I got caught short there once—and there's night service—and no one will think anything of it—and first thing to-morrow morning I shall move on. Don't ask me where. Even if I knew I wouldn't tell you. You aren't cut out for a conspirator, much too nice, not like me who's up to all the tricks . . . the only thing is I must have the rest of that five pounds you offered me, and perhaps a little case—it won't matter if there's nothing but newspapers in it—something that won't be traced back to you—that's why I've come back . . .'

'Caro!' He sounded desperate. 'It's no use. The news will be in the morning papers, and then you can't pretend you didn't know.'

'You do believe in making things easy for the police, don't you? If I go rushing back into their arms they won't even try and hunt for clues. Whereas if I lie low for a few days they may find some clue that will guide them to the real criminal. I can tell you this, Con, Toby was in no end of a stew to get me out of the house. Which means he was expecting someone else. And if the police find out who that person was they'll probably have solved the whole business. Unless, of course, he just wanted me out of the way so as to do a bolt.'

'He doesn't appear to have made any preparations,' Con pointed out wretchedly. 'By the way, what time did you leave the flat?'

'I didn't look at my watch. Does it matter? Oh,

all right, Con, I know you're trying to help me really. Well, it was about the quarter past when he suggested airily I should drift round and hold Gerry's hand. We had our up-and-a-downer—say ten minutes, it's wonderful what a lot you can cram into ten minutes when you give your mind to it—say about half-past six.'

'I suppose no one saw you?'

'I don't know. I didn't see anyone if that's what you mean.'

'No porter?'

'He goes off on the tick of half-past five and even when he's on duty he only sees what he's paid to see. I never quite knew how he stood with Toby. Toby used to spoon a bit with Mrs. P.—it didn't mean a thing, he'd have flirted with a nightcap on a bedpost if nothing better offered—other times they seemed to be getting together.'

'And—there was no one else?'

'No one I saw. I wasn't looking for people anyway.'

Con couldn't move her and was forced to agree to her demands. He knew it was crazy, he knew that if (when) the facts came out he was done for; but he wasn't a sedate young man in the legal profession any more, he was a madman in love with a girl oblivious to reason. He knew that what she was proposing was insane, yet he saw the point of her argument, though he doubted whether there was another lawyer living who would agree with him. What he feared was that she would go to ground and leave it to the police to dig her out, like some fox from its earth. He'd lived in the country as a boy, and he knew how much chance the fox has against the determined digger. But he couldn't move her.

'If I go back now,' she reiterated, 'I'm simply playing into the hands of the police. It's all very well to talk about the authorities being unprejudiced, but they're no more angels than you or me.'

Arthur Crook, that odd unscrupulous lawyer (the Criminals' Hope and the Judges' Despair they called him) who was going to be dragged into the case by someone whose name neither he nor Caro had yet heard, would have nodded his big red head at that and observed: 'And how!'

Then she was gone, 'Remember, you haven't seen me since you left the flat. Stick to that like glue. I can promise you they won't get anything out of me. I don't want to do you any more harm.' Her voice trembled suddenly into tenderness. 'Oh Con, no one's been good to me like this without wanting something in return since Aunt Laura died.'

6

In her room at 16 Devon Street old Miss Elliott shuddered like some ancient night-bird beside her closed window. Very funny goings-on on the bombed site this evening, she thought. Lovers were one thing, and bad enough, but this was—sinister. Peering between the curtains she'd distinctly seen a figure cross to the trees and hand over a bag and something else—stolen jewels perhaps—to a second party who contrived to remain invisible. Now what did that mean? And ought she to telephone the police? She wanted to be a good citizen, of course—just because you were old you weren't necessarily useless—but even good citizens didn't want more truck with the police than they could help. And Mrs. Fairfax would perhaps give her notice if she brought the force round at this hour of the night, and you have to think of yourself, don't you? She tried to tell herself she was being silly, it was all right really, it's a free country. Only—suppose it was a case of burglary and it turned out she could have been of use. Why, they might even think she was in the plot as a—what was the word?—a look-out girl.

She heard the front door close, stole to her own door and looked out through a crack. That nice quiet Mr. Gardiner was coming softly up the stairs. He saw her light and stopped.

'Oh Mr. Gardiner!' She clutched her lounging robe (we called them dressing-gowns when I was young, her scornful married sister, Millie, told her) about her skinny form. 'I'm so glad it's you. I was wondering . . .'

She explained her dilemma and he was so kind, not laughing at her or being rude like so many young people.

'I wouldn't bother,' he said. 'And anyway there aren't any burglars here. We aren't worth their trouble.'

She smiled gratefully, all her fears at rest. Such a reliable young man! And quite a little adventure to tell Millie on Saturday.

In his own flat the reliable young man leaned against the wall, feeling like someone at the wheel of a car dashing down a dangerous hill, with all the brakes out of action. Any minute now he'd crash, he and Caro. It was odd how much satisfaction he could derive from the thought that they'd be in it together.

CHAPTER TWO

1

When he had watched Con out of sight Mason turned into the telephone box and dialled the police station.

'Latest development on the Graves case,' he said. 'I haven't got positive identification yet, but I don't think there's much doubt this is Toby Graves. The wife—widow—hasn't turned up yet and I've no reason to suppose she will. But I've had another visitor.'

He explained the situation.

'I want a man to go round to the Hat and Feather and see what he can find out there. If this chap's story is true Graves was going to meet someone there to-night, and as he didn't turn up questions may have been asked. Anyway, they may know something about him there. I'll wait for the porter. He sleeps on the premises so he must be back some time, and he'll be able to say if this really is Graves or not.'

He rang off and slowly climbed the stairs to the second floor. A rum story from that fellow, Gardiner. Mason wouldn't be surprised to learn that he knew more than he cared to say. In the meantime, he had plenty to brood about. The safe had revealed a revolver for which it seemed highly improbable the dead man possessed a licence—anyway there was no sign of one among his papers—and a small parcel of drugs. Nothing, so far as he could learn at present, was known of Toby Graves as a drug merchant, but it was always the small men it was hardest to trace. He hoped a good deal from the inquiries at the local.

2

The Hat and Feather was one of those houses that aren't troubled by the police, except when they drop in during their off-duty periods to have a pint like other men. It had been taken over about a year previously by an ex-Commando and his wife, Joe and Rosa Bates, who were making a success of the job. Rosa, like all good publicans, kept her clock five minutes fast, and as the hand approached half-past ten she began her usual chant—'Drink up, gentlemen, please. Time, gentlemen, time.' And in the crowded bar men hurriedly finished their drinks and slid the glasses along the counter. As the reluctant customers began moving out Rosa exclaimed to her husband, 'There now! I clean forgot. He never came after all.'

'Who never came?'

'The one they call Toby.'

Joe Bates's tough face creased in a scowl. 'Expecting him?'

'He telephoned, didn't he?'

'First I've heard of it.'

Rosa considered. 'That's right. You were out taking that delivery. And a nice time you took, too. Nearly swamped with that charra from Longstone. And Bob taking a night off to go to the hospital.'

Joe's expression didn't change. 'Anyway, we can do without his sort.'

Rosa smiled, a wide charming smile that lit up her round gay face.

'Say what you like, Joe, he's a pushover for the girls.'

'Then let him push 'em in some other bar. Chap like that ought to have got himself born a Turk.'

Rosa's smile faded a little. 'What have you got against him?'

'Chap's got a wife of his own, hasn't he?'

'That one must be the original icicle.'

'Maybe if you had to go around with a husband like Toby Graves you'd feel the same.'

'What she comes for I can't think. She never enjoys herself.'

'And I don't enjoy having 'em in my bar, which makes us quits. All the same, she's a lot too good for him. What Mr. Lessing sees in him I don't know.'

'It was Mr. Lessing who was asking for him to-night. He was expecting him at six-thirty. Tried to get him at seven, but there wasn't any reply.'

'I thought you said he rang up.'

'That wasn't till some time later, said he'd be coming along. But he never turned up.'

'Mr. Lessing went off early, too.'

During this exchange the Bateses were clearing up the bar and putting everything in order for the morrow. Caro's ideas of housekeeping would have given Rosa a heart attack. Even Joe thought sometimes she overdid it.

'Leave it till the morning, girl,' he would urge.

But Rosa never would.

'Suppose I was to die in my sleep? It 'ud haunt me in purgatory to think of my bar in a mess.'

They were hard at it when the knock came on the door.

'Don't take any notice,' Joe advised. 'We're shut.'

'Wonder who doesn't know that,' Rosa speculated. 'Ghost, p'raps.'

'Ghosts don't knock, they walk right in.'

The knock sounded again. Joe looked troubled. 'Sounds like the police. What have you been up to, Rosa?'

She shook her head. 'Nothing. Unless they passed a new law this morning and it hasn't gone the rounds yet. You better open up, Joe.'

Joe slowly pulled back the bolt. 'It is the police,' he exclaimed. 'Sure it's the right address?' he added.

The policeman came in. The instant he mentioned Toby's name the dark look returned to Joe's face.

'Chap seems in the news to-night,' he observed.

'Nothing to what he'll be in the morning,' the newcomer assured them. 'Been here to-night?'

'No.'

'He was expected, though,' said Rosa. 'I was just telling my husband . . .'

She repeated what she'd just told Joe.

'What time was this?'

'Oh, about half-past seven. When I told Mr. Lessing he . . .'

'Chap didn't speak to Mr. Lessing himself?'

'No. Sounded in rather a hurry. Said to tell him he couldn't make it till later, but it 'ud be all right.'

'Didn't say what would be all right?'

'No. And to tell you the truth I hadn't the time to ask.'

'Often meet Mr. Lessing here?'

Rosa looked across to her husband. 'Three or four times, would you say?'

'Something like that, I suppose.'

'His wife come with him? Mr. Graves's wife, I mean?'

'About a couple of times.'

'What's happened to him?' Joe enquired.

'He seems to have got himself knocked on the head,' said the policeman.

'Not before it was due,' commented Joe crisply.

The policeman lowered his note-book. 'You didn't care for him much?'

'How did you guess? Not that that's anything against me. I've seen prettier things than Toby Graves under a flat stone.'

'Don't take any notice of him,' Rosa advised. 'It's you, Joe, not Toby Graves that should have got himself born a Turk.'

'What's happened?' Joe repeated. 'Got himself murdered?'

'What put that idea into your head, Mr. Bates?'

'Well, if he'd been bowled over by a lorry you wouldn't be here; and if he was where he could talk he'd be talking. Never knew a chap with such a gift of the gab. And then there was the little matter of his being expected here.'

'Seems as though he had a visitor first,' the policeman acknowledged.

'Good luck to him,' said Joe, heartily. 'If I knew his name he should have a drink on the house every night from now till Christmas. Come on, man. Open up. How was it? Someone got into Toby Graves's place and crowned him?'

'I didn't say anything about his place.'

Joe groaned. 'Ever heard of cats?'

'Cats?'

'Always take the longest way round.'

'All right,' the man agreed. 'Have it your own way. That's about the size of it. Seeing a chap can't very well hit himself over the head . . .'

'How bad is he?' asked Joe. 'Able to talk?'

'Corpses don't, as a rule.'

Joe stiffened. 'You mean—murder?'

'I call that awful,' murmured Rosa in subdued tones.

'If ever a chap asked for it . . .'

'I don't know why you took so against him,' she protested. 'He was always very pleasant to me.'

'I don't want men round here being pleasant to my wife.'

'About this Mr. Lessing.' Their visitor dragged the conversation back to the rails. 'Know anything about him?'

'He's all right,' said Joe unenthusiastically. 'Not exactly my cup of tea, perhaps, but nothing against him. Comes in most nights, has a couple of pints, plays a game of darts. Goes home to his wife at week-ends. And that's a funny thing,' he added meditatively, 'we don't generally see him of a Friday. Pushes off before we open. Must have been something pretty important to keep him in London that late.'

'Happen to notice when he arrived?'

'He said he was expecting Mr. Graves to meet him here at half-past six,' Rosa contributed. 'It was about seven when he asked if there'd been a message, and tried to ring through but couldn't get any reply. Then about half an hour later Mr. Graves rang up, and I told Mr. Lessing.'

'Say anything?'

'Simply that he couldn't wait much longer, he'd got a long motor drive. Left a bit before eight, I think. Said when Mr. Graves came to tell him to ring him up in the country; he had the number.'

'And he never turned up?'

'No.'

'No idea why he was coming, I suppose?'

'To meet Mr. Lessing.'

'That all?'

'In my job,' said Joe politely, 'you soon learn it's not healthy to poke your nose into other people's affairs. Anyway, you have your own health to consider.'

'Meaning?'

'Work it out for yourself,' offered Joe.

'You've probably gathered my husband didn't like Toby Graves much.'

'Chaps like that don't do a house any good,' Joe contributed.

'Any evidence that he was mixed in anything—crooked.'

'Not a sausage. Just my natural sense. They taught you more things in the Commandos than how to break a chap's neck without making a sound. Was that the way of it?'

'Mr. Graves? No. It looks as if someone hit him on the head with a blunt instrument.'

The policeman put one or two supplementary questions and departed.

'You are awful, Joe,' said his wife. 'Even if you didn't like him he's dead, and say what you like—murder—it's not very nice.'

As she turned to complete the work of tidying the bar the clock struck eleven.

3

It was just past the hour when Don Price, the porter at Morris House, returned in a morose state that was not improved when the policeman outside the flats told him the authorities were in possession upstairs and would be glad to see him.

'Get this, copper,' said Price belligerently. 'I'm off duty.'

'So's the chap in No. 8 by all accounts,' retorted the constable. 'Permanently.'

'You don't say.' But he went upstairs rather more smartly than he'd come in.

Detective-Sergeant Mason felt he'd been on duty in this flat half his life, and he was ready to welcome anyone, even Don. He saw a tough youngish man with the sort of face that tells you nothing except that if you want the price of a drink—and no pun intended—you might as well save your breath. If Don had been in charge of earthly affairs he'd have requisitioned air and siphoned it out at so much a breath, and if, like Caro, you'd left your purse at home, that was just too bad. He was smartly dressed in a dark suit, with a wilting flower in his buttonhole and the latest thing in check caps. A nasty piece of work and Mason wouldn't be surprised to hear he knew what prison looked like from the inside, but it didn't follow he knew anything about Toby Graves's death.

He made his attitude clear from the word Go. Whoever was going to shed tears for Toby Graves, it wasn't going to be Don Price.

'Yep,' he agreed, apparently under the impression

that he was the British Humphrey Bogart. 'That's Graves. What was it?'

'That's a nasty lump he's got on his head,' said Mason smoothly.

'Spoilt his beauty a bit, hasn't it? P'raps all his admirers would think twice if they could see him now. You know,' he went on lighting a cigarette—no respect for the dead man or for any living ones either, if Mason read him aright—'he had it coming to him. No laundry's going to make its fortune washing tear-stained handkerchiefs for him, and certainly not Mrs. G. By the way—she nowhere around?'

'She's not come home yet. I suppose you didn't happen to see her go out this evening?'

'I go off duty at five-thirty, and she wasn't showing up then. Maybe it was the one he was expecting.'

'Who was that?'

'How should I know? I can only tell you he came strolling in about—oh about three, I should think—and said, "If anyone comes for me, shove 'em up." That was the way he always talked. Then he said, "Be seeing you," and that's the last I saw of him.'

'Did his visitor arrive?'

'Not while I was on duty. Still, he had plenty, all shapes and sizes, coming at all hours. Can't think myself what the women saw in him. But they did. Even my wife thought he was a knockout. "What do you see in him?" I asked her once. She said he could always arouse a woman's curiosity and no woman can resist that. You married?'

Mason said nothing, and Don, quite unabashed, continued, 'Who brought you in?'

'Tenant in the flat below rang through to the station just before eight.'

Price whistled softly. 'You don't say.'

'Anything wrong with that?'

'Only that there isn't any tenant in the flat below. Moved out the end of last week and the landlord's doing a bit of decorating, and not before it was wanted. Did you try knocking the chap up?'

'Yes. But he'd told us on the phone he and his wife were going out.' He frowned.

'Bought that one,' Don pointed out juicily. 'Want me for anything else?'

'Was three o'clock the last time you saw Mr. Graves?'

'Call him Toby,' suggested Don. 'Yes, that's the last I saw of him, but I heard him again, at seven-fifteen. Another bull and cow,' he added.

'What makes you so sure of the time?'

'The tenant in No. 15 wanted a pair of curtains rehung and she couldn't do a job of work herself, not her. Would I come up at half-past six. She had a date at seven o'clock. These women!' He brooded. 'Think they own the earth. I got there at six-forty-five, and the way she created! "I've been ringing your flat," she said—all the flats have a house 'phone, see, just put in to give the porter hell—"I told you I had an appointment." "That's all right," I said, "I've got one myself at half-past seven—anyway, I've got to be off the premises by then. It won't take me more than a quarter of an hour to put your curtains up. Everything'll look smashing by the time your friend arrives." "I'm going out," said she. Well, I put 'em up, and what do you think she gave me? *Two bob!* Two perishing bob! This is overtime, I told her, and my price is five bob. The way she carried on—you'd think she earned her own living instead of having her rent paid for her by someone who ain't Mr. Benyon—then she pretended she hadn't got any change. "Come along in the morning," she said. "Oh, I can oblige," I told her. She didn't like it but she had to hand over a quid, and I gave her the balance. If she could have swopped it for a cup of cold pizen she'd have thought it cheap at the price. No sense, these dames. It 'ud pay her to keep in with me, knowing what I do.'

Mason made no comment. 'You came away from her flat—what time?'

'Seven, might have been a minute past. I went across to the flat at the end of the passage. The tenant was away for the week-end, and I'd promised to shut it up for him, do one or two little jobs. Might have been there ten minutes.'

'Reading his letters?' wondered Mason. Chaps like Don Price were as common in his experience as dandelions on an untended lawn, the little men of the underworld. Mason hated the expression—the little man—as much as anyone in England.

'So it would be between ten and a quarter past when you came down?'

'That's right, and they were hitting the high lights all right in this flat. You can hear everything—walls are only made of plywood—and neither of them ever thought to lower their voices. Sidelights on Marriage. The B.B.C. might have bought up the rights. She had a tongue made vitriol look like mother's milk.'

'Did you hear any individual sentences?'

'I heard him. "You're slipping," he said. And then he laughed. He had the sort of laugh you don't want to hear behind you in a dark passage with a brick wall the other end.'

'That all you heard?'

'I didn't stop. You're like the tenants here. Never expect a chap to have any private life of his own. Still, I didn't need more than one guess to know who he was talking to. The number of times she's told him she'll run out on him—and I for one wouldn't blame her if she did. The Greeks had a name for chaps like Toby. I can tell you this—any rent that was paid came out of her pocket. Not that he wasn't flush sometimes, but he liked to spend his money his own way. She had jobs from time to time and in between she used to hock her rocks.'

'You mean, she pawned her jewellery?'

'The last word from Oxford College,' said Price in mincing tones. 'Yes. There was a nice ring she had—sapphire set in diamonds. I've seen that in Mortimer's myself. She used to get a cheque the first of the month, and then she'd get the ring out of pawn. There were some ear-rings, too . . .'

Mason looked up sharply.

'But I hadn't seen those just lately. Could be they were in hock, too.'

'Remember what they looked like?'

'Pearls set in diamonds. Daise—that's my wife—was always on to me about them. You never give me anything decent, she said. Still, as I say, she's only been wearing something out of the half-crown tray lately.'

'Would you recognise Mrs. Graves's ear-rings if you saw them?'

'Well, I'd know if they looked the same.'

'Might this be one of them?'

Don looked at the little object lying in his palm. 'If

you found that on the premises, I'd say Yes. I'm no jeweller, mark you.' He looked up, sharp as a ferret. But Mason was in no mood to satisfy his curiosity.

'You're sure you didn't hear her voice—any voice but Mr. Graves's—this evening?'

'I told you, I was in a hurry. It's rush, rush, all the time. First Daise—that's my wife—to get off to her mother. She didn't go till six. "I'll take the late train," she said. Daise's Mum was having one of her turns; she has 'em regularly, just to spite me, I believe. If ever I marry again it'll be an orphan. By the way, I suppose you've looked under the floor-boards and all that.'

'For . . . ?'

'Mrs. Graves. It wouldn't surprise me if they found half a dozen bodies in pickle in the store cupboard. If the directors knew as much as I do about the private lives of some of the tenants . . .' he shrugged his shoulders, and spread his square powerful hands.

'It's Mr. Graves who was knocked out,' said Mason.

'Well, good luck to him, whoever he was. Spending the night here? Well, good luck to you, too. There's only the one bed.'

And, still chuckling, he took himself off.

4

Shortly before midnight Helen Lessing, opening the front door of the country house she'd refused to abandon for the flash town flat Gerald Lessing wanted, exclaimed almost before her husband had opened the door of the car, 'At last, Gerry! Have you any idea how late it is?'

Lessing frowned. He was a big, fresh-faced fellow, some years younger than his wife, whom he had married for her money. It had been one of his plunging speculations that hadn't quite come off. He hadn't realised that in marrying Helen he was also taking on her cousin and legal adviser, Bob Gatesby. Innocently he had imagined that any woman of thirty-five would be so grateful for a proposal of marriage that she'd be prepared to let her husband handle her cash, and it had been a shock to discover how tough—there was no other word for it—Helen could be. She always quoted Bob as her authority.

'Bob doesn't think . . . Bob doesn't approve . . .'

'I wonder Bob didn't marry you,' he said, sharply once. She looked down, her small fair face colouring.

'I think he meant to . . .'

'Pipped on the post?' said Gerald, and she coloured more than ever. Gerry picked up such extraordinary expressions.

'Care killed the cat,' he added. He was a plunger by nature. Take a chance was his motto. One foot in front of the other, one foot in front of the other and so to the top of the mountain was a creed that never appealed to him. Put on a pair of wings and try to fly and if you crash, well, that's just too bad, or go up in a crate and jump and if your parachute fails to open, well, you've bought it—that's how he saw life.

'Why did you marry me, old girl, if you weren't going to share my interests?' he'd asked her once.

She had married him, of course, because she was infatuated, he'd seemed almost too good to be true, and she wouldn't listen to Bob who'd warned her he was after her money-bags.

'Gerry could marry anyone,' she said, indignantly.

That was five years ago and passion had cooled. Each secretly believed he'd bought a pup, but Helen had no intention either of letting her husband play ducks and drakes with her money or pay out good cash to buy a freedom she didn't want. She knew nothing of his life in London, and asked no questions.

'So long as I don't know,' she told Bob.

But secretly she thought of London as a place packed with women all agog to trap Gerald into mortal sin.

* * *

Gerald, who had been thinking of very different things on his way down, started at the slightly peevish tone of her voice, and said mildly, 'It ain't twelve yet, old girl. I told you I might be late.'

'I thought late meant eight o'clock or possibly half-past. I should have thought you had enough of gasoline and fogs during the week. Country air must be a heavenly change.'

Gerald thought of the country as a nice place to be buried in if you were the fussy type, butterflies hovering over your gravestone, birdies singing . . .

'I should have been earlier,' he said rather sulkily—couldn't women understand a man hates being nagged? 'I had an appointment . . .'

'And I suppose you've been drinking for hours. What happened?'

'Chap didn't turn up. By the way, was there a message for me? A call from London?'

She shook her head. 'No.'

'Quite sure?'

'Well, I've been in since about six-thirty.'

'It would be later than that. Funny. I left a message.'

'Where?'

'At a pub.'

'Oh Gerry, do you ever go anywhere except pubs?'

'I come to church on Sundays to please you and I go to pubs during the week because you meet all the best people there. Toby was to have been there to-night at . . .'

'Toby? What an extraordinary name for a man. It sounds like a dog.'

'Gerry sounds like something worse than a dog.'

She let that pass. 'Was it important?'

'Everything to do with money's important. Surely Bob's told you that.'

'And he didn't come?'

'That's what I said. He was coming later, but I couldn't wait. I thought you might be anxious. So I left word for him to ring me here.'

She glanced at her watch. 'Is it too late to get him now?'

'As you've just reminded me, it's nearly midnight. And he's a married man, too.'

The familiar pangs of jealousy smote her. 'Do you know his wife?'

He grinned. 'Not as well as I'd like. She's like you. Doesn't think her husband's friends are good for him. Come to think of it, though, perhaps she stopped him coming to the Hat and Feather to-night.'

Helen frowned. 'I suppose you're sure he's—reliable?'

'I'm damn' sure he's not. Only, if he thinks he can double-cross me he'll find he's bitten off more than he can chew. Oh well, let's wait till the morning. There might be a late post letter—give the chap the benefit of the doubt. In any case, I'll be seeing him Monday.'

Only, of course, as it happened, he didn't.

CHAPTER THREE

1

All the morning papers carried the story from the three-line paragraph in the *Post* to the cheerful query:

ANOTHER COSH CRIME?

in the *Record*. If anything could brighten up crime it was the *Record*, though even that enterprising organ had to give pride of place to the disreputable *Daily Fizzer*, whose ship always sailed so close to the wind it was the marvel of Fleet Street that she hadn't sailed into Davy Jones's locker long ago.

The *Fizzer* seemed to know more about Toby than the rest of the press put together, though when you came to examine the report you found it was a brilliant fandango of hint and report and innuendo. But it made exciting reading for people whose daily lives were pretty devoid of colour and who had to get their thrills by proxy.

And among these was old Miss Fennimore

who had the ground floor flat at 16 Devon Road.

When she had digested those remarkable columns the old lady exchanged her bedroom slippers for what were advertised as Loungers and beetled up to the next floor where her equally old friend, Miss Elliott, had her one-room apartment.

'Mabel! Have you seen this? The most extraordinary thing. I saw a girl answering to the description in the paper talking to Mr. Gardiner outside the house last night.'

Her voice rose with each word, so that the sentence ended like the blast of a trumpet.

Miss Elliott stared. 'May! Are you sure?'

'My dear, I remember thinking—Still waters run deep—always such a *quiet* young man . . .'

'That's what I thought. But—do you know what time he came in last night, May?'

'Oh, this was before the nine o'clock news.'

'I don't mean then. I mean the *second* time.'

Their voices had dropped now; the conversation sounded like a colloquy in the Larger Snakes Enclosure—hiss-hiss.

'Mabel, whatever do you mean?'

Oh, there could be no doubt about it. Here was a plum. A plum? A peach, a nectarine, a hothouse melon. It wasn't long before they were wondering: Should we? Must we? Shall we?

The answer came with one voice. Nodding like a pair of mandarins, their hearts singing as tunefully as a brace of vultures scenting the flesh that dies, they donned their British Museum bonnets and set out for the Police Station.

* * *

Joe Bates picked up a couple of papers at the newsagent's at the corner who opened at six a.m. and glanced quickly at the front page of each. There it was—Toby's death—six lines in one paper and a couple of paragraphs in the other—and that, thought Joe savagely, was more than he deserved. He wondered how many hearts were singing this morning because Toby Graves was dead.

Rosa heard him come in and poked her head out of the door of their room; her face was soft and rosy with sleep, her fair hair rough like a child's.

'For pity's sake, Joe! I thought it was the end of the world.'

'I'm always up round about this time,' Joe defended himself.

'That you're not. Hullo, got a paper already?'

'Had to take the dog out,' explained Joe, nodding towards Jessie, the half-bred collie bitch.

'Oh get along,' exclaimed his wife. 'Putting the blame on the woman. Since you are up you might put the kettle on. I could do with a cup of tea.'

2

Don Price read the *Fizzer*, propped against the teapot; when Daisy was away he didn't set a proper table, just made himself some tea and put out the butter in its greaseproof wrapping and ate the bacon out of the pan. Daisy believed in having things nice—'You'd have finger-bowls, I suppose, if you had your way,' he jeered at her. 'Why not?' retorted Daisy. 'My Mum says . . .' Don was sick of Daisy's Mum. 'Wonder the old girl ever let you marry me,' he remarked. 'She was against it from the start,' Daisy assured him. It had been one of their bad weeks. Two evenings when he'd come down from his job she had gone out leaving a note—the pictures, she said. She'd developed a regular craze for the pictures, but when he offered to take her it was a different pair of shoes altogether. More than once he'd come across her and Toby Graves on the stairs or meeting (by chance?) at the street corner; and once he'd found Toby leaving his flat. 'Looking for you,' he'd said. 'You know where to find me,' Don told him. 'I know where you ought to be,' Toby agreed. As though a fellow hadn't the right in a country they still called free (and that was a laugh) to go along to the corner to find out what won the 3.30. 'Why don't you tell that chap to stop on his own premises?' he'd demanded, when Toby was out of earshot. Daisy had tossed her head. Nothing in it, just a civil word, makes a nice change for me. That was the burden of her reply. He didn't believe her; he'd noticed a marked change in her of late, she was evasive, unaffectionate—'give over messing me about, Don, do, I'm tired.'

'I suppose you think he's a sort of Clark Gable,' he had sneered.

'Be your age, Gable's had it,' she'd retorted.

The fact is theirs had degenerated into a cat-and-dog existence, not unlike that of the Graves themselves; this flight to her mother (he suspected she'd sent herself the telegram) was just another bit of calculated spite. Heaven only knew where it would end.

Murder? He thought consolingly she wouldn't dare.

3

Helen Lessing was also an early riser. She took the dignified *Post* and by the time Gerry came down to breakfast she'd stripped it to the backbone. It was a gay sunny morning and Gerry looked as new-minted as an Elizabethan shilling. The morning suited him, which was more than you could say of a lot of men. No one seeing them together would have believed they were husband and wife. The same thought was in his mind and he didn't conceal it quite carefully enough.

''Morning, Helen. Had a bad night?'

'Certainly not. Why on earth should you think so?' She handed him his coffee.

'Any letters?' Memory seemed to strike him. 'Nothing from Toby?'

'No. There won't be.'

He put the coffee cup down. 'Why not? You don't mean to say the chap's turned up here?'

'Not here. In the mortuary.' Her anger, because she had so accurately read his thought, made her bitter.

He had just lifted the cup; now he set it down and a little of the contents slopped over into the saucer.

'What are you talking about?'

'It's in the paper.'

He came round to the head of the table. 'Let's see, old girl.'

He took the paper from her hand.

Summoned by a telephone call shortly before 8 o'clock last night, police found the body of a man identified as Toby Graves in his flat in Morris House, W.11. The deceased had head injuries. The possibility of foul play is not excluded. The police are anxious to interview Mrs. Graves, the dead man's widow.

Gerald handed the paper back.

'No wonder he didn't ring up,' he said. 'Does it say what time? At all events he must have been alive at half-past seven, because that's when he rang the Hat and Feather. Wonder if he got round there, after all.'

'It seems pretty obvious he didn't,' said Helen, who read detective stories because she liked to pit her wits against the authors, and would have written them, too, and much better once, if only she'd had the time. 'He didn't meet you because he had someone in his flat, who saw to it that he didn't go out again.'

'You watch your step,' her husband advised her. 'You said that as pat as if you'd been there.'

'It's common-sense,' retorted Helen, severely. 'Gerald, was there a great deal of money involved?'

It took his slower brain a moment to get abreast of her.

'Good grief, Helen! You're a cold-blooded fish,' he exploded. 'Here's a chap found dead, probably murdered, a chap I knew and did business with, and all you're concerned about is have I lost much money?'

'Have *I* lost much money?' she contradicted.

The blood flowed sharply into his face, bright against his fair hair.

'This was my money. Roughly, a hundred pounds

of it. It didn't say anything about the place being ransacked, did it?'

'You read the paragraph,' she told him. His money! What did *that* mean? Gerry up to some monkey-trick, no doubt. Her colour rose, too. What right had he got to be engaged in private business about which he'd told her *nothing*? Her financial superiority was the only holds he had over him; if he was going to start becoming self-supporting he was as good as gone already.

'I wonder what happened,' Gerry murmured. 'He was a queer fish, but . . .'

It seemed to strike him for the first time that Toby Graves, the crooked chap, the charmer, with whom he'd done some business he'd just as soon the police didn't know anything about, was dead. Which meant the authorities would go through his flat with a fine-tooth comb. He wondered uneasily how much they were going to learn about the deceased's relations with Gerald Lessing.

After breakfast he took the car and drove down to the village. Helen's choice of daily papers was austere, he wondered what the more highly-coloured rags had to say—in a word, he wondered if there was any mention in any of them of a chap called Lessing.

He bought the papers and was glancing through them, sitting at the wheel of his car, when he heard his name spoken and looking up he saw Davidson, the local constable.

'Hullo!' he said, laying the paper down. 'Want me for something?'

'It's the Inspector, sir. He's come over from Waylands. There's been a message from London . . .'

'About me?' But this after all was only what he'd anticipated.

'He was coming up to the house, but seeing you're here, sir, it might be more convenient . . .'

Gerald put down the paper and locked his car. The inspector from Waylands was a man called Norris, and no waster of words.

'You've heard about Mr. Graves's death, Mr. Lessing?'

'My wife called my attention to it. She got at the papers before I did.'

'She knew Mr. Graves?'

'No. But she knew I was expecting a message from him last night. In fact, my first question when I arrived was whether it had come through.'

'And—it hadn't?'

'No. Of course when my wife drew my attention to the paragraph in the *Post* I realised why. I came in to see if there was anything fresh—more, rather—in any of the other papers. I rather anticipated being called on . . .'

'How was that, sir?'

'Well, they knew at the Hat and Feather that I was expecting Graves last night.'

'You had an appointment with him?'

'Six-thirty. When he hadn't turned up by seven I tried to get through to him, but the line was blocked or something. About seven-thirty Rosa—she's the publican's wife—told me he'd sent a message—wouldn't stop and speak to me himself—to say it was all right but he couldn't get away yet.'

'Did that reassure you?'

'Frankly, it didn't. But I couldn't wait. My wife expects me home for week-ends, and anyway so far as I could make out he hadn't given any indication of when he would be coming round. I had another shot at ringing up after I left the Hat and Feather, with the same result.'

'Telephone's cut off,' said Norris.

'Oh? I wondered if perhaps he'd removed the receiver . . .'

'Not wanting to get in touch?'

Norris's voice was sharp. Gerald said, 'It seemed a bit queer to me. Why not speak to me when he got through to the local? Rosa said she asked him to hang on but he cut off at once. That should have warned me.'

'And you say you expected a message at your own house?'

'I told Rosa if he came in to tell him to ring me. He didn't, because my wife was in all the evening and no one came through, at least, he didn't.'

'If he'd come through before you returned, could Mrs. Lessing have handled the business?'

'No. But it would have been proof that he was on the level.'

'You didn't try and ring him again last night?'

'It was too late, and I thought he might have put a letter in to catch the late post. It doesn't go till after ten from the Leicester Square office—and I daresay there are others.'

'Nothing?'

'Nothing. Well, this morning's news explains that.'

'Was it an urgent affair, Mr. Lessing?'

'It was, rather. I don't quite know where we stand now.'

'Had you known Mr. Graves long?'

'A few months. I only knew him in the way of

business. I met him quite casually—in another pub as it happens. But then in my line you make a lot of your contacts that way.'

'What is your line, sir?'

'I run a small—at present almost an experimental —car hire service from London. Mainly for the Continent. Chaps who want to go abroad and haven't got cars of their own—or only family or business cars that aren't available—but want to be free and drive around as they please. I got the idea through talking to some fellow who wanted to do that very thing. Of course there are big agencies, but it's not always easy to get a car just when you want it, and there's a lot of red tape, and naturally they charge more than I do—have to, they've got big overheads, whereas mine are cut to a minimum. Operating on such a small scale, I don't need a large office or a staff. I've got four cars at the moment, and they're generally in fairly brisk demand. When the summer comes along I hope to branch out a bit.'

'And—where does Mr. Graves come in?'

'He is—was—a queer sort of chap. He gets around, people like him, he's the kind that always has a tip or knows the man you want; and he got orders for me. Couldn't put up any capital, he hadn't got it; well, I haven't a great deal myself which is one of the reasons I'm only working on a small scale. Besides, as I told you, it's an experiment. If I do well this summer I can branch out a bit next year. And, of course, there are bound to be the flat periods, out of the holidays, though I hope there to touch some of the chaps who put up their car for the winter. But about this last deal. Graves came to me and said he'd met a fellow called Robinson who wanted all the arrangements made in a hurry. I had a car—a

Morris Minor—which fitted the bill, so I agreed. Graves was to see the fellow and get the money. I booked a place on the night ferry—he didn't want hotel accommodation, they seldom do, because at this time of year you can get in anywhere, and at a pinch you can sleep in your car. I told Graves I'd get his ticket and see about his currency, if he wanted me to, and I asked about his passport, naturally. He said that was all right; but I was to get the currency, which I've done, it's in my office now, and he'd get the payment. I asked a fairly healthy deposit on the car, naturally, which is repaid when it comes back to me in good condition, and there was the hire fee—the total amount was something over a hundred pounds—say, a hundred and twenty.'

'Which Mr. Graves was to collect?'

'Yes.'

'Is that the way you generally work, sir?'

'We don't actually have any rule of thumb. Sometimes the fellow comes to the office, and Graves gets a commission for the introduction. Sometimes it's all done through him, and he gets the cash.'

'Cash? Would that be literally cash, sir?'

'In a case like this, yes. I couldn't risk a stumer cheque at such short notice. When there's time to get one put through the Bank naturally I accept that. But in this case it was to be money down.'

'So that there should have been between a hundred and a hundred and twenty pounds in Mr. Graves's flat that evening?'

'If this chap had brassed up—yes.'

'You think perhaps he hadn't?'

Gerald frowned. 'I don't really know. If I'd spoken to him myself—what Rosa said was, more or less, "He told me to tell you he'd not be round for a while, but it was all right." He said that part of it twice—"it's all right." Which sounds as though he'd got the money.'

'Or was sure of getting it.'

'You mean he was waiting in for Robinson?'

'If he had the money on him, why didn't he bring it round? Or ask you to meet him at his flat?'

'Funny thing,' said Gerald meditatively, 'I never went round there. He never suggested it. I used to think it might be on account of his wife—perhaps he wasn't taking her into his confidence. Well, nothing in that. Lots of husbands don't tell their wives all their business affairs. But later he brought her along a couple of times.'

'When you were talking business?'

Gerald paused again. 'Now I come to think of it, I don't believe we did. Or only just in passing. I took it that she'd come along with him to have a drink, as wives do. On those occasions we hadn't met by appointment, we just happened both to be in the same bar. I'm there most evenings during the week, and I gathered Toby—Graves—went in pretty often, too. He seemed to know the landlord quite well, used to lean over the bar and talk to the wife rather more than Joe Bates approved. But I always thought Toby was a bit of a womaniser. Nothing to do with me, of course.'

'No, sir. All the same—what impression did you get of the relations between Mr. and Mrs. Graves?'

'We-ell.' Gerald hesitated. 'Hard to say. I don't think she thought a pub-crawl was an amusing way of spending the evening, and then there's no doubt about it, the old boy did put the comehither on all the females within range. I daresay wives don't look too kindly on that sort of thing. I know mine wouldn't.'

'Quite, sir. You wouldn't say you knew them very well, then?'

'Only what I've told you. I've hardly exchanged half a dozen sentences with her. A good-looking wench,' he added. 'By the way, I see they hadn't found her by the time the papers went to press. Any fresh news?'

'I couldn't say what London knows,' said Norris. 'Now, about this man, Robinson. You haven't any actual proof that he ever existed.'

Gerald looked startled. 'Come to think of it, I suppose I haven't. But . . .' he paused. 'I'm rather in the dark as to where we all stand now. I don't know if he and Graves ever met, and, if so, what happened.'

'You mean, if he paid up?'

'Precisely. Did they find any money on him?'

'A sum of roughly twenty pounds. But it seems that Graves told the porter he was expecting someone who hadn't arrived when Price—that's the porter—went off duty, and as we haven't yet located Mrs. Graves we don't know whether anyone called between 5.30 and 6.30 when, according to Mr. Gardiner's statement, Mrs. Graves left the flat. Of course,' he added, 'she might have been out that afternoon until, say, six o'clock. How about tickets for Mr. Robinson?' he added.

'He'd get those when he collected the car. According to Graves, that would be on Monday morning.'

'He'd come to your office?'

'Yes.' He gave the address. 'It's not a very

pretentious place, just a room and a small garage behind for the cars.'

Norris didn't conceal his distaste for the general set-up; but then, come to that, Gerald didn't care for it much either.

'Mind you,' Norris added, 'I'm not suggesting at this stage, that everything isn't above-board so far as Robinson is concerned . . .'

Gerald laughed shortly. 'It's obvious you didn't know Graves.' He looked a little uncomfortable. 'I mean—well—the fact is—I hadn't been quite happy for some weeks. I thought I'd make this a test case. If it was all straightforward I'd forget one or two rumours that had come to my ears; if it wasn't, then I'd close up the connection. You see, I didn't much like the affair of the telephone call. If there was no hanky-panky why didn't he speak to me himself? Or it wouldn't have hurt him to take time off to come round to the pub and explain. He's only about a couple of minutes away.'

'We don't know what happened at the flat that night,' Norris reminded him.

'No. I suppose not. By the way, is there anything to show when . . . ?'

'We haven't a witness yet who admits seeing Mr. Graves alive after the telephone call. And the police were in the flat soon after eight.'

Gerald whistled gently. 'And we know he was all right at seven-thirty. You know . . .' he stopped, and Norris said, in an inviting voice, 'Yes, sir?'

Gerald looked uncomfortable. 'Just an idea that came to me. I suppose there couldn't have been anyone with him in the flat *making* him send that message? I suppose that sounds like the pictures . . .'

'A lot of things in our line sound like the pictures,' said Norris, 'but no, I don't think it was that way. I don't see how it could be, all things considered.'

4

Daisy Price was one of the *Daily Fizzer's* most ardent readers. It was wonderful what a good story they made of Toby Graves's death. When she'd finished reading it Daisy went to the window and looked out. It was a lovely morning—a shame to be going back to London—the sun shining on the sea and all the birds crying and swooping. Like a ballet, thought Daisy, watching those white wings flash in the shining light. Still—Don was like all men—unpredictable.

She turned as the door opened. 'There's been a murder,' she announced, and her heart was shaking her to pieces. She held out the paper.

'What of it? You didn't do it, I suppose?'

'What a thing to say! Anyway, I'll have to be getting back.'

'What, to-day? I do call that a shame, Daise, you said you'd stay till to-morrow. You know how I feel . . .'

'Don'll expect me back the minute I hear of this. Well, it's only natural. I don't want him sending telegrams, making trouble. Come to think of it, I'll send him one myself. Oh, can't you understand?' The words broke passionately from her lips. 'This is murder—someone we know . . .'

'You only got down last night, I thought . . .'

'I know. I know. Turn it up,' she begged. 'It's on Don's account, see? That's a husband all over.

Spoil all your fun. Why girls get married at all beats me.'

5

Con was up early, too, wishing he could sneak across the Park and have a final glimpse of Caro, even if it would be too dangerous to try for a word with her. But common-sense warned him that very likely his movements would be watched, and he didn't want to be the one that led the police to their quarry. He went out before breakfast—it was a Saturday, when he didn't have to go to the office—and put temptation behind him by taking a bus in the opposite direction and walking over Putney Heath and Wimbledon Common until such time as he was convinced Caro must be safely away. It was almost eleven when he returned and Mrs. Fairfax came trembling out to meet him. It was becoming quite a habit, he reflected.

'Mr. Gardiner! Did you see them?'

'Them?'

'The police. I'm sure it was the police. And what's more I believe it was the police who rang up last night.'

He maintained a calm air. 'Did they say they were the police?'

'No. But you can tell. They came round quite early; seemed very surprised you were out already. Asked if you always went out so early. I said well no, not on Saturday . . .'

He interrupted, 'Did they say anything about coming back?'

'They left a telephone number. I rang it to make sure, and it was.'

'So you know they were the police? Why didn't you say . . . ?'

'I'm upset and that's a fact. It's not very nice for me having the police come here. It's not as though you had a car—anyone can get in trouble with a car.'

He wanted to tell her you don't need a car to get into trouble, but glancing up he distinctly saw a shape glide away from the banisters and heard the soft closing of a door. The house was all ears.

'You'll find your picture in the papers yet, Mrs. Fairfax,' he said, and was suddenly filled with an enormous irrational rage.

This sustained him when, a little later, he found himself face to face with the police. They didn't try to hide their feelings.

'Mr. Gardiner, you were asked by our representative last night to give information as to the whereabouts of Mrs. Graves if any such information should reach you. Have you, in fact, seen Mrs. Graves since you left Morris House yesterday evening?'

A layman might have wondered about denying it, but the thought never went through his mind. He might be a poor sort of lawyer, but the profession had its responsibilities.

'Yes.'

'By appointment?'

'No. I had no idea . . .' He supposed Miss Elliott had been doing some arithmetic. Twice one are two and twice two are four, but twice two are ninety-six if you know the way to score.

'You didn't attempt to get in touch with us?'

There was nothing he could say to that.

'Where is Mrs. Graves now?'

'I don't know. If she had any definite plans she didn't tell me.'

'Why did she come back if she wasn't going to ask for your help?'

'She wanted money when she found Mrs. Ryrie had left her old address.'

'She must have told you something. Mr. Gardiner, if a criminal charge should result you won't be held free from responsibility.'

He laughed shortly. 'Accessory after the fact! But you'd have to prove murder against Mrs. Graves first. As to where she is, she spoke of leaving London.'

'Where was she proposing to spend last night?'

'At one of the main line stations.'

'Which one?'

'She spoke of Paddington. I didn't follow her there and we've not been in touch since. It may have been a blind, since she must have realised you were likely to come down on me again. I don't know.'

But he didn't believe it. Of course she'd gone to Paddington, and equally of course she had left it hours and hours ago. As to where she was now, that was anybody's guess. He tried to picture her, cowering somewhere as he'd cowered in the alien jungle in another spring. He pulled himself up. Caro cowering? More likely kicking some police officer in the teeth.

The questions went on. Con said that Caro's first intimation of her husband's death had been his own story of the previous evening. When the police tried to pull the one about innocent people having no need to fear the law, he said shortly,

'Don't make me laugh,' recalling Oscar Slater and Adolph Beck and—the police stopped him there. He felt convinced they'd tap his telephone, though even Caro wouldn't be mad enough to ring him up on a trunk line. It did go through his mind for a minute that she might remain in London, but he dismissed that idea. She wouldn't subject him to such a risk. He took it for granted that her reaction to last night's meeting was identical with his.

The police didn't ask for any further undertakings, but Con knew that from now until Caro was found he'd be under perpetual supervision. He wondered if there was any way of tampering with his letters. And in the meantime what was Caro doing? where was she? and what, oh what for her did the future hold?

CHAPTER FOUR

Caro got the *Post* and the *Morning Sun* and read them in a third-class carriage travelling non-stop to Reading. Con would scarcely have recognised her this morning, so little relation did she bear to the haggard, distracted creature of the night before. When she left him she had gone to the all-night chemist in Piccadilly Circus and bought the necessary cosmetics and toilet articles; in the underground lavatory she combed her hair and made up her face, turned her mackintosh which was of the reversible variety, and came out in a black coat with a yellow-spotted scarf round her head. Her very poise of the head, her walk even, seemed to have changed. So smooth, so trim, there was confidence in every movement. She travelled by underground to Paddington and spent a reasonably comfortable night on a deep settee in the lounge, all the rooms, as she had surmised, being occupied. A night-staff waiter brought her coffee and sandwiches and later she slept. Con couldn't have done it; at any minute he'd have expected a policeman to poke his head round the corner, but Caro said sensibly, 'Well, staying awake won't keep him away,' and so she slept. Next morning she caught an early train, being fortunate enough to find an empty compartment. She was sorely tempted to ring Con up, but decided she'd made trouble enough for him already. If she had had any doubt as to her own situation, this was dispelled by the newspapers. She could hear through the carriage's thin wall a couple discussing Toby's death, automatically holding her responsible.

When the train was well under way she stripped off the mackintosh and untied the scarf, placing both articles inside Con's little zipper bag; and then she tore off her wedding ring and flung it out of the window.

'That's a thing I've been wanting to do for more than two years,' she said, with a sigh a relief. The morning sun illuminated the carriage, rolled away a faint early mist, and enlarged the horizon. And as the light strengthened and the train widened the distance between her and the mortuary where, no doubt, Toby now lay, her hope grew. Incredible as it was to seem to everyone whom she subsequently met, she really did cherish the idea that she could leave the unfortunate Caro Graves behind her, and begin again.

The first thing, obviously, was a new name, and she decided to revert to the one she had borne before her marriage, that had been Aunt Laura's also. Charlotte Maxwell. That's how she would register at the hotel or boarding-house where presumably she would spend to-night. There were disadvantages, of course. She couldn't present a ration book in the name of Charlotte Graves, which meant she must be perpetually on the move; you could stay three nights—or was it four?—at a boarding establishment without your book being asked for. Well, she told herself, here's my chance to know my own country. She still couldn't make herself believe that the liberty she longed to embrace was a chimera, that every day would bring her closer to the morning when her secret would be known.

At Reading she handed in the little case at the Left Luggage Office, immediately destroying the ticket, so that it couldn't be reclaimed. Poor Con, it was never likely he'd see that again, but most likely he had others. Men always appeared well furnished in this respect. She went into the town, a tall slender girl with a bare head, wearing a grey suit and red shoes, with a red bag slung from her shoulder, and bought herself some breakfast at a Self-Service Café. Coming out her glance fell on a B.R. poster, advertising cheap day tickets to Bath. The name awoke memories.

'If ever you're on your uppers, Caro,' Aunt Laura had said, 'make a bee-line for Bath. There are always aged tyrants there hanging out the flag for slaves.'

'Slaves!' sniffed the independent Miss Maxwell. But that had been before she married Toby.

Bath was as good a place as any to hide, and surely the police wouldn't think of looking for a suspected husband-killer in the guise of a meek companion to some dictatorial old trout! Yes, let it be Bath by all means, particularly as a train went within the hour. When she had paid for the ticket she hadn't a great deal of Con's five pounds left, not enough to start a new life if she didn't tumble into a job at once; and dictatorial old trouts expect their companions to have at least a change of underwear. All of which added up to one thing—Aunt Laura's ring. It was a very beautiful and unusual design, a square sapphire of great depth, set in diamonds; the most travelled ring in London, Caro had once described it. There could scarcely be a pawnbroker's in the metropolis where it wouldn't feel at home. But now, she decided, she must sell. Pawning was too dangerous. You had to supply a name and address. It was a shock to find that if you sold you had to do the same thing, though, of course, there was nothing to show that you were giving the true facts. The first two jewellers hummed and ha'ed, it was a bad time, things were very quiet, they had heavy stocks and couldn't offer much. But a third, called Taylor, made a fair offer, and agreed to pay in cash. Caro had thought up quite a passable story about losing a purse, and it being Saturday—and Mr. Taylor could see at once from the mark on her finger that she was used to wearing the ring. He saw, too, that until very recently she'd been wearing a wedding-ring, and decided in his mind this was an elopement. But the young person's morals were nothing to do with him, and she gave her name as Miss Maxwell and a London address that was later proved to be fictitious, and he paid out in pound notes and locked the ring into his safe. Caro stuffed the money into her bag and did a lightning round of the ladies' outfitters, getting underclothes, a plain dark dress, shoes and a hat. She felt that tyrannical old trouts would expect a hat. She still had a comfortable wad of notes left; she'd have to go to an hotel over the week-end, but that would give her a chance of going through the local papers and discovering where her best opportunities lay. There still remained the worry of the ration book, but that could wait till Monday. She had bought a second-hand suit-case for a small sum, and she looked like any other girl going away for a week-end. The queer thing was that already Toby seemed to belong to a vanished world. As for the future—Providence had already sent her one saviour in the person of Con Gardiner. For all she knew to the contrary, it might have another trump up its sleeve. And, in point of fact, so Providence had.

At Bath she booked a room at the Avonlea Private Hotel, for a couple of nights. It was unobtrusive without being squalid and most of the inhabitants looked as if they were taken off the shelf every morning, dusted and put back again. They had so little individuality for the new-comer that she didn't even notice them as people. She bought the latest edition of the *Evening Sun*, but there was nothing fresh. Thank Heaven, she reflected, that Toby in one of his tantrums recently had gone round the flat tearing up all the photographs of herself; the only other copies had belonged to Aunt Laura and had been destroyed after her death before the silver frames that had housed them were put into the sale.

She dined alone at a small table, her face concealed by a book, and she went up to bed early. After breakfast on Sunday she walked about Bath, remembering that time—in another world, it seemed—when she had really been Miss Maxwell staying in Bath with Aunt Laura. She revisited some of their old rendezvous, noticed with pain the damage done by German bombers, and managed to get a copy of the local newspaper. A few of the residents tottered off to Church on Sunday, but none of them spoke to Caro, and she went out of her way to be unsociable.

The Avonlea didn't do teas—Miss Parker explained that the Catering Wages Bill made that impracticable, and really most of her 'ladies' were quite pleased to go out for this fussy little meal. It made a change, you saw different people, and Bath supported so many cafés. On Sunday afternoon Caro went into one of these, called The Seven Sisters, with seven little dolls all dressed alike, in the window. She chose it mainly because it looked empty, and she didn't want to be inveigled into conversation by anyone. She had heard the Graves Case discussed in the Avonlea Lounge while they were waiting for lunch; everyone took it for granted she had whanged Toby over the head—and that without even knowing Toby. The Sunday papers had spread themselves over the case. There were photographs of Toby that wouldn't have disgraced a film star and, rather to her dismay, a picture of Con Gardiner. It looked as though poor Con was being put through it. It was a situation that sounded so romantic on the stage, but was corny, not to say sordid, in real life. She sat back at her table at the Seven Sisters, marvelling at the photographs of Toby. Most press pictures aren't flattering to the sitters. Toby's wasn't. She'd seen him look like that a thousand times, an attractive young man saying, 'Cheese' as all experienced sitters do to give the mouth a pleasant curve without making the subject look as though he were grinning through a horse-collar. She threw the paper down and was just pouring out a second cup of tea when a chirping little voice said, 'Do you mind if I sit here?'

Politeness is a grand thing, but there's no doubt about it, half the time it's just a veneer. Caro wanted to say, 'Why the hell can't you choose an empty table?' but as she glanced up to mutter insincerely that she didn't mind a bit she saw that all the tables were now occupied. The owner of the voice matched it to perfection, a little bird-like woman, dressed apparently in last year's bird's-nest, a nebulous brown mixture suit that a self-respecting bird would have blushed to own, topped by a bright red hat like a cock's-comb that's seen better days.

'My pet table,' the voice chirruped. 'I haven't seen you here before, have I?'

'No,' said Caro briefly, snatching up the paper again. 'I'm only passing through.'

There was nothing she hadn't read except the back page, so she turned to that and learned that Marshall and Snelgrove were having a special show of twin-sets for personal shoppers only. She read the advertisement with the utmost care, though she never wore twin-sets; she said they made her look like a camel. She was aware of her companion diligently reading the paper's front page, and thought irritably, 'Why can't she buy herself one? If she can afford to have tea out, she can afford a paper.' She was wondering how many people relied on reading the news over a neighbour's shoulder in the train or in a newspaper discarded by an earlier traveller, when the little voice said triumphantly, 'There, I knew I couldn't be wrong. I'm like an elephant,' a statement so startling that Caro instinctively lowered her sheet. The little face that seemed all angles, pointed nose, pointed chin, spiky little sandy lashes, little pointed teeth like a cat (and she never got those out of the National Health, reflected Caro) were as unlike an elephant as anything could be.

'Never forget,' amplified the little creature, beaming. 'I always remember a face, and I was certain I'd seen you before, but I couldn't think where. And then when you didn't seem to know me—but then I'm not used to being noticed. Like a gadfly, you know, you only realise it's there when it stings.' She laughed merrily. 'But I used to notice *you*. Mrs. Graves.' She said the name proudly. Caro felt she might swoon at any moment.

'I think there's some mistake.' She glanced round. Those flute-like tones would carry as clearly as a blackbird's note. Fortunately everyone else seemed completely engrossed in gossip, argument or the cakes provided. 'Very small for threepence,' she heard someone say. 'My name is Maxwell. *Miss* Maxwell.'

'Really!' The little tawny brows drew together. 'I wonder if you have a twin sister.'

'I'm an only child.'

'Extraordinary. Quite extraordinary.' She paused and the cretonne-overalled waitress (one of the seven sisters?) came up and dumped some apple-blossom china on the table.

'Toasted or plain?' she asked.

'Toasted what?'

The woman stared. 'Bun, of course.'

'Neither. Plain bread and butter, strawberry jam—yes, of course you have some—no milk but plenty of hot water.'

The woman looked sulky. 'The set tea . . .'

'I didn't ask for the set tea.' The sullen woman took herself off. 'Really, one has to be quite firm sometimes. Now, Miss—Maxwell, did you say?—are you quite sure you don't suffer from loss of memory?'

'Look,' said Caro desperately, 'if I were Mrs. Groves . . .'

'Graves.'

'Graves I should know it, shouldn't I?'

'That would all depend—on whether you do suffer from—is it amnesia, I mean? I can never be sure—well, but tell me, where have you come from?'

'Reading,' said Caro in a sulky voice. 'I told you, I'm only passing through.'

'And how long have you lived in Reading?'

'Why should you suppose I live there at all?'

'My dear, you must live somewhere. And if you're not sure, then don't you see the likelihood is that you are Mrs. Graves, as I have no doubt at all that you are. You see, I've seen you in London. Now, you do remember being in London at some time, don't you?'

'Yes,' agreed Caro with an immense show of patience and wishing she had the fatal cosh at her elbow, 'I have been in London.'

'Now, think for a moment. Does the name Morris House wake any echo in your mind? No, don't answer at once. Just let it sink in. Morris House.'

'Morris House,' repeated Caro, expressionlessly.

'Yes.'

'Is that where you think you've seen me?' (Who the heck was the old girl? She didn't look like one of the tenants. Perhaps she ran a Savings Branch and came round every week selling stamps. She'd got to be put off somehow. She looked more than half dotty and capable of anything, as dotty people are.) 'Look,' she said again, quite desperate now, 'it's awfully easy to make mistakes.'

'Exactly. Oh, don't think I blame you in the least.'

'Blame me?'

'Well, my dear, you may be Miss Maxwell now, and even in this regulation-ridden country I suppose we still retain the right to call ourselves whatever we please, but I was always observant, even as a child, and I can see you've been wearing a wedding-ring for some time.'

Caro glanced instinctively at her left hand.

'I'm sure no one could blame you for wanting to go back to your own name,' the little voice chirped on. 'All this changing is most unsettling. So inconsistent, too.'

'Perhaps,' thought Caro, charitably, 'they only let her out one afternoon a week and Sunday is it.'

'I used to see you with your husband,' the determined little creature went on. 'He was very good-looking, but they say handsome is as handsome does and it does a good many people.' Here her tea arrived and she felt the sides of the jug to make sure the water was really hot, and said severely she hoped it was butter and not margarine. As the waitress withdrew the little woman hurried on, 'I remember . . .' and then her eyes fell on the paper Caro had tossed down. 'Why, there he is,' she began. 'Toby Graves. He . . .' She stopped dead, her eyes popping. 'My dear,' she apologised in a low gentle voice, 'I've done it again. Put my great foot in it.' She stuck it out; it was about as large as a good-sized fairy's. 'The things that foot's done in its time,' she said, regarding it mournfully. 'An elephant couldn't be more destructive. Oh, no wonder you've forgotten who you are. I couldn't agree with you more, as they say nowadays. So clever of you to have thought of it straight away. It shows you have a head on your shoulders.'

'Thought of . . . ?' Caro was absolutely at sea.

'Not remembering you were ever Mrs. Graves. Just what I should have done myself, if I'd had the wit to think of it.'

'Well,' said Caro, with a grim little laugh, 'there's a telephone in the lobby. I saw it as I came in.'

'Telephone, dear?'

'Yes. To inform the police. They're looking for me, you know,' she added explanatorily, wondering which of them was the dottier.

'You suggest I shall inform the police, which clearly wouldn't square with your plans, as otherwise you would have gone to them yourself already? Can you tell me a single reason why I should go out of my way to oblige that body of men? I've found them remarkably disobliging, I can assure you—once over a pearl necklace—and what if it was found in my house later? Anyone can make a mistake. And then my little dog when he was lost—Terry his name was—and when at last the poor darling was found and no thanks to them they refused to hand him over until I could produce a licence. Well, naturally I hadn't got a licence for him, as if he were a motor-car or a wireless set. When I told the policeman that he said, "Well, I've got a licence for my wife"—as if there was any comparison. Oh no, I wouldn't go a step out of my way to help the police. If I were a writer of detective stories I should have a policeman for the murderer and all his colleagues would be accomplices. But I suppose it wouldn't be fiction then.' She had gone quite purple in the face. Clearly the police were her King Charles's Head. 'Now, my dear,' she went on after a moment in a voice appropriate to a pantomime Wicked Uncle, 'what are your plans? Can I help you in any way? They say two heads are better than one, but it's my belief that the person who invented *that* motto was the man in charge of the guillotine. It all depends on the quality of the heads . . .' She rippled and chattered like Lord Tennyson's famous brook. 'Now, where are you staying? The Avonlea? Oh dear, I wonder who recommended that. A friend of mine stayed there last year, and she ordered mushrooms on toast, and do you know what the last mushroom turned out to be?'

'A toadstool,' suggested Caro, intelligently.

'No, my dear. A beetle. Yes, a poor pulverised beetle. Moira said she'd have eaten it—she's rather short-sighted, you see—only its legs stuck up in the air and she did think that rather odd in a mushroom. Now, my dear, I have a far better notion. At all events, think it over. Why not come and stay with me? I'm living down here now, you know. Yes, a legacy. I can hardly believe it. Can you?'

'Well,' said Caro, 'it's always easier to believe it of someone else. But I don't see how I could come to you. I've involved enough people in my affairs as it is. And the police . . .'

Miss Crisp ('that's my name, Emily Crisp,' she said) leaned across the table.

'My dear, it would be a pleasure to annoy the police. But quite apart from that I really do need a companion. My brother-in-law came to see me the other day and he said, "Emmy, you can't live in this house by yourself, you must get a companion." He pretends it's because he's afraid I shall starve myself if I have to think about food, but the truth is he thinks I'm a little—you know,' she nodded and tapped her forehead, 'and he's terrified I might waste my substance on riotous living in what he'd call a nut-house. As his children are my only nephews and nieces one does see his point,' she added, mildly.

'But you can't imagine he'd approve of me for the job,' exclaimed Caro.

'Well, perhaps not. No, of course he wouldn't. It would be like one of those plays we used to get on the wireless before we had a Third Programme, where the beautiful mysterious girl takes a humble job, is half-killed with overwork, but finally—er—scoops the kitty. Seriously, though, you'll do much better for yourself by coming to me. You haven't a hope of eluding the police unless you have someone to cover up for you. Because if they track you to Bath, and whatever you may think of the police you have to admit they do get there in the end, what happens then? They'll go from hotel to boarding house looking for someone called Maxwell. It'll only be a matter of days before they have you under lock and key. You must remember, they've no sporting instincts, they'd be quite capable of installing one of their spies at the Avonlea, and she'd take a positive joy guiding you into an ambush. Whereas if you're staying with me, well, the police can't make a house-to-house visitation of all the residences in Bath.'

'It's wonderful of you,' said Caro slowly, 'but—suppose it lands you in serious trouble? It could, you know.'

'My dear, it'll make a delightful change. Life has become sadly monotonous during these last few years. I'm afraid the war spoilt us for quiet living. And I do assure you, you'd be perfectly safe with me. I do so much deplore all this interference with the liberty of the individual, playing the buttinski as my nephew puts it between husbands and wives.'

Caro laughed for the first time. Like Con, Miss Crisp looked startled.

'My dear, with a laugh like that you should be on the stage. Do you laugh much?'

'It depends how much encouragement I get.'

'You shall have plenty with me. Well, as I was saying, I'm quite sure you had excellent reasons for doing whatever you did do. I shan't ask you to tell me anything, because it's far better I shouldn't know. Then I can truthfully say I have no information.'

'I didn't kill Toby, you won't be harbouring a murderer,' said Caro bluntly. 'On the other hand, I haven't shed any tears over him, and I haven't the faintest idea who else might have thought him worth the risk. And it's perfectly clear,' she added dryly, 'in which direction the police are looking.'

'Oh, I understand a wife is always the first suspect,' replied Miss Crisp, cosily. 'Such a comment on marriage. No wonder the wise women of the Bible were all virgins. I never heard of a wise married woman except the one who got up in the night and staked a claim on her husband's behalf by walking round miles and miles of fields, and I don't call that wise at all. A woman with any sense would have stayed in bed and let her husband do the prowling if he wanted the land all that much.' She broke off and waved a small imperious paw at one of the seven sisters. 'I said plenty of hot water, and I expect it to arrive in a covered jug. And we want some cakes, and don't ask me what sort because we want all sorts. No private enterprise left,' she confided to Caro. 'You're expected to order everything in triplicate. Not that I should mind some of those chocolate éclairs in triplicate. I wonder if they're real cream.'

Over the éclairs they perfected their plan. Since Caro was due to leave the Avonlea to-morrow it seemed unnecessary to attract attention by leaving a day early. They laid their plan with unnecessary elaboration. Crook would have said all women do. Caro was to have a taxi to take her to the station, and at the station she'd get another to take her to Miss Crisp's house.

'Then that's settled. I shall write to my brother that I have a companion. Have you ever noticed—good heavens, is that the time? I have to go to a meeting on Dog Protection.'

'Protection against what?'

'Oh, general interferingness. We have to have it on Sundays because that's the only day our chairwoman can be certain of having the drawing-room to herself. And after all,' she was back at dogs again, 'they're God's creatures as much as we, and who's to say He doesn't like them a lot better?' She called for her bill and went off, her skirt hem a bit uneven, her yellow hair, that clashed with the hat as well as the eyebrows, vivid as a Van Gogh sunflower. At the door she turned and hurried back. 'Forgot you didn't know where I lived,' she said. 'Here's the address.'

And then she really was gone.

CHAPTER FIVE

1

Meantime the police, who unlike the Crooks and Crisps of this world, don't rely on hunches but on evidence and the result of painstaking inquiry, were losing no time. They had a good start, thanks to the two beldames of Devon Road, and the facts they'd twisted out of Con. They traced Caro to the Station Hotel—she wasn't, as Con had realised instantly, a young woman easy to overlook—and they knew one of her first steps would be to disembarrass herself of anything that would point to her identity. In this case, of course, it would be the mackintosh. They inquired at Paddington Station, having wrung a reluctant description from Con of the zipper bag ('Not that that helps much,' Mason observed grimly, 'there can't be more than about two million of them in the country and according to its owner there's nothing individual about this one, and he wouldn't tell us if there were'), but it wasn't there, so it seemed obvious she would shed it a bit farther down the line. They tried the Lost Property Office in case she had taken the line of least resistance and left it on the luggage rack, but they drew a blank here, too. Still, with the forces at their command, it wasn't so immensely to their credit when they found what they were looking for at the Reading Luggage Office.

'Reading was the obvious first stop for someone on the run from Paddington,' Mason observed. 'Possibly the most intelligent thing would be for her to double back to London, but there'd always be the chance of someone recognising her. And then, if she's got any sense at all, only people trying to jump the law haven't as a rule, she'll keep as much distance between her and Gardiner as she can. It seems pretty clear she has no friends in London, or she'd have gone to them sooner than beg a pound from a stranger; she couldn't go abroad without a passport, and hers was in the flat.' She couldn't, in fact, go anywhere far without more money than she possessed, and she hadn't tried to get funds from her London bank. So it followed either that someone was hiding her up or she had contrived to 'raise the wind' on her own account.

Mason recalled the porter's evidence about the ring. If she raised money on that in London it seemed probable that she would repeat the performance wherever she now found herself. A description of the ring was obtained from Mortimer, the jeweller to whom it had been most often entrusted, and this was circulated to all jewellers, with particular attention to those in Reading. And, since both the ring and its owner were distinctive, that brought them pretty soon to Mr. Taylor of Reading.

Mr. Taylor had not so far disposed of the ring. He had put a good price on it, and he was prepared to wait for the right purchaser to turn up; and before that day dawned he learned from the authorities of its previous owner's probable identity and turned it in. It was easy to get Mortimer to identify it, even if there hadn't been a monogram on the inner side—L.M. intertwined, being Aunt Laura's initials—and now the police were a step on, because they knew the name Caro had been using.

'Of course she may have changed it again,'

Mason agreed, but on the whole he thought not. So inquiries went round Reading for a young woman clocking in on the day following the murder in the name of Maxwell.

2

'My dear,' announced Emmy Crisp in enthralled tones, 'they've traced you to Reading. Listen to this. Oh, it's obvious you weren't cut out for a criminal life. Giving your own name. Now if you'd said Dalrymple-Montmorency . . .'

Her little green eyes were bright with excitement. Whoever else was in the red over Toby's death Miss Crisp was having the time of her life. Every morning she came down and dived for the papers—she took four instead of her usual one, and Mason might have said this showed she wasn't really cut out for a criminal existence either, pointing the spotlight on herself in this reckless fashion—and devoured every syllable connected with the Graves case to see how much the situation had changed since the night before. As for the *Daily Fizzer*, she couldn't speak loud enough in its praise. If it could do that on virtually no information at all—words failed her.

'Really, dear Mr. Churchill should make that editor Chancellor of the Exchequer,' she announced, when she had recovered her breath. 'He'd conjure up money from the air.' She put up her skinny little arms and waved her little mole's hands about, catching no end of imaginary bank notes.

'Reading?' exclaimed Caro. 'What does it say?' She came across and took the paper from her benefactress's hand. 'You know, Emmy, it's no use. Sooner or later you'll hear the bell ring and discover a fine fat policeman on your doorstep. This is only putting off the evil day and it's not fair to you.'

'Not fair to me?' Emmy sounded shocked.

'Of course not. If—when—they track me down here, as sooner or later they will, because the police always do, they'll never believe you didn't know who I was.'

'Well, of course I know.' Miss Crisp sounded indignant. 'I daresay my precious brother goes round telling all and sundry I've got a screw loose, but I was very well brought up—too well, seeing the sort of world we're expected to live in nowadays—and I shouldn't dream of taking on a companion of whom I knew nothing. But even the police can hardly expect me to forget what I owe to my upbringing.'

Privately she thought it a shade ungrateful of dearest Caro to look so pale and drawn, and to have such dark lines under her eyes.

'If it was me,' brooded Emmy wistfully, 'I wouldn't mope, I'd get something out of it. But she seems to be losing heart.'

'They're getting warmer,' she informed her guest thirty-six hours later. 'They know you've been in Bath. That sourpuss from the Avonlea told them. Still, all is not lost. Miss Parker told them you left Bath on Monday. They're probably halfway back to London by now.'

'All the same, this can't go on for ever,' argued Caro, who was in one of her desperate moods. 'I can't spend the rest of my life crawling out under cover of darkness, wearing a black veil or an eyeshade . . .'

'My dear, you're not thinking of *leaving* me?' Emmy sounded horrified. 'Take my word for it, the station will be swarming with police, and all the hire-car agencies will have been warned.'

'There's Con,' began Caro, but Emmy swept Con away like a vacuum cleaner dealing with a pencil chip.

'Fiddlesticks! A young man who isn't prepared to put up with a little inconvenience for the sake of the woman he loves—yes, of course he does, dear, there wouldn't be any story if he didn't—isn't worth much. And I daresay he was never happy in that office anyhow.'

'You mean—he's lost his job? On my account?'

'I mean he's severed his connection with his firm. Well, if they can treat a promising young man like that it shows they'd never have treated him right.'

'It was his living. If I had any guts I'd go round to the police this morning, only . . .'

'Only what?'

'Just that I don't want to hang,' finished Caro, simply.

3

The next morning Emmy received a telephone call. Any telephone call was likely to prove a precedent to adventure, she even welcomed wrong numbers.

'Who? Sally? Oh, of course, Sally Wright. Yes, of course I do. What? Well, naturally. Oh dear—rather alarming, though. Still, we can die but once. One o'clock. I'll be there.'

She hung up the receiver and turned to Caro to

say, 'Now, isn't that like life? Always some new interest. That was Sally Wright—well, of course you don't know her—my old friend, Frances Pinnegar, has suddenly appeared in Bath. Something to do with a Nursing Convention she has to address. Address? More likely devour them all. Getting on for 70, Fan, I mean, but the heart of a lion. A lion in a dragon's skin. She got herself kidnapped a year or two ago, she was in all the papers, so enterprising. Anyone else would have died, but not Frances.'

'Is she coming here?' asked Caro, when she could get a word in.

'Oh no, dear. That wouldn't be at all wise. Fan's the soul of rectitude, she'd probably think it her duty to get in touch.'

'With the police?'

'I fear so. Anyway, you oughtn't to put temptation in anyone's path, ought you? Now, Caro dearest, don't look like that. You haven't put the smallest temptation in my path. I wouldn't help the police in any circumstances. In fact, you've been a perfect godsend. I was getting quite old and set, and you've positively rejuvenated me.'

The odd thing was it was quite true. Emmy looked smarter and more alert than she'd done for years.

'But that's our danger these days. After all, what's a grave but a rut, and why go into your grave before you need? I'm sure we shall stay there long enough. Now you've jerked me out of my rut and I shall always be grateful to you. I daresay getting kidnapped jerked Frances out of her rut, too. You can't help being grateful to Providence—people don't really take much interest in us old girls—so when they do you feel, well, rather as if it were a feather in your cap.'

'Me being your feather?' suggested Caro, unsmiling.

'I'm afraid you're feeling the lack of fresh air,' said Emmy regretfully. 'It must be very tiresome for you being cooped up like this. The only thing is a cell would be even more restricted. And you mustn't lose hope, my dear. Why, salvation may be just around the corner. That's what makes life so interesting. I can never understand why people get so tired of it they want to throw it away. It's the unexpectedness of things—like meeting you at the Seven Sisters. Just like Frances opening her door—she lives in a very respectable block of flats in South Kensington—and finding the wolf on the threshold. Now, my dear, I'm going out to lunch. There's half a pound of pork sausages in the refrigerator, the best kind, and some potatoes and—if I'm back a bit late don't worry. Fan and I may get together. We old girls are dreadful like that. I was always so sorry for Mrs. Noah in the Ark—so early in history there was really nothing to talk about. I haven't seen Frances for years . . .' She chattered her way round the daily duties. 'So lucky Mrs. Jones broke her leg last week, though I didn't think so at the time, tiresome creature, I thought. I've none of the womanly virtues, my dear, can't see any romance in a duster or one of these dear little washing-up mops—but really it was a blessing in disguise. These women do *talk* so. Really, when she's here I can hardly get a word in edgewise.'

'And of course,' admitted Caro, 'it does help to pass the time—chores, I mean.'

In fact she was doing more housework now than she'd ever done in her life. Toby would have been staggered to see her polishing furniture and scattering Vim in the sink.

Miss Crisp went off about 12.30. 'See you at tea, I expect,' she said, 'unless Fan wants me to go back with her. I'd bring her here, nice company for you, but perhaps it would be a mistake.'

'I daresay she doesn't mix much with the criminal classes,' offered Caro.

'Oh, my dear, that's all you know. She spent most of her life somewhere in Dockland and they had some amazing adventures there. And then the war! Oh, you can't say Frances has lived a sheltered life exactly, but—well, it's just as well to play safe, don't you think? I mean, she really has a respect for the police, wouldn't think she ought to deceive them . . .'

All of which went to show how little Emmy knew Miss Pinnegar.

Emmy hurried into her bedroom, tying on a tulle scarf, probably the last of its kind in England if not the world, jamming an amazing jet-headed hatpin into the upturned bird's-nest she stuck on her head, draping herself with an amber chain and snapping a bracelet of coloured stones round one wrist. 'There, do I look grand enough? I always think it's a compliment to your hostess to put on your *best* things . . .'

When she had gone the house seemed very quiet and empty. The sun had gone in, too, and the sky was a uniform grey. Caro dusted the dining-room and replaced the postcard of Jane Avril by Toulouse-Lautrec that Emmy had once bought at an exhibition and kept in full view—'An awful warning, dear,' she explained. 'One might so easily get to look like that oneself. Yes, I daresay he thought a lot of her, but we know artists are odd and French artists . . .' and up went her little hands. The dining-room done, it was time for lunch but Caro couldn't face the four beaming pink sausages on their white shelf. She found some biscuits and cheese and ate them, walking absently round the house, shedding crumbs everywhere. She washed up, taking as much time as possible, and wandered back to the living-room. She felt as though she had lived in Bath for years. What would it be like, she wondered, to sit once more in the window at Charbonnel's drinking chocolate and smoking a Turkish cigarette, watching the busy Bond Street traffic passing under the window, seeing the new hats, hearing snatches of conversation? Or window-shopping at Aspery's or Finnegan's? She thought of turning into the big travel association headquarters in Berkeley Square, collecting the coloured leaflets, staring at the huge posters on the walls—Come to Dalmatia—Find summer in winter in Sunny Spain—Visit the Austrian Tyrol. Funny, she thought, leaning her forehead against the glass, how cows in an English meadow are just cows but cows in the Tyrol or a Swiss upland are romance. She remembered a day before her marriage, walking up a slope above Wengen, stopping at a shed and getting a glass of milk warm from the udder. It seemed like another world.

4

Miss Parker of Avonlea Private Hotel clapped on her best hat and hurried out. They were having an auction sale at The Grey House and she had marked down some china and a carpet that would be uncommonly useful. She hoped she was in time to bid. The street seemed very empty, positively nobody about. She turned her head and saw someone standing at the window of a house, looking vacantly out. Miss Parker's heart gave a great leap. There was no mistaking that face. So the deceitful creature hadn't left Bath, after all. Poor Miss Parker! She was on the horns of a dilemma. Conscience (and inclination) said, 'Let the auction rip. Go to the police at once.' Common-sense said, 'An hour won't make any difference, and you do want that carpet. She doesn't know you've seen her.' Common-sense won. Miss Parker, having quickly noted the number of the house, hurried on. She wouldn't stop a single minute after the carpet and the china had been bought. Poor woman—she meant Emmy, whose name wasn't then nearly as well known as it was going to be in the next few days—fancy having a murderess under your roof unbeknownst!

But Caro had seen her, realised immediately that she had been recognised and supposed that Miss Parker was making tracks for the police station instanter.

'Here we go,' thought Caro, and in a way it was quite a relief. At all events, it broke the monotony, and much more of this underground existence would have driven her to the police herself.

5

Emmy meantime was enjoying herself immensely. Her hostess was one of those fortunate women who have a perfect cook who really enjoys visitors. Lunch was a dream, and it wouldn't have occurred to Sally Wright not to have wine with her meals. She even has it when she's alone, Emmy reminded herself reverently. Her other guest was a tall thin old woman, with the face of an ancient horse, but a Derby winner in her time, Crook had reflected at their first meeting. Her clothes were as old as Emmy's, but less eccentric. Emmy found herself wondering if dear Fan had bought anything since the outbreak of the second war. They were a mossy green with a brown fleck and really looked as though they'd grown on her, as bark grows on a tree. But the eyes were as keen, the mouth as dauntless, as when Frances Pinnegar went to combat suffering and misery in the Docks nearly fifty years ago.

It was Sally who brought up the case of the missing Miss Maxwell. 'Or Mrs. Graves I suppose I ought to say. I do wonder where she is. It must be horrid to think everyone's after you. I do hope she's got some friends. She seems to have had so much bad luck. But I suppose the police will get her in the end.'

Miss Pinnegar, with one of her sub-acid smiles, said, 'There are times when you're quite pleased to see the police. I know I was that day in Brighton,' and Emmy chipped in, 'Ah, but, Fan, you hadn't killed your husband. That makes all the difference.'

'We don't know that she did,' exclaimed Sally.

'Well, no, we don't, but you'd need to be very strong-minded not to kill a husband like that, I should think. He really was a most horrid person.'

Miss Pinnegar sent her a queer look and deliberately changed the subject. Emmy went a little pink. She'd been indiscreet again. Of course, Fan would naturally be on the side of law and order.

'I don't believe she ever left Bath,' contributed Sally, bypassing Miss Pinnegar's tactful efforts. 'That would be the best plan, I'm sure. Let them think you've gone. It really would be very funny if she were just round the corner, wouldn't it?' She chuckled. 'Perhaps Emmy's hiding her up,' she suggested. 'We all know she'd do anything to annoy the police.'

Emmy felt very cross. Sally shouldn't give you shocks like that, it was enough to bring on a heart-attack. But Miss Pinnegar, true to type, saved the day.

'It's by no means easy to hide nowadays,' she said, severely. 'Even if you changed your name and looked for employment, you'd be asked for your National Health Card to say nothing of your ration book.'

'They think of everything to make life difficult, don't they?' agreed the rebellious Emmy. 'It doesn't give fugitives a chance.'

'One really wonders if her best plan wouldn't be to reveal her whereabouts,' Miss Pinnegar went on. 'She needs an alternative criminal, and how is she going to provide one if she continues to remain hidden? Unless, of course, that young Mr. Gardiner is at work in what might be called the underground movement.'

That was a new idea to Emmy. 'I wonder if he is. But—how would he set about it?'

Miss Pinnegar's long old mouth looked a little scornful. 'My dear Emmy, people achieve what they wish to achieve. If he really has any strong feeling for this young woman there is nothing to prevent his setting the wheels in motion.'

Then the maid came in with a heavenly French pancake and the subject was really changed this time, and none too soon, thought Emmy. Fan would get through my defences if she kept on long enough. Coffee—and what coffee—was served in the charming drawing-room looking over the garden.

'It's like being back in the days of Jane Austen, being with you, Sally,' Miss Crisp sighed. 'Don't you envy her, Fan?'

But Miss Pinnegar had never envied anybody.

It was after three o'clock when the party broke up.

'Do you come my way?' Frances asked, as they stood in the hall, wearing their ancient ulsters, for there was a brisk spring wind in spite of the sun that was trying hard to break through the clouds.

Emmy rather hoped not. Frances was too like a human gimlet to be comfortable company to someone with a guilty secret. But they set out together and Emmy began to gabble admiration of their hostess's way of living.

'My dear Emmy, if you wish to live in a cotton-wool environment I have do doubt Sally's is ideal. Personally, I am not an invalid.'

'Oh, you're wonderful, Fan. I suppose that's why things always happen to you. I should probably have died if I'd been kidnapped.'

'I should have died if it hadn't been for Mr. Crook. A most remarkable personality. You should try to meet him some time. Such a hard worker, Emily. If he isn't to be found in his office in 123 Bloomsbury Street you can always be sure he's prepared to receive visitors at any hour—*any hour*—in his flat in Brandon Street, just round the corner from Earl's Court Station, the house with the china cow in the window. And you'd have so much in common. You both like to—er—wipe the police's eye, as I have heard him put it. Such a pity Mrs. Graves didn't know of him. So much more sensible to have him working for her than wasting all this time lying hidden in a cellar somewhere. He'd find an alternative to put in the dock in no time.'

'If—that is to say, assuming there is one,' murmured Emmy, who had her doubts.

'Of course there'd be one, if Mr. Crook had the case in hand. I only work for the innocent is his motto. Didn't I hear that this young Mr. Gardiner is a lawyer?'

'Yes. Yes, he is, only he seems to have lost his job through this.'

'Temporarily suspended,' said Miss Pinnegar, firmly. 'No more. You mustn't believe everything you read in the papers, Emmy. You're so impulsive, but there's a text Miss Barclay used to drill into us at school. Surely you remember. "He that putteth his hand to the plough"—you know the one. Naturally it makes things more complicated if you're trying to plough a stony field, but one should think of that before one takes the plough out. It seems a little—chicken-hearted—to desist because it may do the plough a little harm.'

They turned a corner. Emmy's brain was whirling. 'Let me see,' murmured Miss Pinnegar, 'I think our ways part here.' There was a sign-post, To The Station. 'Your road, I believe,' said Frances.

Emmy began to say: No, it wasn't. She lived . . .

'Dear me, how stupid! I quite thought . . .'

Emmy nearly fell down with shock. Who'd have thought it?—Of Fanny, that pillar of rectitude. Oh well, Miss Crisp had never been very good at sums, it took her a long time to get the right answer.

'I'm the stupid one,' she acknowledged. 'Losing my wits altogether, I'm afraid. Of course you're right, Fan. And I ought to hurry, oughtn't I? Quite a long way when you come to think of it. Shall I—shall I give Mr. Crook your love?'

Something like a frozen smile dawned on the long horse-face.

'As I said, Emmy, always so impulsive.' She held out a hand in a woollen glove. 'He was a horrid young man, wasn't he?' she added. 'Take care of yourself, my dear. Don't dash under the traffic. Remember, no man liveth to himself alone, and of course no woman either.'

And then she was gone, marching off like an old Grenadier, her flat pancake of a hat on her grey bun of hair, her umbrella, with its gilt duck's-head handle (because dear Fan suffered from arthritis a bit these days), acting as a support, never looking round . . . You couldn't, reflected Emmy, with a suppressed giggle, help feeling a bit sorry for any plough those capable hands guided. They'd drive it up the side of a house or down a precipice.

'But I do wonder,' thought Emmy, rushing across the road and being missed by a car by inches, 'how she *guessed*! I'm sure *I* never said anything to give it away.'

6

Con Gardiner was preparing to go out to dinner. He didn't go to the Live and Let Live any more, he attracted too much attention, but went to a different place each night where he wasn't known. He was wondering which of them to sample when the bell of his flat began to whirr and went on whirring as though the button had stuck.

'Who on earth?' he wondered, releasing the automatic catch. 'The police?' He wasn't much troubled with other company these days.

But when he heard the feet that came scurrying up the stairs he knew they never belonged to the force. Another woman in trouble wanting his help, he thought ironically, never dreaming that he was right. He opened the door of his room and an odd little creature looking like last year's Christmas tree virtually fell into his arms.

'I'm afraid,' he began, meaning to say, 'I'm afraid you've come to the wrong address,' but she broke out at once, 'Oh nonsense, there's no time for that. You and I are the only friends she has—you can't count Fan—we can't afford to be afraid. And anyway, what are you afraid of? The police? Nonsense, they're only men like you and me (the absurdity of that statement didn't appear to strike her) and out of their uniforms they can look remarkably silly. I know. I met a plain-clothes man once. I was so nervous in case you mightn't *be* here still, and I didn't dare take a taxi, in case I was being followed.'

Con, having no more idea than the man in the

moon what was going on, produced a bottle of sherry and poured out two glasses.

'Do have something to drink, Miss . . .'

'Crisp. Emmy Crisp. Dear me, I am going it. Wine for lunch and now sherry with a young man. You are Con Gardiner, aren't you? Of course you are. Dear Caro's told me so much about you.'

'Caro!' The glass tilted and the sherry spilt over his thumb and down his wrist. 'You mean you know where she is?'

'Yes, of course. But I don't think I'll tell you, because if the police come asking questions, and applied the thumb-screw, and I wouldn't put anything past them . . . you see?' She sipped her sherry and began to explain the situation. 'It's obvious that we ought to have some theory to set up against the official one. That's what Fan made me see. (He hadn't the ghost of an idea who Fan was.) The police are sure to think she killed her husband, and of course her disappearing like this will increase their conviction. Now, if we mean to show she didn't, because somebody else did, and if she didn't someone else must, mustn't they, there's no time to be lost.'

What price the nut-house? thought Con privately, but aloud he said of course Caro must be legally represented.

'I don't know if she has a solicitor . . .'

'It wouldn't matter if she had half-a-dozen, there's only one man who can really help us. His name is Crook. I thought we might go and see him to-night. I'd have gone there straight away, only you are involved in this and I didn't want to seem to go right over your head, and then being a lawyer yourself you might know him personally, and though I have a sort of introduction from Fan . . .'

He managed to insert a few words. 'Of course I know who he is. Everyone does. Everyone in the legal world, that is, (including those who thought he ought to be struck off the Law List, he added silently) and most people in the underworld. He's a bit unorthodox, you know.'

'Of course I know. That's why we must have him. Orthodox ones wouldn't be any use to us at this stage. I wonder what time he has dinner.'

'Dinner?'

'I thought we might go round straight away . . .'

'I really think it would be better . . .' began Con, appalled at this precipitancy. Lawyers don't like being rushed, any more than dowagers do.

'Nonsense. I must go back this evening or Caro will be all alone, and she's been alone practically all day. I don't mean she'd do anything desperate, of course, but she is my guest, so I do feel responsible, and there's no getting away from it, she is becoming a little low-spirited. She might do something foolish.'

'You don't think she'd try and put an end to things?' Con's heart contracted.

'Oh, not in the way you mean, but she might go to the police, because she thought she was putting too much responsibility on my shoulders. Dear Caro, she'll never understand the police wouldn't be in the least grateful to her for saving them trouble. Gratitude's a word you'll never find in a policeman's dictionary.'

'Crook's address,' Con began, but once again she swamped him.

'I have it here, Earl's Court, the house with the

cow in the window, so convenient, and he's sure to be back by now. If not, of course we must go to Bloomsbury Street. No, no, we won't telephone. I've always found that if you're on the spot people find it's quicker to do what you want than go on arguing about why they can't. And if you let people know you're coming you give them a chance of going out and forgetting to come back. Now then, what are we waiting for?'

'I feel as though I'd been run down by a tank,' said Con, frankly. 'You do realise, I suppose, that Crook's regarded as something of a rogue elephant by the profession? He's known to undertake any case that attracts his fancy and not to pay too much attention to the evidence.'

'We've been over all that,' snapped Emmy impatiently. 'Too many lawyers worry about kudos or their own precious consciences and nonsense of that kind. We don't want a man who wastes a lot of time weighing up the evidence and perhaps having doubts. We're not paying good money—oh, I forgot to say it doesn't matter about expenses, and you can't expect that sort of man to be cheap, but I've quite a lot of my legacy left, and I can't think of any better way of spending it, and even if it takes it all, well, what are we paying taxes and insurance for, except to enjoy the benefits? I daresay one would get quite a lot of pleasure out of life in an Eventide Home. You know what they say, life is what you make it.'

She'd make it a riot in any circumstances, Con reflected. It was odd, seeing the difference in their age, build and appearance (experience, too, come to that) but she reminded him irresistibly of Caro.

'I agree with Mr. Mell, no time like the present,' Emmy continued as a dazed Con found himself walking with her towards Earl's Court. 'But I suppose you young people don't read Dickens any more. All this television. And don't go on saying we ought to have telephoned. Never give people a chance of refusing you. A lot of men must have taken that to heart when I was a girl. I never had the chance of refusing even one, and though I never actually wanted to be married it's nice when you're older to be able to say you had the opportunity. Though, come to that, I daresay no one would believe me.'

Con suggested taking a taxi but Emmy wouldn't hear of it.

Another witness against us, she said.

Con didn't attempt to sort that one out.

'Dear me, life gets more and more interesting as you get older. Mine really was very blameless and boring when I was a girl. But now—with a suspected murderess lying hidden up in my house, and me coming up secretly to London and going to see a—a rogue elephant lawyer—with a young man I never met before to-night—oh, I wouldn't call the King my cousin.'

CHAPTER SIX

1

Crook was drinking beer and laying a plan of campaign for a man who had escaped more prison sentences than anyone living when his bell rang and feet came up the uncarpeted stairs. He flung open the door and went out on the landing to greet his visitors, a big red-headed man with brows like a hedge and a face as square as a box, and an eye so bright and beaming you could have lighted a candle at it, even at that hour of the night.

'Welcome to Castle Dangerous,' he said. 'Who is it?'

Emmy Crisp never gave Con a chance. She broke into a spate of words out of which Crook managed to dredge three or four.

'My friend, Miss Pinnegar . . .' and he threw up his hands, crying, 'Don't tell me she's on the rampage again. Once was a privilege, but a second instalment would turn even my hair grey.'

'Of course not,' said Emmy. 'It's Mrs. Graves. You must have read about her. Dear me, what a charming flat. So unfussy.'

Crook beamed; she couldn't have said anything to please him more. He began to expatiate on its virtues. Con quite simply thought they both had a screw loose. But it wasn't long before they got down to brass tacks. Miss Crisp told her story, with emendations, and Crook observed in a reverent voice, 'The day we have women judges it'll be good-bye to justice.'

'I'm not interested in justice,' stormed Emmy. 'I want you to get Caro off. I'm sure if she did hit her husband over the head he fully deserved it, but as that sort of reasonable argument doesn't go down in a court of law you must show that she didn't.'

'I see,' beamed Crook. 'As simple as that. Well, then, let's consider alternatives.'

'I told you he wouldn't waste time.' Emmy turned on the speechless Con. 'Yes, let's see who's most likely, and then get up a case against them.'

'I can see you and me talk the same language,' approved Crook. 'Now, let's put our cards on the table and see what sort of a pattern they make. Yes, I know the police have done that already, only our pattern 'ull be different, see?'

Con murmured grimly, 'And how!'

* * *

'Ever hear tell of the Israelites?' asked Crook a little later.

Both his companions stared at him.

'Set to make bricks without straw,' Crook amplified. 'Well, take it from me, they had a kid's job compared with us. Why, do you realise that apart from dear Toby's death we haven't got a fact between us?'

He had astonished them by his intimate grasp of the situation, before he had any notion that he might be involved, but this statement brought a cry of indignation from Emmy Crisp.

'We've got heaps. We know Caro marched out of the flat at six-thirty, and we know Toby was having a row with somebody at seven-fifteen, and we know he rang up the Hat and Feather at half-past and someone rang the police just before eight, giving a false address—I should have thought that was enough to be going on with.'

'Facts,' said Crook patiently, 'are things that can be sustained by proof. We can't prove any of those things you've just said, barring the last. They're statements—but if I said I was the Shah of Persia it wouldn't make me the Shah of Persia. Take that first statement, about Mrs. Graves walking out of the flat at six-thirty. Anyone see her go?'

Con was looking troubled. 'No. If they had she'd be all right.'

'I wouldn't go as far as that because she could have walked back again. She hasn't got any alibi between six-thirty and the time she met you, which is roughly two hours. I just walked about. Well, I've heard worse.'

'That's what I like about you,' beamed Emmy. 'You're like me, an optimist.'

'Should have been under the daisies long ago if I wasn't,' Crook assured her. 'Oh yes, she might have said she'd gone to the pictures, that's a favourite one, that 'ud have put her in Queer Street right away. Because if she hadn't got any money, how did she pay for her ticket?'

'I should never thought of that,' acknowledged Emmy.

'Lots of chaps don't. They try swinging it, and in the end, of course, they do the swinging. Well, that's Point One. Point Two. Price says he heard dear Toby shooting his mouth off to some buddy, but d'you think any jury's going to buy that one? Suppose it suited Price to have heard him? Or suppose X had done his little job and heard Price coming down the stairs, all he's got to do is fake a dude accent—chaps see what they expect to see and hear what they expect to hear. Mind you, I don't say Price isn't on the level. I just say I don't know. No proof, see?'

'That brings us to Mrs. Bates's story,' said Emmy excitedly. She had the whole of the evidence by heart, Con realised. 'Now there can't be any motive for her to invent the telephone call, can there?'

'Not that we know of,' agreed Crook cautiously, 'but then our trouble is we don't know much. Still, no more does she. A chap rings up and says he's Toby Graves—but I could ring up, you could ring up,' he butted his big red head in Con's direction, 'and say we were Toby Graves—or could have done a week ago—and—well, we ain't got T.V. on the telephone yet . . .'

'You mean,' unconsciously Emmy's little hands were clasped in a quite theatrical gesture, 'it might have been the murderer telephoning. Well, wouldn't that prove it wasn't Caro? Mrs. Bates said a *man* rang up.'

Crook didn't look convinced. 'Not having met Mrs. G. I couldn't say, but some of these dames with deep voices can swing it. And then if someone rings you up when you're doing the work of two people and says, "I'm Toby Graves," and she knows Lessing's waiting for Graves, it ain't likely she's going to stop and ask herself if it really was Toby Graves on the wire. For one thing, voices often sound a bit different on the air, and for another she's got no reason to suspect everything ain't hunkydory.'

'It would mean that whoever was telephoning knew of the arrangement between Lessing and Graves,' put in Con in thoughtful tones. 'That should narrow the field.'

Crook groaned. 'My dear chap, use your loaf. You're Toby Graves, X is beating up for a storm, you say, "Well, that's how it seems to you, I daresay, very interesting and all that, but sorry I can't stay, I'm meeting a chap called Lessing at the Hat and Feather."'

'Or, of course,' Emmy's voice rang with triumph, 'he might simply say he had an engagement—Toby, I mean—and X says, "Well, ring through and say you can't make it." He might be in a position to make Toby take his orders.'

'We-ell,' said Crook judiciously, 'I don't think that's the way of it.'

And he told them why.

* * *

He said there was nothing more to be done until Caro really was under arrest, and, 'Don't count on the police doing the obvious, because every now and again they do something quite different just to fool you'; in the meantime he'd put Bill on the trail to discover the nature of the tie-up between Lessing and the dead man, and added that when it came to dealing with headaches the chaps who invented aspirin hadn't got a thing on Bill Parsons. Then he insisted on running Emmy to the station in his famous (infamous, said the purists) little red car, the Scourge, and she delighted him afresh by admiring her whole-heartedly.

'So original,' she cooed. 'And such a nice cheerful colour for Coronation Year.'

'Oh, she don't need a coronation to set her off,' replied Crook, looking at her affectionately. 'She flies the red flag all the time.'

2

It was quite late when Emmy returned to Bath; she wouldn't take a taxi from the station in case 'They' were watching, disguised as a couple of lamp-posts. But all her diplomacy was thrown away, because on her arrival at her house she found 'Them' on the doorstep. The police were represented by a man in plain dark clothes, looking remarkably like everyone else. As she put her hand on the gate this man seemed to bob out of the ground at her side, causing her to exclaim, 'Who on earth do you think you are? Nellie Wallace?' She was fumbling for her latch-key, remembering not to ring the bell since the house was officially empty, and noting with satisfaction that Caro had had the sense not to show a light.

'Miss Crisp?'

'Well?'

He produced a card. 'I'm Inspector Bennett.'

'Oh, a policeman. I might have known.' Her heart jumped into her mouth, almost suffocating her. 'What can I do for you? How many laws have I broken now?'

The inspector said quite pleasantly, 'I couldn't say, I'm sure. I began to think you weren't coming back,' he added.

'Well, my goodness,' exploded Emmy, standing there with the key in her hand, 'whatever next? It's news to me there's a law about what time a person can come back to her own house. Or did you pass a curfew when nobody was noticing?'

'That's all right,' soothed the inspector. 'Don't let me keep you standing. But if you could spare me a few minutes . . .'

'What does it matter if I say I can't? You'll walk straight in.'

'Oh, no, we aren't allowed to do that, not without a warrant, and I haven't got one. We have to wait till you give us the word.'

Emmy looked for a moment as if she were going to refuse to give it, then sensibly realised he'd simply beetle back to the station and get a warrant, because she hadn't a doubt she had to thank Caro for his visitation, so she fitted her key into the lock and opened the door on to a darkened hall. At least, she thought with a breath of relief, Caro had had the good sense not to leave the hall light on.

'It's rather late to be collecting for the Police Orphanage,' she observed jauntily, to show that she hadn't a thing on her mind, not a thing, 'but I suppose inspectors leave that sort of thing to police constables. Oh come in, come in. What are you waiting for?'

Bennett stepped over the threshold. Emmy snapped on the light in the living-room.

'I can't offer you anything to drink,' she explained. 'I don't keep anything.'

'I shouldn't be drinking on duty in any case,' he said, taking off his bowler hat. Emmy looked wildly round. At any minute, she supposed, Caro would come charging down the stairs. But there was no sign of her, only some letters that had come in the afternoon post. Emmy glanced at them. A letter from Amy Martin, a picture postcard of Jane Avril, two circulars. She threw them back. Amy could wait till the morning; her letters always read like five-finger exercises, anyway.

'Come in, Inspector.' Emmy raised her voice so that she could have been heard all over the house. 'I can't imagine what a police officer can want with me at this hour of the night. Or have you come to tell me that someone's broken in while I was away?' She looked about her more wildly than ever. 'Not that I'm used to late visitors,' she chattered on, without waiting for any reply to her question. 'I'm an early bird. Only I've been seeing an old friend and we've been gossiping. You know how it is.'

The inspector said politely, 'Yes, indeed,' and they went into the living-room. Emmy's eyes had to do the work of four, looking in every direction at once.

Caro would be sure to have left some trace of her presence. Still, whatever it was, Emmy could say it was hers and how could a bevy of inspectors prove anything different?

'Well?' She threw off her hat, 'to what do I owe the honour, etc?'

'I expect you know as well as I do,' said her companion, still good-humoured, still cool. 'We have received information that Mrs. Graves was seen here this afternoon.'

'And I was out,' mourned Emmy, swiftly. 'It has happened and I was not there. That's a quotation, but nobody recognises a quotation these days.'

'I don't think she came while you were out, Miss Crisp. I think she's been here for some time.'

'Disguised as a coal scuttle perhaps. Well, they say the person concerned is always the last to know.' She felt like that frantic creature, the hen lapwing, dashing desperately up and down, trying to deflect the attention of possible marauders of the nest.

'She was seen at the window by Miss Parker. She has no doubt at all of her identity.'

Poor silly Caro, thought Emmy. 'She must have mistaken the number of the house,' she said aloud.

'I don't think so. Miss Crisp, you don't need me to tell you that concealing a person wanted by the authorities will make serious trouble for you . . .'

'If I'd wanted to avoid trouble all my life I'd have been a still-born child,' retorted Emmy, scornfully. Could Caro realise what was going on? And hide—somewhere? Get out on the roof through the trapdoor? Oh, but you could rely on the police to have a helicopter floating just above the house for precisely such an emergency. 'Well,' she continued in the same defiant voice, 'you can see for yourself she's not here.'

'I should like your permission to see the rest of the house.'

Emmy stood up. It was no good, but oh what luck that she'd seen Mr. Crook already. Most likely they'd have tried to prevent that. (They wouldn't, of course, but Emmy, like Crook, never even tried to be fair in this connection.) They went patiently from room to room, Emmy still chattering away at the top of her voice. No one in the dining-room, no one in the kitchen, no one in the scullery or the coal-cellar. No sign that anyone had lunched here, every plate washed and put away, every cup on its appropriate hook. The inspector laid a casual hand on the tea-kettle, but it was as cold as his own heart. Upstairs she flung open the doors one after the other, bathroom, box-room, her own bedroom.

'And that door?' said the inspector.

'That's the spare-room.' She rattled the handle. 'Perhaps it's locked. I haven't used it for so long . . .'

'The key's on the outside,' the inspector pointed out.

She juggled hurriedly with the key. 'That's it.' No one here either, blankets neatly folded under the coverlet, eiderdown on a chair. Emmy dropped on her knees. The inspector looked startled.

'Looking under the bed,' she explained. 'Electric fire here, so she can't be up the chimney. There's the wardrobe, of course.' She ran across and flung the door wide. The empty hangers swayed in ghostly fashion. Nothing else there at all. The inspector had raised the counterpane, was poking about among the blankets. 'You couldn't hide the smallest body there,' exclaimed Emmy, puzzled. Then she realised he was looking for the bedlinen. Now where had Caro put that? She looked round. There was a laundry basket in the corner and the inspector lifted the lid. But like the wardrobe it was empty. No trace of powder on the dressing-table, no tell-tale pad of cotton-wool in the basket, nothing. Clever Caro! Of course she'd seen Miss Parker, had known the game was up, and somehow she'd managed to get away before the police arrived. Gone out by the back door into the lane and escaped that way, no doubt. On the top landing the Inspector paused.

'That's a trapdoor.'

'So it is. It only leads to a loft, though, and the cistern.'

'How do you get up there?'

'There's a folding ladder. You know the sort of thing.'

She watched the ladder's descent and all the time something flickered in the back of her mind. Somewhere since her return she'd seen a clue, but she couldn't identify it. Caro had left a message but—what? If she didn't discover it soon Bennett might get there first. She watched the man climbing out of sight, her heart almost suffocating her. If Caro was there . . . Where, oh where was the message? Suddenly a light clicked on in her mind. Now she was hurrying down the stairs as though a wolf pursued her. Oh let him break his neck on the ladder, she pleaded. Let me get there first. She dashed into the hall and snatched up the letters. Of course. The picture of Jane Avril. She left the three envelopes and disappeared into the downstairs cloak-room. A few lines had been hastily pencilled on the back of the postcard.

I'm going, Emmy. Miss P. saw me at the window. Can't leave any address. Thank you a million times. Don't get further involved. Will get in touch as soon as it's safe. Bedlinen in clean linen cupboard.

She tore the card into minute fragments and flushed them away.

The inspector was waiting when she came back to the hall.

'You shouldn't have done that, Miss Crisp.'

'Well, really!' She turned pink. 'What will the police try and stop us doing next?'

He said, nodding towards the envelopes, 'There was a postcard there.'

'Was there? I really hadn't time to see.'

'And it's not there now.'

'I shall have to pay a little visit to my oculist,' muttered Emmy. 'So convenient this National Health. Otherwise I should have to queue up at an eye hospital, and that takes simply hours. Did you ever—but I expect being a civil servant you get preferential treatment.'

'Those letters must have come by the afternoon post.'

'Did they? I expect so.'

'And you went out to lunch?'

'Oh dear! More regulations?'

'So someone must have picked them off the mat and put them on the table?'

'Oh, I just dashed in after lunch to pick up a scarf.' She twirled the tulle rag at him. 'I didn't stop to look at the post. It didn't seem very interesting.'

'You will be asked to give evidence on oath in due course,' Bennett warned her. 'False statements

131

constitute perjury. It would be better for you to make a clean breast of it.'

Emmy stuck out her hand. 'Hold lighted matches under my finger-nails,' she suggested. 'I still shan't be able to tell you anything different.'

He looked as if he thought she were mad. Suppose she could persuade anyone she was—would that help?

'If you take my advice, Miss Crisp, you'll consult a lawyer, and if you're wise you'll tell him the truth. And if you think we can't prove that Mrs. Graves has been here you under-estimate us.' He looked round. 'Where did I put my hat?'

'You don't mean you're going?' Emmy's surprise was quite genuine this time.

'There doesn't seem much point in staying any longer to-night.'

'Say au revoir but not good-bye. I understand. Will it be all right for me to lock up now, or will anybody else be calling?'

But though she put a brave face on it inside she was ice-cold. 'This is it,' she was saying. She locked the front door and put on the chain, shut and bolted all the windows and drew the curtains. The house that had always seemed so cosy and welcoming was bleak to-night; she opened the door of the guest-room but it was as chill as a grave.

'Caro's spoilt me for living alone,' she thought. She couldn't settle, couldn't sleep, didn't dare use the telephone, not only because of the lateness of the hour, but because most likely the police would be listening. In fact, after a little, she removed the receiver. It wasn't likely Crook or Con would ring her up during the next few hours but there was no sense taking more chances than you must. She went dispiritedly into the kitchen and boiled some milk. Bringing it back she remembered she hadn't opened Amy's letter. It would be as dull as tombs but it was the next best thing to talking to someone. But when she reached the hall table her heart seemed to fall right through her body. It was like going down in a very quick lift. Because though Amy's letter was still there, both the circulars had disappeared.

3

'They always forget something,' remarked the inspector to his subordinate, throwing down a couple of cheap manila envelopes. 'That girl thought of a good deal, even remembered to hide the linen she'd used, but she forgot about finger-prints. Mind you, I could probably get a dozen from the room she's been using, but this is simpler. I suppose it's second nature to pick up the post when you see it on the mat—old lady doesn't sport a letter-box. Have these tested for prints and then have 'em checked with the prints in Graves's flat. If there aren't some common to both I'm a Dutchman, and though I've been called a lot of things in my time I've never been called that before.'

Emmy had a sleepless night, tossing and turning and wondering how best she could help Caro. But as it happened it was all a waste of effort, because when she opened her paper next morning she saw the flaring headline:

MRS. GRAVES FOUND IN LONDON.

CHAPTER SEVEN

1

After all, Inspector Bennett could have saved himself his trouble, because by the time he was putting Emmy through it Caro was already in safe custody. Miss Parker's desire for the carpet, that went to a more lavish bidder, had given her that margin of time that saved her from the final humiliation of being hauled out of her hiding-place as a fox is dug out of his earth by terriers. Working faster than she had ever done in her life she had slipped out of the house by the back door, bought a ticket for London and was in the train before Miss Parker left the auction rooms. She wanted desperately to see Con, but feeling she had already done him harm enough, she went by underground to Notting Hill Gate and marched into the nearest police station. A constable was on duty, who glanced up and said in a strong Scots voice, 'Yes, ma'am?'

Caro announced her identity. 'I think you want to see me.' Her voice sounded dry and unnatural.

'Mrs. Graves, now? Did we write or would it be . . . ?'

'Don't you read the papers?' demanded Caro, feeling this was anti-climax indeed.

The Scotsman's tawny brows lifted. 'Oh aye, that Mrs. Graves. Take a seat, ma'am . . .' It was less tense than a visit to the dentist. But things warmed up all right when Mason appeared. Before she could speak he told her she need answer no questions and make no statement until she had consulted her lawyer, and indeed he strongly advised her not to do so.

'Lawyer?' repeated Caro. 'There's Mr. Gardiner . . .'

Mason shook his head. 'He's going to be a witness. He can't act for you . . .'

'I never thought he could, but he might recommend someone—that is, if there are any philanthropists among the profession.'

'You can be allotted a lawyer if you're unable to pay for one yourself.'

'They think of everything, don't they? As a matter of fact, I don't see what use a lawyer would be at this stage. You haven't actually accused me of my husband's murder yet, have you?'

'We can't do that without a statement—or at least a refusal on your part to make one.'

'Well, I'm ready. Yes, I realise I've been cautioned, you're doing everything according to Cocker. And I've had enough of this hanging about. Anyway, I didn't kill Toby, he was perfectly well and waving the gun at me in the most energetic way when I bounced out . . .'

'Did you think he would use it?' inquired Mason, woodenly.

'He never had before. No, I wasn't really nervous. It was just one of his ham acts.'

'Did you know it wasn't loaded?'

'How should I? I never handled it in my life; and I don't know anything about firearms. I was too young for the A.T.S.'

'They didn't arm the A.T.S., they weren't combatant troops,' Mason told her dryly. 'Well, Mrs. Graves, you didn't believe you were in any danger from the weapon?'

'I wouldn't go as far as that, because you never could tell with Toby. He was so—unpredictable.'

'But you knew on Friday night you were in no danger, because, in fact, the weapon was in the safe.'

'In the safe? You mean, that's where you found it?' She threw back her head and, to his amazement, began to laugh. 'Don't you see, that lets me out? Dead men can't return weapons to safes . . .'

'There hasn't been any suggestion yet that that is what happened,' said Mason. 'It's suggested that there was no sign of the gun when you left the flat.'

'You mean, he chucked it back in the middle of the conversation? Why should he?'

'I'm asking the questions, Mrs. Graves. You must realise there's no proof at present that the weapon was ever produced on Friday night?'

'Why, I've told you . . .' she caught herself up. 'Oh, I see. You're going to play it that way, are you? Well, it'll be for the jury, I suppose. I say he waved the gun about, and I don't see how anyone can prove it, if you found the gun in the safe. But—*it wasn't there when I left the flat*. If he didn't put it back in the safe, someone else did, and you'd better find that other person and see what answer you get from them.'

Mason let that pass. 'Mrs. Graves, when you read of your husband's death on the Saturday morning, why didn't you come to us?'

'You'd simply have arrested me, anyone would. But if I went away I thought you might go on scratching around and unearth the real criminal.'

'If you didn't kill your husband, Mrs. Graves, you won't be found guilty.'

'So your idea is I should put my head down and have a nice nap?' Enormous incredulity and rage struggled in Caro's voice.

She insisted on making a statement, stopping short at her final scene with Con on the bombed site. 'Toby was dead by then and I was out of London next morning. I've been out of London ever since, so nothing that's happened since Saturday morning can be of any importance.'

When Mason applied some pressure, she flared up. 'You can't expect me to do all the work for you. Besides, you're only trying to see if I tell you the same story as you've heard already.'

She repeated her version, and at the end learned that she would be detained in connection with her husband's death. If she had a lawyer she could send for him; if not, one could be nominated by the court. She would not, of course, be admitted to bail. Caro put her silly proud head high.

'That's all right. I haven't anywhere else to sleep anyway. I'll never go back to the flat. And to-morrow we'll send out an S O S for my Fairy Godfather . . .' but there her courage almost collapsed, as if the truth had only just struck home, the fact that in the morning she'd be taken before a magistrate and formally charged, and later she would stand trial, and afterwards she might . . . even . . . hang.

Hang! she whispered under her breath.

The final indignity was being taken to her prison accommodation under close guard. She'd be brought back in the same state the next day. She felt her control slipping.

'To-morrow,' she repeated. 'To-morrow will be the brightest day of all the Bright New Year . . .

To-morrow and to-morrow and to-morrow . . .
What will the morrow bring?'

2

In point of fact, the morrow brought Arthur Crook,
a great bustling red bear of a man, tumbling into
her cell like a north-east wind. She found her hand
clutched in one about the size of a leg of mutton,
heard a voice like a tornado shouting, 'Crook's the
name, Arthur Crook. And I only work for the
innocent. Just bear that in mind and you can stop
worrying,' and began to smile.

'That's the ticket,' approved Crook, heartily.

'Are you—did the police send you?' His vitality
almost swept her off her feet.

'Tell them that and hear them laugh.' He laughed
himself, a kind of fee-fo-fum laugh. 'No, it's your
pal, Emmy Crisp, you've got to thank for pulling
me into this. She's quite a girl, isn't she?'

'I'd feel more guilty about getting her involved
if I didn't know she was really enjoying herself,'
admitted Caro, frankly. 'This has been one big
thrill for her.'

'That's the best way to take it,' Crook assured
her, earnestly. 'Don't let them get you down. Well,
maybe it has been a bit tough this past week, but
now you hold the ace for a change . . .'

'Do I?' Caro's big grey eyes widened. 'Thanks for
telling me.'

'Well!' Crook being coy was like an elephant
trying to polka. 'Your danger's my danger from
now on, and you don't see Arthur Crook sticking

138

his neck out. Now, let's have the facts from the horse's mouth.'

'I ought to have had a gramophone recording made,' suggested Caro. 'The story's the same every time.'

'Remember, I haven't heard your version, sugar, and I never had much opinion about second-hand goods.'

So once more Caro repeated her story. 'There's one thing I didn't know till last night,' she added, 'and whatever the police may think, I feel it's important. Did you know they found the gun—Toby's gun—in the safe?'

Crook nodded. 'Your point bein' it was still lying around when you bounced out.'

'It was in Toby's hand.'

'Turned against you?'

'I didn't notice particularly. I don't suppose for a minute it was loaded, it was just part of Toby's usual phoney set-up.'

'Licensed?'

Caro stared. 'You and Con are alike in one thing, you do ask the most extraordinary questions. Of course it wouldn't be licensed. I doubt if Toby's ever paid for a licence in his life. He even borrowed seven-and-six off me to buy one for our wedding.'

'If it wasn't loaded and he didn't mean to use it, what was the sense in keeping it?'

'Perhaps he thought it would impress people. Or perhaps he belonged to a secret society. I was his wife for nearly three years, but I seem to know rather less about him than anyone.'

'Any idea what he kept in the safe in the ordinary way?'

'It wasn't our safe. We took it over with the flat.

I don't know why the last tenant wanted it—stolen property, I shouldn't wonder. I doubt if Toby ever had anything worth putting inside.'

'Like that, eh? Interest you to know that the police found a sizeable packet of drugs with the gun?'

Caro didn't appear put out. 'So that was it? I told Con you could bet it was something crooked.'

'What was crooked?'

'The link between him and Gerry Lessing.' Then she frowned. 'No, I don't believe that's right. After all, if he'd been going to do a deal in illicit drugs he'd hardly have pulled me in. If I'd been at the Hat and Feather I should have seen what was going on.'

'Not necessarily,' said Crook. 'Nothing to prevent them strolling off to the Gent's, or one going to the Gent's while the other was at the bar. Just a momentary pause—back in a sec. You know, and the packet could have changed hands. Drugs ain't like bricks. They don't take up much space.'

'All the same, it would have been easier still not to have pulled me in. But then I feel certain he didn't expect me to go. I've had time to think during these past few days, and I believe all he wanted was me out of the way. He wasn't bothering about Gerry. And you see what that adds up to—that he was expecting someone to come to the flat, and he wanted to have the place to himself.' She warmed to the theme. 'The door of the safe wasn't shut when I left, I feel sure of that, but if there had been anything valuable inside it it would have been.'

'So you think he was waiting for X, his partner in the drug market and it was X who put out his light?'

'What's wrong with that?'

'It don't add up,' said Crook. 'That's all. If he had

done for Toby why leave the drugs on the premises?
And Toby wasn't expecting trouble, because he'd
put the gun away.'

'Unless X did that.'

'He'd be more of a fool than most criminals if he
did. If the gun was still lying around, with only
Toby's finger-prints on it, mark you, X might try and
put forward a defence along the lines of self-defence.
He threatened me with the gun and I picked up the
nearest object, which happened to be the cosh, and
lammed out. But if the gun was put away that
wouldn't hold even a thimbleful of water.'

Caro sighed. 'We seem to be going round and
round in circles, don't we? Of course, there's no
proof that anyone came round. Toby could have
collected the drugs during the day and put them
away to deliver, turn in, whatever the word is, the
next morning.'

Crook nodded. 'Any idea about hubby's financial
position when you marched out?' he inquired.

'He hadn't got the price of a bottle of gin on him
in the morning. He asked me to buy a bottle, as we'd
run out, and when I asked what I used for money he
said surely I could lay hands on a couple of pounds,
he was cleaned out.'

'When he was found he had over twenty pounds
on him. And nobody in the crooked world where
drugs are passed in the dark parts with the goods
without he gets his cut first. Well, that's common-
sense. I know all about honour among thieves, but
you can take my word for it most of the honour's in
the breach. So—Toby had more than twenty pounds
to start with. Twenty pounds is what he had left
when he paid for the drugs.'

'How did he persuade anyone to give him the

cash?' Caro marvelled. 'Unless, of course . . .' She hesitated.

'Well?'

'I know they say you shouldn't blackguard the dead, but Toby had a code of morals, if you can call it that, quite different from most people's. I mean, he really did think only fools worked a forty hour week for forty hours' union pay. And he did manage to worm his way in and out of the most unexpected places, and naturally, since he had to eat like the rest of us, he was always on the lookout . . .'

'Let's cut the cackle,' suggested Crook in a cosy voice. 'You mean, he might have been doing a spot of blackmail. Yes, I daresay he might, though the police didn't find anything on the premises to back up the idea. Still, you don't always need your evidence in writing. Just knowing is often enough. But I doubt whether blackmail would help him here, because they were in it together. X wouldn't dare trust him for his money, because if Toby said, "You've got a shocking memory, old man, I handed you your share when you brought the stuff round to the flat," X hadn't a leg to stand on. You don't give receipts for that sort of thing, and X 'ud know as well as the next man that he couldn't go to the police and say he'd been choused, because the police are such curious chaps, they'd want to know the details, and—well, you see.'

Yes, Caro saw. 'He must have got the money from someone.'

'I'll say. Besides, we know he had some money because of Robinson. Not heard of Robinson?' He told her. 'Nothing to show yet that Robinson ever existed, but it's quite on the cards he did and, like X, couldn't make trouble or come into the open.

Still, Lessing spoke of a sum of £120 Toby was to hand over that evening. And when the police found him he was a hundred smackers short.'

'You mean, he never meant to meet Gerry?'

'Well, not on the Friday. He knew the chap went down to the country every week-end, so if he could stall him for two or three hours, that gave him a couple of days to get himself in the clear. My guess 'ud be he had a date with someone else who prefers darkness to light who was going to take the drugs off him and pay him back his hundred plus a bit extra, and on Monday he could cook up some yarn about Robinson coming in late or not turning up till the Saturday, pay over the money and everything would be rumpty-too.'

'Between us,' suggested Caro politely, 'we're supposing enough to write a book.'

Crook looked a little injured. 'No one,' he assured her, 'can knock up a cake with fewer ingredients than yours truly, but even I must have something. Once we put a theory together we can set to work to get the proof.'

'And if there isn't any?'

'We manufacture it, of course. That's what you've got me for.'

Caro looked astounded. 'But—but you're a lawyer.'

Crook frowned. 'Don't overplay your hand, sugar,' he warned her. 'That honeychile stuff's out of date. Mind you, we shall know a lot more in a day or two when we know what exactly was cooking between Lessing and the dear departed.'

'Do you expect Gerry to tell you? That sort of faith's out of date, too.'

'You don't know Bill,' Crook told her. 'Bill

Parsons is my A.D.C. He's like the Angel of the Revelations, has a foot in both camps. He was one of the meteors of the underworld in his time,' he brought out the words with an immense beam of pride. 'Now he's working for Arthur Crook and on the side of the angels.' Astoundingly, Caro laughed. 'What's so funny about that?' Crook demanded. 'Don't you remember the bit in the Bible about entertaining 'em unawares? They come all shapes and sizes and don't you forget it.'

'You seem to know a lot about the Bible,' murmured Caro.

'Ah!' Crook looked complacent. 'That comes of having a good upbringing. Well, if you knew Bill as I know Bill, you'll know it won't be long before he brings home the bacon.'

'If you say so,' said Caro obediently. 'Tell me something else, Mr. Crook. How did the police find out about Toby so early?'

'Had a message from the tenants in the flat below . . .'

'They can't have done. There weren't any.'

'Exactly. But the informant aforesaid didn't know that.'

Caro was frowning. 'Maybe I'm dense,' she suggested. 'What was the sense of calling in the police? Why not just wait . . . ?'

'If you set a scene,' Crook explained patiently, 'you don't want it mucked about before the curtain goes up. Say you'd come back before anyone else had got in, as X had no reason to suppose you wouldn't—what would you have done?'

'I suppose I'd have rung up the police.' Caro didn't seem to be too sure.

'Right away? Without even taking a peek round?'

'Well, I daresay I might. Anyway, while I was waiting for the police . . .'

'And if you found your ear-ring on the floor . . . ?'

'I should pick it up, of course, wondering what on earth Toby had been doing with it.'

'Likely to mention it to the police?'

'I see,' said Caro. 'You mean, I was being framed?'

'Don't it seem that way to you? I mean, where's the sense of jumping out of the frying-pan into the fire? If Toby was in somebody's path and X has pushed him out, he (X) is no better off if he's going to be hustled into the little covered shed before the end of the quarter. No, my guess is that having put paid to dear Toby's account he hurried off and got the police, and then beat it.'

'Making sure he hadn't left any trace? But he had.'

Crook looked at her inquiringly.

'The drugs. Why didn't he take them?'

'Maybe he didn't know they were there.'

'Then why . . . ?'

'The porter, Don Price, told the police he heard Toby bawling someone out at seven-fifteen. You're slipping, he heard him say. That don't give us much . . .'

Caro repeated the words thoughtfully. 'It might have been a woman.'

'Yes. Had a lot of dames to his harem, hadn't he?'

'Oh well, they all came rushing up like deer asking for sugar, the minute he came sidling round a door.'

'And—not to put too fine a point on it—Toby always had an eye for the main chance?'

'I suppose so. Those notes—could they be traced?'

Crook shook his big red head. 'All single pounds. When did you last see him, before Act Three, I mean?'

'In the morning. He went out, and I went to the Public Library to look at Situations Vacant. I really had got to the end of my tether. I couldn't stand him any longer.' For the first time her voice shook. 'I couldn't tell Con, not the worst of it. He's young, and he's probably still got some illusions . . .'

'You're not Methuselah yourself,' Crook reminded her, and she felt his enormous hand on her shoulder.

'Marriage is an ageing experience. Are you married? Ah, then you wouldn't know. But—yes, I'd meant to get out.'

'Take your Uncle Arthur's advice,' Crook urged her, 'keep that to yourself when you're in the box. You haven't told the police already?'

'No. No, I didn't think of it.'

'Praise the pigs,' murmured Crook piously. 'Now, any notion who might have it in for dear Toby?'

'Scores of people, I should think.'

'Ever hear the one about too many cooks?' Crook asked her. 'We don't want scores, we just want one, only it's got to be the right one—see?'

'Mr. Crook,' said Caro, 'have you heard anything about Con? I mean—is it true he's lost his job on my account?'

'Just one more proof that out of evil good may come.' Crook patted her hand reassuringly. 'I know that firm. Two pokers apiece every morning for breakfast. Oh, and Emmy Crisp sent her love.'

'I hope she isn't in a jam on my account. I seem to have mucked things up for everyone.'

For all her direct speech she seemed so young and defenceless that Crook bounced out, wishing with all his heart it was the volatile Emmy who was his client. These old girls were so tough you could hit them over the head with a machete and up they came, inviting more. Not much to look at, perhaps, but they had guts. Roll, bowl or pitch, every time a blood-orange or a good cigar. Emmy now—pure dynamite. He wouldn't care himself to be in her enemy's shoes.

Jumping back into the Scourge he whizzed back to 123 Bloomsbury Street.

3

He supposed he shouldn't have been surprised to find Emmy chatting nineteen to the dozen to Bill Parsons.

'I've decided to take a little vacation,' she announced. 'Having a ringside seat, as it were, it seems a pity not to make use of it. You've seen Caro? Good. I suppose there won't be any objection to my dropping in.'

'It's a prison she's in, not a hospital,' Crook pointed out gently.

'I thought it was an axiom of British law you were innocent till you'd been proved guilty. I might have known. What do they think I might do? Take in a file in a Swiss bun?'

'I wouldn't put it past you,' said Crook frankly. 'Speaking for myself, if I were a prison warder, I wouldn't have you within a mile. Not unless I'd made my will, that is.'

Emmy chuckled. Then, sobering again, she asked how Caro was.

'The sooner you get her out of that stuffy place the better. I'm sure they're not hygienic. Don't they say every criminal makes a mistake? Not that I blame him. I never see how anyone can remember everything. I tried to learn to drive a car once, but it was no good. Too much to remember. Going round corners, for instance.' She hunched her shoulders and clenched her hands on an imaginary wheel. 'Mirror, indicator, hand signal, take up correct position, give slow signal, change down—oh, it's ridiculous to expect you to remember everything.'

Crook grinned at the thought of Emmy at the wheel of a car. Lucifer falling from Heaven wouldn't be in it.

'Anyway, I found I didn't like it, so why should I spend money on something that wasn't any fun? Besides, I haven't got so many wits I can afford to waste any, and really it was cheaper to take an occasional taxi and let someone else take the risks.'

Crook said simply, 'I'd back you against the whole police force,' reflecting that if there should be a crash it wouldn't be Emmy they'd take to the mortuary.

'I was thinking,' the little creature went on, 'about Caro, of course. And I remembered something. You know I had a flat in Morris House for a short time, and while I was there I got quite friendly with Daisy Price. She didn't demean herself to go out to work, of course, but sometimes she'd lend you a friendly hand at three shillings an hour, and once or twice she asked me down to tea, and told fortunes by cards. Well, one afternoon nobody answered when I rang and I saw the door wasn't quite shut, so I pushed it open and—Toby Graves was there with her.'

'Locked in a passionate embrace?'

'Well, more friendly than I'd want to see my wife with one of the tenants if I were the husband,' said Emmy, with unusual caution.

'What did you do?' asked Crook, really wanting to know.

'I just marched in as if I hadn't noticed anything special, and said, "Playing Postman's Knock?" Daisy looked quite cross, not with me, with Toby. He was a most attractive person, of course, only I could never understand anyone taking him seriously. I mean, it was like a lovely picture postcard, all surface and no depths. He just winked and said, "Oh, Miss Crisp's a woman of the world," and out he went. I did say to Daisy she was a silly girl, but she said that being married to Don was like living on Eskimo Island and she liked a bit of warmth herself now and again.'

'I get you, sugar,' said Crook. 'You think there might have been a time when Don pushed open the door? Still, it beats me how any chap can think a dame's worth swinging for. No offence meant.'

'And none taken,' said Emmy, composedly. 'You don't think it would help if I went round to see Daisy . . .'

'She was spending the week-end with her mother, according to Don.'

'I didn't mean she—only we don't want to let the grass grow under our feet.' Crook promised to bear the idea in mind.

'To hear people talk, you'd think dear Caro had a stronger motive than anyone. But that's nonsense. I'd have said she had less motive. I mean, he wasn't keeping her, not even paying the rent, she didn't gain financially by his death, she was independent, she meant to leave him anyway, she wasn't in love with him or with anyone else, and I expect she could have found grounds for a divorce as easy as—as picking up a pin off the floor. So why on earth should she hit him over the head? Only it's no good telling the police things like that, because it's too simple.'

CHAPTER EIGHT

1

It didn't take Bill Parsons long to discover the nature of the link between Toby and Gerald Lessing.

'Oldest game in the world,' he told Crook. 'The Black Market.'

'I thought the bottom had dropped out of that.'

'Out of nylons and butter, but—there's always something in short supply. Just now it's foreign currency. Even though the Chancellor of the Exchequer has bumped up the allowance to forty pounds, that doesn't go far with chaps who want to get away for a month, and whose wives have an idea about bringing home a Paris gown—you know. So a fellow who can supply the little bit extra is batting on a good wicket.'

'Not a bad idea,' Crook acknowledged. 'Lessing's office would be the shop window, and Toby's fabulous charm and social abilities would provide the clients. Where did they get the stuff?'

'There's always a way of getting what you want if you're not particular what you pay for it,' Bill reminded him. 'Plenty of chaps don't want to go abroad at all, but there's nothing to stop anyone with a passport drawing a whack of foreign currency. Then there are foreigners over here without too many scruples, who don't mind smuggling the stuff in if they know there's a hot market for it, and some of our Dominion friends, who get a bigger travel allowance than we do, are prepared to convert a part of it at a profit. Mind you, they're the exceptions, but then so are the customers, and chaps like Lessing and Graves get their living out of the submerged tenth, so to speak. I doubt if they were in it in a big way . . .'

Crook was doing mental arithmetic. 'It 'ud put Toby in the clear,' he suggested. 'Lessing couldn't do without him, and he couldn't boggle too much about terms. This chap, Robinson, for instance. There's no absolute proof that he exists, and Lessing has to take Toby's word for it. If things go wrong Robinson can't surface, because he's in the red, too. Mind you, as I told Mrs. Graves, I think Toby meant to tie up all the ends, in his own time; the way it works out he didn't get enough time. I think I'll go round in the morning and see Lessing, get his reaction.'

2

The next morning, however, proved a heavy one, and it was after midday before Crook could turn his attention to the Graves Affair. Assuming that Lessing would probably have a luncheon engagement he decided to see Don Price first. Don had presumably been on the premises when the murder took place or at all events within a few minutes. Don might let slip something darned useful in his, Crook's, subsequent dealings with Lessing. So, clapping on his horrible brown bowler hat, Crook jumped into the Scourge and shot along to Morris House.

He found the porter looking gloomily at the sort of wristwatch honest men can't afford.

'Have I hit the jackpot or have I hit the jackpot?' exulted Crook. 'Just going off the lot? So am I.' He paid no heed to Don's black looks. 'What's wrong with the Blue Boar?' he suggested. 'Not the beer, because I've sampled it.'

'Are you another of 'em?' asked Don.

Crook explained the situation. 'Now I'm checking through to see where the police made their bloomer,' he added.

It was evident that there was no love lost between Don and the tenant of No. 15.

'To hear her throw her orders round you'd think she was a duchess,' he complained. 'One thing I do know. It's not her name on her monthly rent cheque.'

'You went up to do her a favour,' suggested Crook, in a voice as smooth as cream.

'That's right. Wanted her curtains hung. They'd just come back from the cleaner and of course Her Ladyship couldn't do a job of work for herself. Thinks I'm a sort of machine, if you ask me. If I had a union . . .'

'If you had a union you wouldn't be allowed to turn an honest copper out of hours,' Crook warned him heartily. 'You count your blessings, chum. Well, you went up—what time?'

'Say a quarter to seven, and she didn't half create

because I'd said I'd be as near half-past six as I could. "I've got a private life, too, though you mightn't think it," I told her. "I have an engagement," says she. "I mustn't leave an instant later than seven o'clock. You know what men are."' Don emptied his glass and looked round belligerently. Crook called, 'Same again. Twice.' 'Well, what I don't know about men she can teach me,' Don went on coarsely. '"I've got a date myself," I said. "And fifteen minutes is plenty to hang a pair of curtains." She gave me two bob—can't believe it, can you? "Keep it to buy yourself sweets," I said. "Five bob's my price. And no pun intended." She started to say that was a pound an hour; if she'd carried on much longer I'd have asked her what rate she got. P'raps she saw that because she shelled out, after making more fuss than most people over five pounds. "If you don't like it," I told her, "I can easy take them down again. You won't mind people seeing in. You won't be doing anything you shouldn't."'

Crook was secretly appalled at the venom in the young man's voice. But he covered up nicely, and said, 'So it was seven when you left the flat?'

'Might ha' been a minute after. Anyway, while I was up there I thought I'd just go across and do a little job for the tenant in the flat at the end of the passage. He was away for the week-end, but of course I had my key. That took about ten minutes (five for the job and five for snooping was Crook's unspoken comment) and then I came down and . . .'

'Any sign of Mrs.—Whatsit?'

'Benyon? Not her. She'd beetled off to meet the boy-friend.'

'No sound from her flat?'

'Why . . . ? Oh, you think the boy-friend was coming to see her? I didn't see it that way. Anyway, she'd been putting on her hat and shaking out her gloves. Mind you, she wouldn't leave me the key—mortice lock she's got—to lock up when the job was done.'

Crook didn't blame her; he'd as soon have left a gorilla on his premises. Looking at that tough unscrupulous face made you understand some of the crimes that at first sight were too bad to be believed, like the fellow who knocked an old woman on the head and then dropped her out of a window, or the gangs who put unconscious bodies on railway lines just before the express comes thundering by.

'No sign of anyone else either?'

'Nothing but this voice from Toby Graves's flat. Mind you, I didn't give it a second thought. Always rowing those two. You get used to it in flats like these. There's times I don't blame Daisy saying she didn't expect to come this low. Trash, that's what they are.' He stopped, his eyes slewing round in a cunning fashion.

'Thought of something?' encouraged Crook, remembering the one about not touching pitch without being defiled. He wouldn't have called himself a fussy fellow, but he'd met quite a number of honest-to-God-murderers he'd sooner sit around with than Don Price.

'Well, you'd say it was nothing,' he muttered. Crook knew that, just as there are no small jobs, only small men, so, when murder's in question, there are no insignificant details. Everything matters.

'Give,' he said more encouragingly than before.

'I got the idea there was some chap mooching

around that night, though I didn't think it had anything to do with Toby Graves. Anyway, he was alive and kicking when I went by at 7.15. I went straight down to my flat, I was going out, don't often get a chance, but my wife had gone to her mother—lives in some dead-alive little village where it's an event if the cat has kittens—nothing but fields from one sky to the other—and I hadn't any time to waste.'

'They tell me,' offered Crook, 'it's sometimes a good idea to keep 'em waiting.'

'No married man 'ud tell you that. I didn't want to start a good evening with my eyes scratched out. I'd put everything ready so's I could change out of my working clobber without wasting any time.' He grinned, but not very pleasantly. 'If Mrs. B. had seen me in that get-up it 'ud have put her eye out all right. Might have given her ideas.'

'You were going to tell me . . .' insinuated Crook.

'Oh yes. Well, I went into the bedroom and—oh there wasn't much to go on, but I had the feeling someone had been in there while I was out. I hadn't bolted the door, I was having a new key cut and I'd forgotten to pick it up, so I shot the bolt on the inner side of the door and then pulled it to, the door, I mean, so it looked closed, but of course anyone could get in who had a mind.'

Crook was looking grave. 'Any idea who it might have been?'

'Some chap on his uppers, asking for a job, which means asking for charity, someone selling, which comes to the same thing, any chap on the look-out for a bit of light-finger-work. You see, there's an entrance to the porter's flat down the alley at the back. All the boilers and the coke sheds are out there, and Daisy and me use that way. We know our place, the front hall's for our betters.'

'Anything missing?' asked Crook.

'Well, that's the funny thing. There wasn't. But someone had pulled out a drawer and pushed it back in a hurry. Mind you, it could be someone who heard me coming back . . .'

'Anything like this happened before?'

'Not that I remember. But then I haven't been here long. Or,' he added slowly, 'and this is only an idea, mind, that's come into my head this last few minutes, it could be someone hurrying down the central staircase and not wanting to be seen leaving the building by the front. Why, do you think it's important?'

'In a murder case everything's important,' said Crook. 'But what it means—don't ask me, not yet.'

'It's not as if we keep anything on the premises you'd think would appeal to a burglar,' Don went on restlessly. 'I mean, it's not like one of those stories where there's a box of bank-notes under the bed, anything like that. It was all we could do to get by. Daise cleaned me out before she left. "How do you expect me to go to the dogs on five bob?" I asked her. "You'll get another five from Mrs. Benyon," she told me, as cool as you please. "Ten bob's as much as we can afford to lose." That's a woman all over.'

He told Crook a bit impatiently, No, he hadn't seen anyone on the stairs or in the hall, he hadn't noticed anyone in the telephone box or coming into the building. He'd left the house by the front door at half-past seven, he had a date at 7.45. Crook could check with Mrs. Benyon if he wasn't satisfied.

Crook said, Yes, that was right, he meant to

anyhow. And asked if Price had ever met Gerald Lessing.

'Not me. But then I don't keep track of everyone coming and going.'

Which brought them into another cul-de-sac. Crook decided there wasn't much more to be learnt from this source, and if he did get anything it was as likely to be lies as not, so he said, 'How about one for the road?' and when they'd had that, they parted.

3

Mrs. Benyon was a woman of early middle age—'Long time since anyone gave her a christening mug,' was Crook's way of putting it—with a dark complexion, black hair cut square across her forehead, very large hands and a deep voice. She opened the door of her flat to Crook, and stood staring.

'I don't give at the door,' she said sharply.

Crook pushed his bright brown shoe across the threshold.

'I've no objection to comin' inside,' he assured her. 'In fact, it's more cosy.'

'I've no idea who you are . . .'

Crook soon remedied that.

'Mrs. Graves? I can assure you, she's no concern of mine.'

'She's my baby,' quoted Crook, rapidly. He could hear the inevitable crooner on the wireless set in the invisible sitting-room. 'I have to see everyone who might be able to help me about general movements on the night of Toby Graves's death.'

'The police have made their arrest . . .'

'Made a bloomer, not for the first time,' said Crook, simply. 'Now, what I want from you is—corroboration.'

'Corroboration of what?' She didn't look prepared to give an inch.

'Corroboration of the porter's testimony.'

As though he had uttered some magic slogan— Open, Sesame, say—his companion's whole manner changed in a flash. She drew the door back.

'Come in for a minute, won't you, Mr . . .'

'Crook.'

'Crook. I don't know, of course, what Price has been saying to you, but my advice would be to disregard it. A most unpleasant man and quite unsuited to his position. Dishonest, too, most likely, and quite unscrupulous.' Crook's brows flew up. The lady had something on her mind, not a doubt of it, he reflected. Innocence doesn't protest so ferociously.

'About his call here on Friday night?' he suggested.

'To hang my curtains—yes. And a quarter of an hour late, and most insolent when I objected. Five shillings he asked me for hanging a pair of curtains.'

'Pay him?' murmured Crook.

'I had no alternative. I couldn't hang them myself and I was in a hurry to go out. But—it's no wonder he's so well off if that's his scale of charges. I suppose he'd been mulcting some other tenant before he got to me.'

'Remember what time you left your flat?' asked Crook, patiently.

'A minute past seven, two perhaps.'

'Meet anyone on the way down?'

She stared. 'You mean, someone who might have murdered Toby Graves? Supposing it *wasn't* his wife. What a shocking idea! Fortunately, I didn't see anyone.'

'Or hear anyone? Price swears there was the sound of scrapping going on at 7.15, that is, about ten minutes after you left your flat.'

'I can only say I didn't hear anything, and I didn't meet anyone on the stairs.'

'Or coming in?'

She began to get annoyed. 'I don't go round staring at people. I daresay there were men and women on the pavement. I happened to be in rather a hurry . . .'

'Of course. Your date. Any objection to telling me where you went?'

She looked as if she couldn't believe her ears. 'What on earth is that to do with you?'

Crook looked earnest. 'Process of elimination. The quicker I can clear the impossibles out of the path, the easier it's going to be for me to identify the slayer. The wood and the trees, you know,' he added encouragingly.

'But—you are not surely suggesting I had anything to do with Toby's death?'

Crook spread his big hands. 'I wouldn't know, lady. Only—you were on the premises . . .'

'I left the building by 7.5 at latest. We know he was alive at 7.15 . . .'

'Well, we know someone was in his flat at 7.15.'

His meaning was unmistakable.

'You are daring to suggest . . .'

'Now, sugar, be reasonable,' Crook implored. 'Try and see this my way. My girl, that is, Mrs. Graves, is going to be tried for her life. Say that over and over till it gets into your head. She's going to stand up in court and twelve muttonheads are goin' to decide whether she lives or dies. Whichever she does it ain't to be no picnic. The only person who matters to me in that Court is my client. I don't care if all the rest of you are tarred with the same brush. Say you are! It's up to you to find someone to take care of you, same like Mrs. Graves and me. Now if you can show you were over the hills and far away by 7.15 you're in the clear. You left at 7.5. Car?'

'No,' snapped Mrs. Benyon.

'Taxi?'

'There weren't any. I took a bus.'

'Far to go?'

'The West End.'

Crook practically rubbed his hands. 'That makes it simple, don't it? I daresay they know you quite well at this place, wherever it is' (for himself you could have given him three guesses and he'd have handed you back two on a plate with parsley round the edge). 'So they'd remember . . .' Her glance was murderous, and he tailed off skilfully, 'And anyhow your friend would remember. Yes, I know chaps don't like being bothered, but it 'ud be less trouble for him to remember now than to have to tell the authorities or maybe the Court . . .'

'I think you're out of your mind. There's no question of the Court . . .'

'That's what you think. Now, ease off, lady, it's all perfectly simple really. All I'm asking is proof of your statement that you were off the premises by, say seven-five. If you were at your rendezvous by seven-fifteen or even seven-twenty . . .'

'You mean you expect my companion to remember the precise time I arrived.'

'He'd likely remember if you were late. Do try and get it into your head that a girl's life is at stake.'

'Why should I worry about her? If, as seems most likely, she's murdered her husband? Oh, you can look as black as a London fog but you didn't hear her. And he was a charming person. I do think jealousy's such a vulgar characteristic.'

Crook sighed. 'We are but human, and I daresay with you and all the other dames he met going crazy over dear Toby . . .'

'I didn't say crazy. I just said he was very pleasant and helpful. I've sometimes wondered why he married that half-savage girl. Certainly not for her money, because she had none.'

Crook looked at her out of a deceptively sleepy brown eye.

'That what darlin' Toby tell you? Well, then, you and him must have been buddies of a sort. Even the Tobys of this world don't discuss their wives' "financial standin'"' with strangers. Mind you, he got it wrong . . .'

'You must remember,' the lady was now as smooth as a snake, 'you only have Mrs. Graves's version.'

'Well?' Crook's eyes resembled those of the dog in the fairytale, that were as large as cartwheels. 'She's my client, ain't she? Whose other version would I want?'

'In any case, it was just a casual remark. He'd dropped in one evening for a glass of sherry . . .'

'Mrs. G. accompany him?' Crook's voice sounded sleepier than ever.

'I've told you, I only knew her by sight.

Toby—Mr. Graves—had helped me over a little business . . .'

'Othello's occupation gone,' murmured Crook. 'I mean, it's a poor look-out for the Toby Graves's of this world when any honest-to-God citizen can walk into a shop and buy a bottle of whatever he fancies over the counter at the Government price.'

'I don't know what you're insinuating,' cried Mrs. Benyon sharply, 'but I've always thought people were entitled to what they could pay for. If a thing's too dear for you, well, that's too bad, but it doesn't follow that people who can afford it have got to go without, too.'

She had fine eyes, but Crook was unmoved. 'Lucky the Welfare State provides a burial grant,' he observed. 'If it didn't, the row of stiffs who'd pass out because the black market was way above their heads 'ud stretch from here to Temple Bar. Well, so you did know the deceased?'

'I've told you, just in the way of business, and I always found him perfectly straightforward and above-board.'

'Which only goes to show you didn't know him very well. Have a date with him that Friday night?'

His voice didn't change, but his eyes did. They were now like those of the archangel who shot sparks at his opponent.

'I've told you—no.'

'Too bad the courts don't accept a lady's word without something to back it up. Now, if you had a witness to back up your story . . . All right, all right. Take it easy. There's one murder in this block. We don't want a second. By the way, if you haven't got a nice picture of yourself, how about having one done?'

'I don't know what you mean.' But her breath was coming faster than before.

'Think of the *Fizzer* captions,' Crook suggested. 'What has Mrs. B. to hide?'

But even that didn't draw her. It was evident she had a lot to hide.

'I realise you'd like to think it was me in Toby Graves's flat at 7.15 that night . . .'

'Well, of course I'd like to think it was you. That 'ud let my client out. That's my job, what I'm hired for,' he explained elaborately.

'The burden of proof's on you,' Mrs. Benyon reminded him.

'Oh, I'll get it. Crook always gets his man—or his dame, as the case may be.' He stooped and picked up his brown billy-cock. 'By the way, if you're thinking of going abroad in the near future . . .'

She looked at him in amazement. 'As a matter of fact, I am, though what it's got to do with you . . .'

'I shouldn't,' said Crook. 'Not too healthy.'

'What do you mean—not too healthy? People are going abroad all the time. Mr. Graves . . .'

'Booking through his agency?'

'I don't know anything about an agency. He was giving me some advice . . .'

Crook thought he could guess the shape and colour of it.

'Have it your own way. But leave an address where you can be found. There's something called contempt of court, and you're likely to be wanted.'

'You could talk yourself into a figure of eight, couldn't you?' she snapped, and Crook, glancing down at his comfortably rotund figure, couldn't conceal a grin.

'Arthur Crook, the miracle man. Well, be seeing you.'

He thought she had something to hide, but he didn't see why she should want to cosh Toby or be so eager to hustle Price off the premises if she'd only been going to drop down a couple of floors. Besides, would Toby have made a date for seven o'clock in his own block of flats if he'd been going to meet Lessing at six-thirty at the Hat and Feather?

'It don't add up,' he told himself, sadly. 'I daresay he was getting her a bit extra for her continental holiday, but you don't have to crown a chap for doing you a favour.'

No, the fact was she was some other fellow's fancy bit, and she didn't want to pull him into the affair, for fear of losing her rent cheque. He stepped into the telephone booth in the hall and looked up her number. But when he dialled it he only got the engaged signal. That made him wonder. Was she getting in touch with the partner of that Friday night, putting him on guard in case questions were asked?

That was a question even he couldn't answer as yet.

4

The clock had just struck three and the door of The Hat and Feather was locked till opening time when a visitor came to the side door.

'See who it is, Joe,' said Rosa, who had her own reasons for liking to take time off now and again out of hours.

Joe opened the door to find a big square chap looking as though he'd walked straight out of Music Hall on the step.

'What can I do for you?' he demanded.

Not the sort of chap you'd like to have for an enemy on a dark night, reflected Crook. He explained his position.

'Graves? We've had the police here, I told them all I knew, which wasn't much.'

'Ah, but how am I to know the police are being square with me?' Crook urged. 'Ever meet the lady?'

'Mrs. Graves. She came here with her husband two or three times.'

'To meet Lessing?' Crook insinuated himself into the passage.

'Not that I'm aware of. Just came with her husband. If Mr. Lessing was in the bar, and he's here most nights, he might move over.'

Reluctantly he took Crook into the sitting-room. It was the sort of room Crook liked, with old-fashioned chairs and photographs on the mantelpiece.

'Notice anyone else special Graves talked to when he came?'

'Can't say I did. But then when we're open we don't have much time for noticing.'

'I'll say,' agreed Crook pleasantly. 'Now, you can see how I'm placed. I want to find out something about Toby Graves. I know all the women loved him—excepting Mrs. G. But even so . . .' he spread his hands. 'The most unlovin' wife don't suddenly pick up a cosh and brain her old man just because she's annoyed. I mean, if she was going to end it that way, why wait three years? She must have got his measure in the first three months. And there wasn't any point in it. I know dames don't understand logic, but all she had to do was walk out.'

'I've told you,' said Joe in a tight voice, 'I didn't know Mrs. Graves.'

'Never came here without her husband?'

'I never saw her.'

'You're a married man,' Crook wheedled. 'You can probably size chaps up. How would you say they were shaping?'

But Bates wasn't to be drawn. 'I've told you, you don't have time to notice when you're behind the bar. Rosa'll tell you the same.'

'Your wife? Mind if I have a word with her? Women are supposed to be better at this sort of thing.'

Crook wasn't sure what would have happened next if Rosa hadn't come in at that moment.

'Joe,' she began, but Crook jumped in before the husband could speak. He liked the look of Joe's wife, a plump gay girl, the sort it did you good to see. He thought Joe might have looked a shade less intimidating. A wife like that did you good in the bar business.

'Mrs. Graves?' she said in reply to Crook's question. 'Well, she didn't come often, and when she did she looked as if she was insulted at being asked to breathe the same air as the rest of us.'

'Could be because of the company she had to keep,' cut in Joe.

'Marriage is what you make it,' said Rosa. 'Mind you, he was popular. Made friends all round.'

'Not this side of the bar,' retorted Joe.

'Don't listen to him,' Rosa advised Crook in comfortable tones. 'It's not my fault if a boy wants to hold my hand now and again. There's no harm done.'

'And I suppose,' suggested her husband, 'you'd be quite pleased to see me holding a girl's hand.'

'Get along with you,' said Rosa. 'If I was to have a pound for every girl's hand you'd held we could shut up shop to-morrow.'

'You've no call to say that,' Joe exclaimed.

Crook, the normally imperturbable, knew a pang of unease. 'Anyway, it's one of the things fellows come to a bar for,' Rosa went on. 'Well, if they didn't like the company they'd do their drinking at home, wouldn't they?'

'I'd say Mr. Graves had it coming to him any road,' Joe said heavily. 'And I'm only glad he had the sense to get himself knocked on the head in his own house. That sort of thing doesn't do a public any good. I'm only the landlord here, I haven't any say as to who drinks in my bar and who doesn't. The law doesn't give me any choice. And it doesn't do a place like this any good to have the police on the premises, not so long as they're in uniform, I mean.'

'You don't want to pay too much attention to what Joe says,' Rosa warned Crook. 'There was never any question of police. And you're giving Mr. Crook a wrong idea of the Hat. Don't know why you took such a dislike to Mr. Graves, I'm sure. You were all right at the start. I saw you talking to him one evening by the pillar-box when you were bringing Jess back from her run. You seemed friendly enough then. And I'm sure I found him pleasant enough.'

'I don't want chaps coming into this bar being pleasant to my wife. He'd got one of his own, hadn't he? Why couldn't he do his lovey-doveying with her?'

'Well, you've seen her,' said Rosa simply. 'Lot's wife wouldn't be in it with Mrs. Graves. I call it silly, getting all worked up because a chap's had a row at home and wants someone to tell him what a fine chap he is. That's all he wanted. All most of 'em want, come to that,' added Rosa, the philosopher.

'Women!' said Joe, scornfully. 'They don't know a thing. Chap comes in, tells 'em the tale, war hero—oh yes, he had a medal and I daresay he swindled someone else out of that . . .'

'Joe! That's slander. And Mr. Crook's a lawyer.'

Crook waved a huge hand. 'Think nothing of it. Daresay if I was Mrs. Joe's husband . . .'

'That'll do,' said Joe.

Rosa shook her head. 'You see? Spoiling for a fight. If you ask me the war did a lot more harm than good. You can't teach fellows to go round killing people and giving them medals the more they kill, and then expect them to settle down like a lot of bank clerks for the rest of their days. Government's potty, if you ask me,' she wound up, expressing the view of about ninety-nine women out of a hundred.

The telephone rang from the back premises and Joe went to answer it, throwing a suspicious look at Crook on the way.

'You don't have to pay any attention to Joe,' said Rosa again. 'Silly, too. Why, I'd put all the rest of the world in a sinking boat and push it out to sea sooner than lose him. It's the war, like I said.'

'Joe have a bad time?'

'It's unsettling,' said Rosa. 'Not that he ever had what you could call a home life after he was a kid. And then one of his best friends shot himself because of the way his wife was carrying on at home with an American. You have to make allowances.'

'I reckon Joe's lucky,' said Crook. 'Do well here?'

'Well, we do and we don't. Place is always full and we take good money, but where it goes to I don't know. Some chaps can't hold on to money and Joe's one. But—there's always something, and it's better than being mean.'

Presently Joe came back and in reply to Crook's question gave precisely the same report of the events of the fatal Friday evening as he'd already given the police. Toby hadn't turned up, there'd been a telephone message, Lessing had departed a little later—and the next they heard was that Toby had been found dead in his flat.

Crook couldn't get anything fresh out of that, possibly, he reflected, because the Bateses were telling him everything they knew.

All the same, when he got back to Bloomsbury Street and an impatient new client who wished to be known as Jones, he observed to Bill, 'I have an idea—I don't quite know why—I've seen that chap, Bates, somewhere before. Not one of my cases, of course' (meaning that if it had been he'd have had the necessary information tucked away in a pigeon-hole in his mind), 'and not very recently. I could be wrong—and I don't think he was calling himself Bates then. One thing stands out a mile—he ain't going into mourning for the dear departed. You might see if you can ferret anything out, Bill. It wouldn't do him any good to have something crawl out of his past—or his wife's, for that matter. You know what these brewers are. And now shove this perisher in. Another chap wanting Arthur Crook to work a miracle, I suppose. Ah well, if it means wiping the police's eye, it's a pleasure.'

5

Gerald Lessing was in his office preparing to put up the shutters when the door was pushed open and a brigand of a chap wearing the most shocking brown suit with a billy-cock *en suite* strolled in. He didn't look like a customer, Lessing decided, but still, these days you never could tell who had the money. It never went through his mind that this might be the police; they may come all shapes and sizes but even they, obliging body of men though they are, draw the line somewhere.

In any case, Crook was swift to disillusion him.

'Why come to me?' asked Lessing. 'I've told the police all I know.'

'Well, not quite all,' suggested Crook. 'You didn't tell them the nature of your business with the dear departed. You were expecting him that evening.'

'You're misinformed,' said Lessing huffily. 'I told them everything. I was expecting him to bring me an account he'd collected . . .'

Crook fired a broadside. 'You didn't mention the cash wouldn't be in a currency Joe would have accepted over the counter.'

Lessing's hands tightened on the edge of his desk. 'Really, Mr.—er—Crook, what are you talking about?'

'We can go on like this and meet ourselves goin' to bed,' Crook pointed out. 'Let me tell you the way I see the situation.'

He outlined it with admirable brevity.

'I suppose,' said Lessing, 'you can produce proof of what you say.'

'You don't suppose anything of the sort,' said Crook, contemptuously. 'You know quite well if I had proof I wouldn't be wasting my time here. I'd be polishing my unmentionables in the nearest police station. And don't swing me the one about going through your books. If you were mad enough to put that sort of transaction through the books you'd be in Broadmoor already. By the way, this chap, Robinson? Any news?'

'None,' said Lessing swiftly. Crook could see his mind doubling and turning like a wild thing in a cul-de-sac. He couldn't get out, but he might go underground, and me, Crook reminded himself, I haven't got the figure for tunnelling operations.

'Let's put a few cards on the table,' Crook said, holding out his arm and making a great play of shaking down aces from his sleeve.

Lessing pardonably looked a bit disgusted. He seemed to be tied up with theatrical types all through this case, first Toby, and now this bounder, Crook.

'Don't get me wrong,' Crook was saying. 'It's nothing to me how any chap gets his dough, and my experience is the further you keep your nose out of other chaps' affairs the longer it's likely to stay in the place where Nature put it. Now, don't set up as a continental agency and pretend you can't understand plain English. I'd say Toby meant to meet you as arranged, but something went wrong. Know anything about drugs?'

Lessing looked startled. 'Is that his trouble? Was, I mean. I wouldn't know.'

'I didn't say he took 'em, only dealt in 'em, and even if you don't, and I'm not makin' any suggestions, you must know that if foreign currency's a winner drugs has it beaten on the post.

Now, I don't take it that getting hit over the head was any part of dear Toby's plan. By the way, when did you last see him?'

'He looked in here on the Friday morning. He was going to see Robinson, so he said, and then meet me at the Hat and Feather at half-past six.'

'Who suggested that bit of it?'

'He did. I wanted him to make it earlier, but he said Robinson wouldn't have the money till then.'

'And that didn't make you suspicious? I mean, the banks shut at three. It ought to have been all right for him to meet dear Toby at three-thirty, and he could have come along here by four.'

'He said Robinson had had to go out of London and wouldn't get back till the late afternoon.'

'You have to hand it to the boy, he thought of everything. Mind you, you can't blame him if he didn't keep the date. Death absolves a chap from any promise. Yes, he'd cooked up a very appetisin' little dish—I'd say he was quite a dab in a thieves' kitchen—and you handed over the dibs. Didn't trust him far, did you? I mean, if you were real buddies you'd have said, "Let it ride till Monday."'

'I've already told the police that I'd heard rumours about his—unreliability. Gossip's notoriously untrustworthy, and I had the idea of making this a test case.'

'You like to play it expensive, don't you?' suggested Crook.

'You're not working on the theory that this fellow, Robinson, about whom I'm bound to confess we know nothing, could be in any way responsible for Graves's death?'

'Well—only as a symbol,' allowed Crook, 'and symbols don't get you far in a court of law. No, whoever put out Toby's light knew something about his domestic set-up. And I daresay even that gives us quite a wide field. Another point. Remember that ear-ring they found by the body?'

'I read about it. I can't say I ever saw Mrs. Graves wearing them. But they existed all right.' He laughed shortly. 'If you believed Toby they were worth a hundred pounds.' He looked at his companion speculatively. 'You'll have it all worked out why it was found where it was, I suppose—unless, of course, Mrs. G. had been wearing them that day.'

'She says not—and she's my client, so that must be right.'

'Pity. I mean to say—my wife wears ear-rings—and I can't tell you how many she's lost through the catch getting weak. Of course, they're always insured . . .'

'Very far-sighted of her,' agreed Crook. 'But—well, the ear-ring they found was the one with a clip as fast as the hands of Justice. No, it was planted all right, because Mrs. G. said they were always kept in the jewel-box in the bedroom. Well, come on, let's have it.'

Lessing said, 'Graves 'ud know that, wouldn't he?'

'You mean, you think he swiped himself over the head and put the ear-ring on the floor so as to incriminate his wife?'

'Of course not. But—the women were suckers for him. And say he wanted to make one of them a present . . .'

'Just how well did you know Toby Graves? Was he likely to offer a pair of valuable ear-rings—a hundred pounds, you said, didn't you?—to a dame just for love?'

'That's my point. Not that they were worth a hundred pounds, fifty 'ud be their top figure—but you know the rhyme about big fleas and little fleas. Toby had his finger in quite a lot of pies and some of 'em might have held something less savoury than four-and-twenty blackbirds when they were opened.'

'Hush money?'

'It's only an idea. But—you said something about drugs a minute ago. And he had some pretty rum books on his shelves—quite proud of them, too. Not my cup of tea, I never can see why chaps want to take such chances, though I'm told there's quite a packet to be made that way.'

'That gives us another lead,' Crook murmured. 'Trouble is, this case so far is all leads and no tie-ups.'

But as he spoke he was remembering Mrs. Benyon. No doubt about it, she was a tough nut to crack, and yet—she'd spoken of Toby in an intimate kind of way. He looked up.

'Before we part, there's a client of yours—a Mrs. Benyon.'

'Benyon?'

'Well, she was a client of Toby's. Any record of her on your files?'

Lessing looked through a card-index. Then he said, 'No. One of Toby's specials, perhaps.' His lip twisted.

But Crook was thinking, 'Left the flat at 7.5. Don't want to say where she went. Toby was lending a hand with her holiday. So she says. But—she's the sort that 'ud like a nice pair of sparklers. Say Toby offered them to her—well, then, why didn't she take them? Say he said, "No hard feelings and here's a

parting present." Dames were crazy, every fellow
knew that, inclined to put their private feelings
above a valuable present. Or of course she might
have the wit to suspect they were stolen property.'
He looked up to see Lessing watching him with
perplexed eyes.

'Where have you got to now?'

Crook knuckled his big bumpy forehead.

'Know the slickest thing the Almighty ever did?
He created the human brain and hid it behind the
frailest container imaginable, just a box of fine bone
and skin, a thing that could be crashed by a car
or—or a cosh, say—and yet two chaps can stand
face to face and neither of 'em knows what's passing
in the mind of the other. One day I suppose science
'ull solve that one, too, and may I be in my grave
first. Be seeing you. Happy landings.'

Off he went, leaving Lessing staring after him.

'Chap's barmy,' he decided. 'Who's this Mrs.
Benyon and where does she come in?'

6

That was Crook's problem, too, and one he intended
to solve. Trouble about dames was you couldn't
work by rule of thumb, because they all made their
own rules and every single one was different. If Toby
offered Mrs. B. his wife's ear-rings—she wouldn't
know they were Caro's, would she? She and Caro
never having met—Thanks for a lovely time—well,
a chap being a rational person would probably take
'em and make the best of a bad job; you could
never hold on to someone who wanted to shake

you off. But a dame—Crook had a vision of Mrs. Benyon swiping the ear-rings out of the outstretched hand—'You cur!' Did they talk like that in 1953? He didn't know. And then that fatal jeer—'You're slipping'—and the cosh at hand. Could be, he decided. Of course, that allowed that the lady knew about Toby's date at the Hat and Feather, but—he could have told her, couldn't he?

'Must be pushing along, sweetheart. Time and Tide and Gerry Lessing wait for no man . . .'

And if Caro had really said she was clearing out—he got the feeling she'd regard a pair of valuable ear-rings a small price to pay to be rid of her husband—yes, you could make quite a pattern there. It all depended on the sort of female Mrs. B. was. If it was true that there are nine-and-sixty ways of constructing tribal laws and every single one of them is right, it was equally true that if you had one situation and nine-and-sixty females you'd have nine-and-sixty solutions.

Oh well, he told himself, turning the Scourge in the direction of Bloomsbury Street, it's all grist to the mill. He was prepared to put the Archbishop of Canterbury or the Duchess of Whatsit in the dock if it would save his client.

CHAPTER NINE

1

After that several days passed. Bill was still tracking down Bates's past, Crook was engaged with other clients. It rained persistently. Emmy went storming round to Bloomsbury Street.

'Hullo,' she said, pushing past Bill into Crook's derelict office. At least, it was derelict by modern standards. It looked all right to the chap who worked there.

'Hello yourself!' said Crook, cordially. 'How's the girl?'

'That's what I've come about. How much longer has she got to eat her heart out in prison?'

'Oh, she must be used to that, being married to Toby for three years,' was Crook's unsympathetic come-back. 'Now she's on her way out.'

'Seems to have got into a No Through Way Street,' said Emmy.

'Ever had a garden?' inquired Crook, who'd never planted a seed in his life.

'Where have you jumped off to now? You're behaving like a flea, and you don't look like one. It's very disconcerting.'

'If you put in a seed you don't expect it to come up next morning,' Crook pointed out.

But he suspected that he was wasting his breath. Emmy was like the child who, seeing a flower in process of blooming, decided to help God to blossom it.

'It isn't the next morning,' insisted Emmy sturdily. 'It's two weeks. Do you know who killed Toby Graves?'

'It isn't what I know,' Crook assured her, 'it's what you can get the jury to believe.'

'Can't you lay a trap?' asked the unscrupulous Emmy.

'That's not the way it's done. If your enemy sees you laying a trap he'll avoid it. If you give him time he starts getting hot and bothered and is sure you must have laid one and trying to avoid it he falls into the pit.'

'But you haven't digged a pit.' Emmy sounded quite frantic.

'Never do anything you can persuade anyone else to do for you,' murmured Crook, reproachfully. 'Given time, he'll dig his own. They always do.'

'This one might be the exception that proves the rule.'

'I've got my lines out,' Crook told her in what he meant to be a soothing voice.

'And I suppose when you pull them in you'll find an old boot or something on the end. Well, if you won't move, I will.'

'You take care X don't force you underground for keeps while you're trying to force him into the open,' exclaimed Crook, looking really alarmed.

Emmy shook herself and bounced out. Crook watched her departure from the window. All her feathers ruffled and as mad as a lady coot. He looked a bit put out. He had trouble enough on his hands without Emmy shoving her oar in.

* * *

It wasn't only Emmy who was getting frantic. Con couldn't sleep of nights for thinking of Caro, with her odd boyish defiance, her free walk, her lonely courage.

'You're all I've got,' she'd told him, and if that was true, he thought miserably, she hadn't got much.

Sometimes he deliberately let the thought invade his mind—suppose she had given Toby Graves his quietus? Naturally she couldn't tell anyone, because it would make her confidant an accessory after the fact. But it would be lonely to have to hug that knowledge to yourself, while never seeing anyone but wardresses. What did they think? Or didn't they have any opinion? Of course they wouldn't let her guess. And did she imagine the rest of them had forgotten her, taken up their individual lives?

Because he couldn't settle he went out for a walk. It was raining as usual, proper spring weather, people said. The city had a desolate look; it was early closing-day and the shops were all shuttered and barred, and the pavements were empty. Sensible people went to the pictures in weather like this, or stayed at home and read a nice book. The emptiness of London appalled him—like a deserted stronghold, an empty grave, an unloved woman . . . His similes were getting wilder and wilder. At the pub on the corner they were delivering beer. An elderly man wearing a green baize apron went down a flight of steps and turned and stood looking up at the murky grey light.

'Let's 'ave it, Bert,' he called.

Con realised that he was in the way, and moved off hurriedly. He went down to the Embankment and leaned his elbows on the wet concrete. The water had a flat oily look, there was a dispirited barge creeping past Battersea Power Station, a woman went by wearing a plastic mac and calling to an indeterminate dog. A red car flashed by with a noise that must have set the teeth of every television set in the neighbourhood on edge. Con abandoned his contemplation of the river and turned into the little garden where Thomas Carlyle surveys Chelsea with an aloof air. A pigeon surveyed Thomas Carlyle with disapproval, and showed its feelings in the usual manner. Con laughed abruptly.

'That's better,' said a voice. 'You've been looking even wetter than the day.'

He turned sharply. It was another woman in another plastic mac, but this one hadn't got a dog. And it wasn't exactly another woman, it was Emmy Crisp.

'I've been looking for you,' she announced.

'What made you look here?'

'I went to your flat and your landlady said you often went for a walk by the river.'

'Did she?' Con was staggered. Confound it, could one preserve no privacy?

'Perhaps she stalks you. Perhaps she thinks you have a secret life. Or perhaps she thinks you mean to throw yourself in. Not that it matters—what she thinks, I mean. I've been talking to Mr. Crook.'

'Anything fresh?'

'Of course not. I'll tell you what, the poet who wrote about serene I fold my hands and wait, I know my own will come to me, would have had Crook in mind if they'd happened to meet. Oh, I know Fanny says he saved her life, but if he'd been as good as she says he'd have prevented her being kidnapped in the first place. Now, I want to tell you something, if you promise you won't pass it on to him.'

'What is it?' asked Con cautiously.

'I'm tired of waiting. I think our case is like one of those touch and go medical affairs, you've got to make up your mind to take a chance, it may be life or death, Caro's life, perhaps my death, I don't know, but Crook's not the only person to have hunches, and I have a hunch this is the right time for me to make a move.'

Con looked instantly alarmed. To him Emmy seemed about as sane as a confirmed Bedlamite.

'What does that mean?'

'We've reached the point where, in a detective story, there'd be a second corpse. Well, I don't want the second corpse, because most likely it would be me, but we've got to trip X up. I'm going round to see Daisy Price.'

'Why Daisy Price?' Con was all at sea. 'Or do you think . . . ?'

'It's not what I think, it's what you can persaude a jury to believe.'

Emmy's parodying of Crook was astonishingly lifelike. 'I just thought I'd mention it, so if you don't see me around in the next day or two you'll know where to look. And I'm going right away.'

2

Don Price had recently come off duty. He came up the narrow alley leading to the back entrance of the flat to tell his wife he was going out.

'Don't drink yourself silly,' returned Daisy in her most wifely manner.

'Wouldn't I like to have the chance,' exclaimed Don with feeling. 'To see some of these chaps at the Hat and Feather or the Coach In Hand—must put down a cool quid during the evening.'

'Next thing I suppose they'll be asking the State to give them beer tickets. Men, they make me sick.'

'You stay at home and be sick by yourself,' said Don, disagreeably.

'You'd like that, wouldn't you? Not me. If you're going out I'll go along and see Alice for an hour or two.'

'Uncommon struck on Alice lately, aren't you?'

'She's my only sister.'

'She's been your only sister for upwards of twenty-five years and you don't seem to have minded much one way or the other.'

'You could give me one of those quids you were talking about before you go. I'll need something.'

'It won't cost you a quid to visit your sister Alice.'

'We might go along to the Albert and have a drink. Alice is used to a bit of life. She and Jim always went out of an evening, and she's not one to sit at home and mope because her husband's been taken.'

'Goes out to celebrate it at the Albert six nights out of seven I shouldn't wonder,' agreed Don in the same hostile voice. 'What's wrong with a nice cup of tea at home?'

'I notice you don't want to stay at home with a nice cup of tea,' flashed Daisy.

'Don't know what you women get married for,' said Don. 'Mum and Alice—Alice and Mum. Anyone 'ud think you hadn't got a husband to look after.'

'That's you all over,' flashed Daisy. 'Grudge me having any relations, I suppose.'

'And if you're so set on seeing your sister to-night, she can buy you a drink for a change. She did very nicely out of Jim's funeral, so I've heard.'

Daisy seemed convulsed with rage. 'Of all the mean miserable skinflints! Can't spare me the price of a pint, but you don't stint yourself—oh no! Moment my back's turned out you go with one of your fancy women—red carnation in your button-hole and all, scent on your handkerchief, I shouldn't wonder.'

'What the hell's this?' Don's voice was suddenly dangerous. 'What time are you talking about?'

Daisy seemed lost to reason. 'Time I went home to Mum. I thought you raised less dust than usual about me going. But when I wanted a taxi-fare, oh no, you hadn't got it, not you. You only had five bob and whatever you could touch Mrs. Benyon for. Well, all I can say is it was enough to take you and your—friend' (no toad spitting venom, if indeed they do, could have surpassed Daisy in this instant of supreme malignity)—'to somewhere more posh than you ever take me! When did you last buy me as much as a bunch of violets?'

Don came a little closer. 'You know a lot, don't you, Daise? For a girl who was staying in the country, I mean.'

'These things get about. Someone saw you . . .' Her voice was suddenly shaken by panic.

'Fancy that! Happen to mention where? Come on, you bitch, let's have it. What were you doing? Trailing me? Well?'

''Course not. How was I to guess . . . ?'

'And who was it saw me? You, p'raps. Come on, Daise, I'm your husband, I've a right to know. Were you with Mum that week-end? Or—just where were you sleeping that Friday night?'

His hand came out and caught her arm; she uttered a cry of terror and pain.

'I don't know what you mean.'

Deliberately he twisted her arm. '"I've got to go to Mum Friday, Don. Her heart . . ." It wasn't Mum's heart you were thinking about so much as . . .'

Daisy screamed. The whole world had shrunk to the little patch of carpet on which they stood. Neither had noticed the door pushed softly open

and the diminutive and by now trembling figure of
Emmy Crisp peer round it. Emmy felt incapable of
movement. If this was marriage, oh thrice blest to
wither on the virgin thorn.

3

Mr. Crook was right. Caro could have told them
something, too. And now Don and Daisy Price?
Don was speaking again.

'Perhaps you'd like to do a bit of explaining,
Daise. How come you know about the button-
hole and all that? Seeing you was with your
Mum, that is.'

Daisy was white to the lips. 'I told you—these
things get about.'

Abruptly the telephone rang. 'That's all right,'
said Don curtly. 'Let it ring. We're not at home.'

Daisy tried to push past him, but he held her off
with one arm. The telephone rang and rang.

'You'll have one of the tenants down,' Daisy
muttered, with the air of someone who hardly knows
what she says.

Don put out his free hand and jerked the receiver
off its stand.

'Hullo!' piped a little voice, like the voice of a
ghost. 'That you, Daisy? Or Don?'

Don put the receiver to his ear. Daisy made an
ineffectual grab at it.

'It's for me.'

'Who's that?' asked Don coolly.

'That you, Don? This is Alice. Daise there?'

'You just caught her,' said Don, his voice smooth

with hate. 'She was just coming along to see you as usual.'

'Usual?' exclaimed the little voice. It twittered and twanged quite clearly on the sombre air. 'That's a good one. Me and Mum were beginning to think she'd be found in a hole in the wall or under a floorboard. Quite fashionable, these days. Not so much as a picture postcard.'

'Well, now, isn't that funny?' said Don. 'You and your Mum must be suffering from loss of memory. Daise was along of her Mum two or three weeks back, and she's been running across to see you a couple of nights a week oh for ever so long. Unless, of course, Daise has kind of got herself muddled. Have you, Daise?'

Daisy Price's face was dreadful to behold. 'You let me speak to my sister,' she croaked.

At the other end of the line Alice suddenly tumbled to the situation.

'Here, half a minute, Don,' she said. 'You're right. I was getting mixed. 'Course Daise was over to see Mum. Only you know how it is, time goes so fast you get mixed, and a . . .'

Don threw down the receiver so violently the whole instrument clattered to the floor.

'So that's the way of it! Your Mum! Your sister Alice. And all the time—why, you're worse'n a whore. At least she gets paid.'

Emmy, appalled, remembered a line from one of the poets of her school-days:

Each eye shrank up to a serpent's eye.

That was how Don was looking at his wife now. He was even moving his head from side to side the way a snake does. His face was so close to his wife's Emmy thought she must be half suffocated by what Shakespeare had once described as a surfeit of stinking breath. Like sulphur it was.

'If you've got anything to think with you'd better use it now, while you've still got a chance,' Don warned his wife brutally. 'And remember, Daise, it better be good. Too bad you haven't got another sister you might have gone visiting. Or a brother. P'raps that's the answer. The one that sticketh closer than a brother. And you don't need to tell me his name, because I know it.'

'You can't,' exclaimed Daisy, trapped by her own indignation. 'He never wrote nor rung up here . . . Let go my wrist, Don. You're hurting.'

'What, that? Why, Daise, I haven't begun yet. The floor's still yours. P'rhaps you found when you got to the station you'd forgotten your powder-puff and you came hurrying back to fetch it. Don won't be there at six-thirty, you thought. He's going up to hang Mrs. B's curtains. Safe for me to come sneaking in, no one about . . . Played it pretty, didn't you, girl, all these months? "Good-bye, Don. Shall I give your love to Mum? Alice says thanks ever so for that half of whisky." I suppose you and him got stinko on it. What a laugh! Hope you enjoyed yourself, Daise, because, you see, your laughing days are over. Over for good and all. You've gone too far at last, my girl. Bein' a common cheat's one thing, being a murderess . . .'

'Have you taken leave of your senses, Don Price? Murderess, indeed!'

'You keep your play-acting for the police, my girl. Well, have some sense. There's only one chap you could have come back for. Wonder I didn't think

of it earlier, the times I've found him slinking out
of my flat. Mind you, I don't blame you. It was
time someone broke his bleeding neck. Only—police
don't see things that way.'

'If you mean I came back for Toby Graves you're
crazier than I thought.'

'Well, why did you come back?'

'I came back for the letters. Yes, of course we
wrote letters. What were we going to do the days
we couldn't meet? Only he didn't send them here.
"Burn them," he said, "they're dynamite." But I
couldn't. They were all I had, see. I put 'em where
I didn't suppose you'd ever think of looking for
them, not in my bag, you're always rummaging
in that; and when I went out of the house they
went with me. Only for some reason, changing my
things into a different bag, I forgot them, and it was
only when I got to the station I found I'd left them
behind. I know you. Minute my back's turned you
go rummaging through everything I've got in the
hope of turning up an odd half-crown.'

'Why not?' inquired her husband. 'You'd cleaned
me out, hadn't you? If there was a half-crown
going . . . I knew someone had been into the flat
that night. I told that lawyer chap. Funny I never
thought it might be you. By the way, got those
letters handy?'

'I haven't got them anywhere. I told Ray—and he
said, "I warned you not to keep them." Made me
tear them up with him standing by. It was—oh, like
treading on my own heart.'

'Very poetic,' said Don, 'and does you credit, I'm
sure. I suppose the gentleman wants to marry you?'

'Don't be so daft, Don. How can he—in his
position and married anyhow?'

'Remember his name?'

Daisy stared. 'Remember . . . ?'

'The police 'ull want to know. What's called an alibi, Daise. Because, you see, when they hear my story they're going to think the same as I do, that your precious Ray is all boloney and you really came back to see Toby Graves. Funny to think I told them what I heard—"You're slipping." If only I'd knocked on the door I might have found you there. Mind you, they can't make me give evidence. Husbands can't be forced to testify, only—there's nothing to stop them, Daise. That's a nice string of pearls you're wearing. Beads you said they were. Seven-and-six in the bargain basement, you said. Bet you and Ray had a good laugh over that. Look nicer round your neck than a rope will. Or—my hands p'raps.'

Someone screamed. A voice cried on a high dreadful note, 'No, no. Not another murder.'

Both Prices turned, whirled, to see the preposterous little figure, jerking as though someone held the strings of a marionette, the gaudy red straw hat on the brilliant metallic hair, saw the sheet-white face, the open screaming mouth. That scream saved Daisy. Her husband's hand fell away from her throat. He stepped forward.

'And who the bloody hell told you you could come barging in without so much as by your leave?' he demanded, taking a step forward. 'How did you get in anyway?'

'You left the back door ajar, the bell's broke,' Daisy muttered.

'I did ring,' whispered Emmy. 'You didn't hear.'

'And how long have you been eavesdropping, may I ask? You know what they say about listeners not coming to any good.'

Like a miracle life returned to Emmy's stricken limbs. Terror lent her wings; she was out of the flat, down the passage and through the alley before either of her companions realised what she was about. She could hear a strange thundering noise, like the feet of horses, she told herself; it was a minute before she realised it was the thundering of her own heart.

'Mr. Crook,' she was thinking. 'A clue. Must tell Mr. Crook.'

She no longer had any doubt as to the truth. It had been revealed to her during the past ten minutes or so, but it would be no good to dearest Caro until it was shared with Mr. Crook. Crook would know what to do. She, Emmy, was helpless. It was going to be touch and go, she was aware of that. Price wouldn't let her contact Crook if he could prevent it, and there seemed every possibility that he could. Still, now that she *knew* the identity of Toby's caller on that last night of his life, she'd practically be a murderess herself if she died without passing on her secret. On and on she ran, feeling as though her lungs would burst, down Morris Street and into the welcome lights and bustle of the High Street. Here she stopped for an instant to look in a plate-glass window; people were moving pretty freely, most of them making for home, since a mist was thickening the twilit air, and the B.B.C. had warned listeners of the possibility of fog later in the evening. Emmy plunged forward again, crossed the road, espied Don some way off on the other side. Her unfortunate hat made her a landmark; she snatched it off and flung it into an empty doorway. Two girls turned to stare after her. Shouldn't have done that, thought Emmy. Made me more conspicuous than ever. An old tramp of a woman came past, saw the hat, glanced surreptitiously to left and right, picked it up and jammed it on her scarecrow curls. Emmy stood in a queue buying evening papers and watched. Don's attention had been distracted for an instant by the bobbing red hat. Emmy put a little hand over her heart, which felt like the ball in the cup-and-ball game, leaping up and down . . . Oh silly me, she thought, showing my hand like that. Why couldn't I have crept out? Mother was right. 'Get a bit of sense, girl,' she used to say. 'Don't go putting all your cards on the table, because you can be certain nobody else is going to.'

Across the road, like a star leading the wanderer home, she saw the lighted doorway of the Hat and Feather and jumping into the traffic and just missing annihilation by a black saloon car, she pushed her way in. Already several people were sitting up on stools at the snack bar, or grouped round little tables with a glass of what-you-fancy in front of them. They looked up as Emmy entered, and most of them didn't look away again at once. Not surprising really, only of course you can never see yourself. She looked as if she'd blown in from the other side of the moon. Emmy was conscious of their stares; she looked round awkwardly. In Bath women of her age and appearance didn't go around on solitary pub-crawls. She felt she'd have given a lot to have Crook's burly form beside her, or even Con's, though naturally he wouldn't make quite the same impression.

Joe caught sight of her and jerked a bandaged thumb at an empty stool. Emmy hurried forward. The stool was higher than she anticipated and she nearly fell off. Another sign of the general inconsiderateness of things, she thought. No one ever dreamed of putting an extra rung for the benefit of people like herself who had short legs.

'What have you done to your thumb?' she asked, as Joe came forward and put a knife and fork and a plate with a paper napkin on it in front of her.

He knew who she was, of course. It was characteristic of Emmy that everybody knew her by this time, everyone who mattered, that is.

'Chipped a bit out of it,' said Joe. 'Doesn't stop me pulling beer-handles, though.'

'What are you going to have, Miss Crisp?' asked Rosa, coming forward. Joe moved up the line to attend to some new-comers.

'Everything looks quite delicious,' murmured Emmy, feeling her heart gradually calm down. She'd be safe here, even Don wouldn't take a chance in this crowd. And what a crowd! A lot of the regulars—she recognised Lessing—and there was Mr. Benson from the chemist and elderly Mr. Raikes from the jeweller's on the corner, and already the boys were getting round the dart-board. Place must be a goldmine, she thought, choosing tunny salad and a glass of sherry, the only drink she felt safe in ordering. Interesting working in a bar, never knowing who might come in, soldiers, sailors, tinkers, tailors, bishops in camouflage, your worst enemy and your best friend. Murderers, too, perhaps. The word sprang unbidden to her mind. She glanced up as Rosa put the salad in front of her and in the big mirror behind the bar she saw the door open and Don Price come in. She picked up her sherry glass, sipped it, saw the brown stuff run down her wrist. Joe came back and began awkwardly pouring out a couple of double gins.

'You and Mr. Crook solved the mystery yet?' he asked.

Emmy stared in the mirror. Don had gone to the farther end of the bar.

'As a matter of fact,' she said confidently, 'it's in the bag. By the way, I suppose Mr. Crook hasn't been in to-night?'

'This is off his beat,' Joe explained rather grimly. 'He only comes here if he wants something.'

'That's true of everybody,' said Emmy, 'but, of course, I know what you mean. Mr. Bates, if he should come in—this might be one of the nights when he wants something—would you say I'd rung him up and it was very urgent?'

Joe looked puzzled. 'If you've rung him up already, he'd know, wouldn't he?'

'That's the point. I haven't. But in case he's out when I do and I don't get another chance, will you tell him?'

'If he comes in,' said Joe. He still looked wary. He glanced round him. Emmy had spoken in low tones, but there was a chance she had been overheard. She was looking very queer.

'You all right, Miss Crisp?'

'Of course. I'm just going to finish this delicious salad and then I'm going to ring him up. There's a box quite near, isn't there? The Post Office is closed, of course . . .'

'One on the opposite corner,' said Joe. 'And if that's occupied, and it mostly is, it's not only the House of Commons that talks all night, there's another in Banbury Mews—you know?'

'Yes.' She managed a little trilling laugh. 'You wouldn't think I'd need to ask, having lived in this neighbourhood. But as one gets older one's memory . . .' She seemed to have forgotten telling Caro she was like the elephant. She felt for her purse. Joe moved off and Rosa came up to say what about a cup of coffee?

'Well, that does sound nice,' Emmy agreed. 'It has turned cold, hasn't it?'

Cold? She was trembling. 'Goose walking over your grave?' asked Rosa.

Over her grave? Silly to think she might even now be tottering on the edge, but then she'd always held that half life's enjoyment resides in the fact that you never know from one minute to the next what's going to happen to you.

The coffee came and was hot and strong. Peering cautiously in the glass Emmy saw that Don was sitting with some fellows near the wall, with his back to her. She paid her shot, said, 'Good evening' to Rosa—Joe was busy, she couldn't see him—and received a cheerful, 'Bye-bye, Miss Crisp.' Then she was on her feet and edging her way towards the door.

As she pushed it open she was sure she heard someone say something about a Belisha beacon—that horrid porter from the flats?—and she was convinced, when she heard the laugh that followed, that they were talking about her. She bridled with indignation. It was her hair, wasn't it? because she knew, that's what they meant. But if she *liked* it that colour . . .

As Joe had prophesied, the box on the corner was occupied, by a languid young woman with black hair flowing to her shoulders and oxblood nails. Emmy hung about, secretly conscious of that over-bright hair, planning what she'd say to Crook when her turn came.

'I *know* who visited Toby Graves the night he died.' That would be a sufficiently explosive beginning. She mustn't dither, mustn't talk too much, make him impatient—when men were impatient they never listened to what you were saying, and this was an occasion where every word was important.

She looked furiously across the road. 'Come out, come out,' she willed the languid girl. But the girl took no notice at all, simply shifted her stance and went on talking. Even when she did put the receiver down it was only to put three more coppers into the box and dial another number.

'It's no good,' decided Emmy, desperately. 'I shall have to try the other phone.'

The streets seemed unusually crowded, and it was only when she heard a girl remark to her companion, 'Thursday night is Family night, I suppose they let 'em all out then,' with an unmistakable glance in her, Emmy's, direction, that she realised she was in one of those districts of London where the shops remain open until a couple of hours later than usual. In Oxford Street, she remembered, that would be seven o'clock. Here it appeared to be eight, at all events for the big drapers and ladies' outfitters, Hunt and Marry, round whose crowded windows the women surged and commented.

'Wonder what the shopgirls think of this late closing,' was Emmy's characteristic reflection.

But presumably they had time off to make up for the extra work. In Miss Crisp's experience, a tank couldn't put much over on the modern girl.

Her little figure, with the bright hair that seemed to her supersensitiveness to be attracting more attention than she cared about, was pushed this way and that till she felt she'd be knocked off her feet. Then the thought came to her that if she bought herself a scarf, something sedate, mind you, she could tie it over her head and escape attention that had become unwelcome, if not actually sinister.

She swam through one of the swing doors of Hunt & Marry with about forty other people and found she'd landed up in the mackintosh department. Scarves were three shops away. She turned to the right and was almost submerged in the crowd, crushed actually against a stand of plastic macs. Plastic in the mass had a queer smell, suffocating in a way. An idiotic rhyme came into her mind, something about not surviving attacks in a forest of macs. She smiled nervously, and a young lady (Emmy was out of date, nobody talked about shop girls any more) moved round the counter, thinking, 'Gosh! Where do they find them? Better serve this one quick before she gets back on her broomstick.'

'Want something, dear?' she asked.

Emmy turned. 'Yes, a mac. I left mine at home and it's turning damp, the wireless warned us of mist, possibly a fog. Yes, a mac, with a hood.'

That would be ten times as disguising as a scarf.

'Baby Bats all right,' reflected the girl resignedly. 'Any special colour, dear?'

'Well, let me see.' If she was going to spend money she might as well get some pleasure out of it. 'Not red, that's too bright. Something more discreet—green say—to match my eyes.'

She laughed perkily. The girl, Maudie, touched her perm. As if the colour mattered when you looked like this one!

'Sorry, dear,' she said without moving. 'Haven't a green, not in your size. You're p'tite, see?'

'Are you sure . . . ?'

'Red's nice,' said Maudie. 'Why not have a red? Cheerful, too. No one could miss you in red.' Though it would be hard to miss this one short of an invisible cloak, she added to herself.

Emmy suddenly recovered her individuality. If she was going to die to-night, and she wasn't at all sure about her chances, at least she could enjoy her last few minutes of life.

'You can't have been listening,' she scolded. 'I said not red. If there isn't a green one on this stand, what about one of the others?'

'All the same, dear. Difficult to fit anyone your size. Have you tried Teenagers?'

'I am not a Teenager,' announced Emmy. 'I should have imagined even you could have seen that.'

Maudie's eyes flew open. What sauce! Talking to her like that. Who did she think she was?

'Well, we haven't got a green,' she said, turning back towards her counter.

Emmy was like a tiger who has smelt man in the neighbourhood. 'Who is the head of this department?'

'She's having dinner. Anyway, she'd tell you the same as me.'

But she was intimidated all the same. Who'd have thought it of the old girl?

Now that her blood was up Emmy, actually forgetting the extremity of her peril, insisted on being shown mackintoshes of every weight and shade. She dragged the (almost) speechless Maudie from stand to stand. She tried on sixteen mackintoshes before she found one in a shade of rather dark blue that satisfied her. She stood in front of the long mirror putting it on, arranging the over-large hood to conceal every scrap of her gay hair.

'Pay at the desk, please,' said Maudie, in a faint voice, giving her the bill. The 'please' was an accident. It didn't do to fawn, but she wasn't herself to-night.

Emmy paid for the mackintosh, pushed the bill into her pocket and marched out of the shop. As she passed Maudie she said, in quite a friendly voice, 'You'll know me next time you see me, won't you?'

Maudie gave her a heartbroken look—she'd no idea how soon she was going to see her peppery customer again.

'If we get many more like that,' she confided to her friend, Marleen, 'I shall give in my notice. I mean, you've got to think of yourself, haven't you?'

Back in the street, the momentary thrill of battle past, the thing that had been lurking in the back of Emmy's mind, something that had bothered her like a lash in your eye or a pebble in your shoe, made its presence known. She realised in a flash what it was.

While she was waiting on the corner for the girl in the telephone booth to stop her clacking—and what a hope *that* had been—someone had come out of the Hat and Feather and walked softly past.

'What of it?' she asked herself. 'They can't live on the premises.'

But the cold tremors continued to run up and down her spine, as, looking this way and that, she darted across the road, like a hen hoping to get a treasured bit of bread before anyone else saw it, reflected a motorist who nearly ran her down, and arrived breathless at the mouth of the Mews.

4

Murder had, in fact, followed Emmy out of the Hat and Feather. Lucky, he'd thought, it was Family Night, plenty of crowds to conceal you. Not too difficult to push an old girl under a bus. But he decided against it. Too much publicity, too many questions asked, and that howling cad, Crook, on the trail, Crook, to whom no holds were barred and who probably had never even heard of the Queensberry Rules. He moved a little farther off, pretended to be looking in a tobacconist's window; there was a piece of looking-glass here, he could see her movements without apparently watching. Then he saw her turn and scurry towards the Mews, and knew his hour was upon him. He dived over the road and reached the entrance while she was still on the other side. His original idea of following her was superseded by a much better one. Get there first—the Mews was a cul-de-sac, no one could approach from the farther end, and in that narrow alley between high factory walls, whose workers had the sense to ban overtime, surely he could find some dark spot in which to conceal himself, and wait.

He hurried along under the shadow of the wall. The lighting here wasn't very good and he threw quick glances over his shoulder; but there was no sign of Emmy by the time he reached the box. He walked past and a few steps farther on he found the ideal hiding-place. Three stone steps led down to a locked wooden gate, forming a recess in which a man could remain invisible. He took up his position and waited.

He waited so long that panic began to assail him. She must, after all, have gone back to the other box, but just as he was preparing to emerge, he heard little quick footsteps pattering towards him and Emmy came down and walked into the box.

'Scarey-cat!' she was apostrophising herself, as she pulled the door open. 'People have got better things to do than trail you.'

But such was her mental confusion that now she couldn't recall Crook's number, and must pull out the appropriate directory and look it up. She dumped her blue plastic bag and wished she had thought to bring her reading-glasses. The pages stuck together, dog-eared, of course. And when she found the right one she was horrified to discover how many Crooks there were in the London area alone. With a gloved finger she moved up the column. Suddenly instinct, that unsleeping guardian of the female sex, caused her to glance up. She saw nothing, yet the impression remained, as of a shadow passing across the face of the moon. She half-turned, but before she could reassure herself there was a faint click, as the door of the booth was pulled open. Her mouth gaped, she prepared to scream, but a hand came over her lips, crushing them against her teeth.

'Take care, they're not National Health,' she wanted to say, but she was most effectually gagged. She struggled, putting up her thin little hands, but she might as well have tried to dislodge a leech. Murder was as desperate as she; he could hear the furious clanging of his own heart as he pressed her against himself and his hands, pitiless thumbs outspread, sought for that thin stringy throat. That infernal mackintosh hampered him, but she hadn't

a chance, poor Emmy Crisp. Still, this was harder
than Toby Graves had been. Of course, Toby had
been caught quite unprepared. That second of
recognition had given Emmy a thousand-to-one
chance. Still, it's only on films and in racecourse
romance that the thousand-to-one outsider finishes
first past the post.

Emmy felt her breath deserting her; darkness
flapped in her eyes like the wings of some ill-omened
bird. No, no, she thought she said, but her voice was
dumb. As for Murder—Ask of the winter rain June's
withered rose again, ask grief of the salt sea—before
you looked for mercy in that dark relentless heart.

Suddenly, all in a minute, the struggle came
to an end. Emmy's head in its monstrous blue
shroud lolled against her attacker's arm, her knees
crumpled, her arms hung limply at her side, life
seemed to ooze out of her. Murder was taken by
surprise by the suddenness of the collapse; she
seemed to fall through his hands like water pouring
over a cliff; as she dropped, an unprotesting bundle
on the floor at his feet, there came from her lips
a long dreadful groan as though life gave him
best, abandoned the fight. He stood, shaking,
looking down at the little wrecked figure that
a few minutes ago had been enterprising defiant
Emily Crisp. As he stooped to make sure—make
sure—he'd finished the appalling job, his heart
leaped madly in his bosom, almost suffocating him.
He was standing, back bowed, facing down towards
the end of the cul-de-sac, and from the lighted area
behind him he heard the unmistakable sound of
footsteps. It wasn't only one pair of feet, but
two. They were clearly distinguished; the tapping
high heels of a girl out with her 'date'. While the

man's steps were sober, ruthless. And they were coming nearer—and nearer. He stood transfixed; then hurriedly grabbing the telephone receiver he began to gabble nonsense down the unconnected line. His other hand crammed the hat lower over his eyes.

'There's someone there,' said the girl's voice. 'I told you . . .'

'Well, wait a minute,' the young man urged. But the girl was impatient and plucked urgently at his sleeve.

'Come on, John. We'll miss the beginning of the big picture. Your call can wait. There'll be a box at the cinema; you can ring up during the News.'

Murder could scarcely believe his luck; they were going away. But their coming had unbalanced his resolve. Now he had only one wish, to get away from here, away from his poor little victim, curled like some winged bird at his feet, back to the bright lights and cheerful faces. But first, first he must arrange such security for himself as he could. He dared not leave Emmy here for the next casual person wanting to make a call. At the same time, it was dangerous, ghastly dangerous. And at the realisation of how very dangerous it was he put up his hand, wrapped in a handkerchief, and twisted the electric light bulb from its socket. This time there was no possibility of rigging the stage, faking the evidence, now the longer discovery could be postponed the better. In short, his immediate task was to dispose of the body. That, said the pundits, was every murderer's headache, but in his own case he had the hiding-place prepared. Down at the foot of those three steep steps, crushed against the door that wouldn't be unlocked before morning, Emmy could lie in the dark till the new day dawned.

★ ★ ★

'Hullo,' said the young man, turning at the mouth of the Mews, 'light's gone out. Chap must have finished.'

'Come on,' urged the girl, impatiently. 'Must be nearly half-past now. You can't go back.' On such trifles may destiny hang!

Inside the telephone box Murder was feverishly at work: the darkness made him clumsy, for the only light now came from higher up the mews, a cold greenish beam; he felt like someone swimming under water; stop, consider, and you were drowned. He stooped and caught Emmy's wrist between his own cold fingers. It was flaccid, not just chill but lifeless. If you put out a lamp you could re-kindle it, but this was different. Without a word, with scarcely a sound he had extinguished an immortal light. He remembered the glimpse he had had of her face in that hideous blue frame, the starting eyes, the cyanosed flesh. Don't think, don't think, he warned himself. If you start thinking you're lost. He had believed life had made him hard-boiled, but it wasn't true. Not that any pity stirred in him, he was moved only by fear for himself, fear of his discovery, fear of his own weakness, fear of the thing that had been Emmy Crisp. A text he had learned as a boy floated through his mind, something about killing the body but not killing the soul. For a ghastly moment he had the sensation of a phantom Emmy at his side.

Stooping, he caught the body under the armpits; she was a little thing, couldn't weigh much more than a good-sized bird. But an inert body, however small, hangs heavy on the hands. And the shape of the kiosk and his own position enhanced his difficulties. He tried to gather her in his arms, but the fallen telephone directory, her curled-up position and his own stance all combined to hinder him, and for one grim moment they were jammed together in the doorway; her head fell over against his foot. Now fury possessed him, he tugged, felt her caught by some obstruction but tore her free; the blue mackintosh caught in the door-hinge, but he freed that, too; and then they were out of the box, he could lift her, thrust her down the steps; she fell with a sickening sound, rolling over against the dank uneven stones.

He waited no longer; only as he passed the box he put in his gloved hand and snatched up her bag. It was a chance in a hundred, but he couldn't afford to let it go. When Emmy was found, if her bag was missing, the police might think it was one of these smash-and-grab attempts that had gone too far. The telephone was swinging, but he forgot about that. He opened the bag as he made his way up the Mews, took out the purse-cum-note-case and pitched the bag over the wall into a bit of bombed ground. When he opened the purse he almost burst into crazy laughter; because there was nothing in it worth risking even a month's imprisonment for, a little silver, a few coppers, but the note-compartment was empty. Still, no one would know that, only he, who wouldn't tell, and Emmy who couldn't, smashed down there in the dark. Near the alley's mouth he became cautious, but luck favoured him. Nobody was passing on this side of the street, and an instant later he had crossed and was mingling

with the crowds. He retained enough sense not
to re-enter the Hat and Feather from the front
entrance, but slipped down the passage to where a
sign said Gentlemen. If he were seen here it wouldn't
matter, but nobody did see him, nobody was there.
A moment later he had rejoined the crowd in the bar.
He looked round him quickly. Had anyone noticed
his absence?

Someone stepped up to the counter.

'Another pint, Joe.'

He heard his own voice. 'Another pint.'

Odd how, after all that had happened, his hand
was steady enough to lift and set down the tankard
without spilling a drop.

CHAPTER TEN

1

Henry Smith was a medical student about to qualify
and qualify brilliantly, who was, on this eventful
night, in a foul temper because his girl had
transferred her attentions to someone with more
immediate prospects. This was a new experience
for Henry, who was accustomed to young women
queueing for his company, and he went romping
round the neighbourhood looking for an empty
telephone booth, so as to call up one of the others.
He remembered the one in Banbury Mews, and
walked towards it. There was no light burning,
but that didn't discompose him. He knew about
the young gangsters who went round leaving a trail
of minor wreckage in their path, and anyway he had

a torch in his pocket. But when he pulled open the door and flashed the torch he saw the bulb where Murder had left it on top of the directory-holder.

'Courting couple?' he wondered. It seemed an odd place to choose, when it wasn't even raining. He picked it up—it was quite cold, must have been there some time, and screwed it back.

It was then that he saw the shoe lying on the floor of the box.

He stooped and picked it up, thinking what an extraordinary thing to find in such a place. It wasn't a cast clout, it was a perfectly good, well-made, well-kept brown leather walking-shoe of the kind known as court. It was small—he found himself irresistibly thinking of Cinderella's slipper. But what on earth was a woman doing leaving a shoe behind in a telephone box? She'd have to walk back up the Mews to the high road, even if she had a Rolls-Royce waiting at the top. And anyway, why only one?

He tracked out of the box, holding his torch low; it hadn't escaped him that there was a directory sprawled on the floor and general signs of a struggle; and so, after another minute, he found Emmy lying in a huddle at the foot of the three steps, her face jammed against the door.

Instantly he forgot all his affections and vanities; now he was the doctor, the dedicated man. In a trice he was down on his knees, was lifting her, bringing her to the level of the street. There was blood on the little gaminesque face, but it wasn't that that troubled him. Holding her against his shoulder he felt for her pulse. At first he thought it was lost, but just as hope wore thin he found it, the merest thread of life, but not gone, not gone. And then, faint as the first light of morning, distant, dying away like a vanishing cry, he discerned the beating of that indomitable heart.

A moment later the police were shocked to hear that a woman had been attacked and seriously injured in Banbury Mews. Their informant described himself, a shade prematurely, as Dr. Smith.

'Get a wiggle on,' said Dr. Smith. 'There's one chance in a hundred you might save her yet.'

And hanging up the receiver he went back to Emmy. As he left the box his foot cracked on something and, stooping, he found a blue bone button with a scrap of blue thread attached. He slipped it into his pocket, and promptly forgot all about it.

2

The clock at the Hat and Feather stood at 10.29. Rosa was chanting, 'Drink up, gentlemen, glasses, please, time, gents, time,' when the door of the saloon bar was pushed violently open and a young man barged in.

Rosa started to say they were closed but he broke in tersely, 'Still a good five minutes. Your clock's fast. Scotch and soda, and you better make it a double.'

As Rosa hesitated, glancing at Joe, he added,

'This is an occasion. You don't get a murder just round the corner every day of the week—at least, it's to be hoped not.'

The men who had been moving towards the door stopped, as though Henry Smith was the Medusa, whose face turns every human thing to stone.

Joe turned sharply, putting down the bottle he held.

'What's that you said?'

'You trying to do me out of my drink?' demanded the young man, belligerently.

'Oh, serve him, Rosa. Yes, go on. You have to take a chance sometimes. Besides, you never know. P'raps he's the police.'

'The police at the moment are sitting round the body in Prince Charles Hospital. They're going to have their work cut out, anyway.'

'Who was it?' asked Rosa, handing the glass across the counter.

'Lady hadn't got a handbag, but there was an envelope in her pocket addressed to Miss E. Crisp.'

'Miss Crisp!' The voices of the two Bates rang out together.

The young man's eyebrows lifted. 'Know her? You're the chap the police are looking for.'

Joe leaned his big hands on the counter. 'That mean anything?'

'All they know at present is that she's a woman of about sixty, whose name may be E. Crisp. Anyone who can identify her—can you?'

Rosa said, 'She was in here to-night. Where did they find her?'

'I found her—tucked away behind a telephone box in Banbury Mews.'

'Yes,' muttered Joe heavily. 'I told her to try that one.'

'Poor old girl!' said Rosa. 'I thought she looked a bit shaken when she was in here. But—murder! Are you sure?'

'Some chap had done his best to strangle her. You can take the word of a doctor-in-embryo. If you've ever seen anyone who's been strangled . . .'

Joe said, 'She was going to ring Mr. Crook. I wonder if she got through?'

'If she got through,' retorted Rosa, sensibly, 'you'd have had him round here long ago. What time did she leave, Joe? Round about seven, wasn't it?'

But Joe couldn't be sure. He'd been lending Bob a hand in the public bar, he said. 'Let's have it,' said Rosa. 'Is she . . .'

'Dead? Well, she wasn't when I left her, but I wouldn't give much for her chances. The police are haunting like vultures in the hopes that she'll come round long enough to give her attacker a name.'

'Is there much likelihood of it?' Joe spoke thoughtfully.

Henry Smith shrugged. 'If it was me and I opened my eyes and saw a crowd of bluebottles round my bed, I'd turn my face to the wall and shut 'em again for good.' It might have been Arthur Crook speaking.

Rosa said, 'Joe, you'd better let Mr. Crook know what's happened. Poor old girl! I wonder why anyone should want to strangle her.'

But if Rosa was puzzled Joe wasn't, and nor was

Don Price, who had been with a number of other men near the door when young Smith came in. He had a pretty good idea what Emmy was going to tell Crook; he decided to go back and have a word with Daise, and while Joe went through to the back to get Crook on the telephone Don slipped out unperceived.

3

Crook was having a late session with Bill Parsons, who was submitting the results of his enquiries in a number of directions during the past few days.

'Nice lot we've tangled up,' Crook allowed. 'Murder—blackmail—dope—it all adds up to a nasty smell. I told you that chap wasn't calling himself Bates last time I heard of him,' he added. 'Saw his picture in the papers and that sort of chap doesn't change much.'

Then the telephone rang and it was that chap, Bates, on the other end. Crook listened for a moment in silence. Then he said coolly, 'Serves her right. Why in Pete's name can't these amateurs leave the job to the chaps who're paid to do it? But I suppose when they do that the rest of us will wake up and find ourselves in Heaven, where there's no crime to be solved, and we shall be out of a job.'

He slammed down the receiver and explained the situation to Bill.

'I knew that lollipop would muck up the works if she had a chance,' he said. 'Well, we've got to move fast now, if we don't want another corpse on our hands.'

Late though it was he hurried round to the Prince Charles Hospital, where he stormed the official ramparts like a stallion going through a fence.

'Crook's the name, Arthur Crook, and don't forget it. It's going to be important. Now get this. Miss Crisp's to have no visitors, not if they say they're the Archbishop of Canterbury or a brother or a family lawyer. Because she don't know the Archbishop of Canterbury and she and her brother don't hit it off, and so far as she's got any family lawyer, that's me. Don't let any stranger fool you that he's the family doctor, don't even let a strange rozzer through without he's been vetted by the inspector. This is murder—and not the first. If Miss Crisp dies I'll see to it the Hospital's put on the spot as an accessory.'

They broke into a storm of protest, but Crook swept all that aside like Gulliver disposing of the Lilliputians.

'That's what I said and that's what I meant, and you ask the police if Arthur Crook's word ain't his bond. How's tricks anyway?'

He asked if he could see the doctor, but was assured coldly that Dr. Martin had gone home. Crook wasted no time.

'I'll be back in the morning, and don't think you'll keep me out by putting padlocks on the doors. Because I mean to see him—what's his name? Martin?—if I have to fly through a window on a broomstick.'

He looked perfectly capable of carrying out his threat.

4

After all, Don didn't have his few words with Daise, because when he got back he found an empty flat and a scribbled note on the table:

I'm off. And this time I shan't be back. I don't want to be found with my head battered in like Toby Graves.
Daisy.

He stood swaying a bit—take it all in all, it had been quite an evening—staring at the letters that wouldn't keep still. They bulged and shot up and flattened themselves. He swore at them.

'Can't you lie down?'

But no matter what shapes they assumed or what positions they maintained, the truth was the same. Daisy had gone—and for good. Well, what are you worrying about? he asked himself. She's no loss. Ah, but it wasn't Daisy who was his headache now, but Emmy Crisp, Emmy who'd beetled out of his flat a few hours earlier hotfoot to pass on to Crook some information Don didn't want to know. He'd seen the inside of a prison before to-day, and he had no illusions. He knew that a person can be virtually crackers (like Emmy) and still jump to the right conclusion. He cursed Henry Smith in terms that would have made even the hardened Crook blench. Why couldn't he have kept his nose out of this? It was no concern of his, and who'd be the poorer if Emmy Crisp had died quietly in the dark? Not Don Price. But there was nothing more to be done this evening. Try and get some sleep now, and perhaps morning would bring the welcome news that she'd slipped away without recovering consciousness.

5

Gerald Lessing hadn't been at the Hat and Feather when young Smith made his dramatic appearance. He'd gone home about ten o'clock, and when he opened his paper the next morning and saw the news about Emmy he was shocked to the bone. There was a picture of Emmy looking as perky as a cat with two tails, the same picture as had appeared after Caro's arrest. It wasn't likely she looked much like that any longer. Lessing put the paper down. First Toby, then Emmy—who next? It might be Gerald Lessing for all he knew.

Con was nearly as horrified as Lessing when he read the news. He dressed quickly, and went round without ceremony to Crook's flat. Crook was in his sitting-room, talking to Bill on the telephone.

'Shan't be a minute,' he said, leaving Con in the hall. His big mouth was tight, his eyes as glazed as brandy-balls. For the first time since Con had known him he looked really dangerous.

Con looked round him, thinking this was a bare sort of place for a chap to make his home. The hall, that was no more than a passage really, had a narrow strip of matting with a varnished surround, a hideous wallpaper (he doubted whether, after all these years, Crook could have described the pattern), an old-fashioned hatstand, with hooks for hats and pegs for overcoats, and spaces on either side for sticks and umbrellas, with a circular fly-spotted mirror above a box for scarves and gloves. Con hadn't seen anything like it for years. He glanced in the mirror and through the open doorway of the sitting-room he could see Crook talking away. His face looked as hard as the Rock of Gibraltar.

'I've got it,' muttered Con to himself. The right expression he meant. 'He's out for the kill.'

He shivered involuntarily; if he'd been Crook's quarry he'd have gone home and taken a nice dose of prussic acid.

Crook slammed down the receiver and called him in.

'Seen about your little pal?'

'That's why I'm here.'

'Expecting it, huh?'

'Not precisely, but I knew she was going to see Mrs. Price; she had suspicions . . .'

'Didn't occur to her to mention them to me, I suppose. That's an amateur all over. Beetle over and put the suspect on his guard. You're a fine lot of allies. What was it they said in the war? When you haven't any friends at least there's no one to let you down. Well, if she does go underground she's no one but herself to blame. Except, maybe, you.'

Con had never seen Crook in a rage before; he was secretly appalled. And indeed it was enough to chill anyone's blood.

But he summoned up sufficient courage to ask if there was any later news about Emmy's condition.

'I'm sure,' said Crook, with devastating politeness, 'it'll be a consolation to her, wherever she may subsequently find herself, to know that the chap who put out her light is going to swing.

I wouldn't care to be in his shoes in the Hereafter, if they should happen to meet.'

'I wonder if the Hospital would give one any news,' persisted Con.

'I'm on my way,' said Crook, ungraciously. 'You can come with me, if you like. At least then I'll know you're not running any other fancy plot to put a spoke in my wheel.'

As he followed Crook down the stairs Con wiped his forehead. What price the piping times of peace? Crook on the warpath was as dangerous as a dyak with a poisoned blowpipe.

At the Prince Charles Hospital they couldn't have been less pleased to see him if he had been a dyak. He pushed his way past the porter and established himself in the corridor outside Emmy's ward. A nurse having failed to dislodge him the Sister herself came along, making clucking sounds of disapproval.

'It's against the rules,' she began.

'So's murder,' said Crook, 'but some chaps manage to pull it off notwithstanding. I just want to make sure X don't get away with it within these sacred walls.' He thought them pretty bare—no *Monarch of the Glen* or *Dignity and Impudence* to cheer the unfortunate patients.

'You can't stay there,' the Sister protested. 'Visiting hours . . .'

'That's just what I'm afraid of. Can't you push her into a private room hermetically sealed for choice?'

There were no private rooms vacant, said the Sister primly, and anyway the Welfare State didn't really approve of privilege. Crook said he wasn't so sure he approved of the Welfare State, so that made them quits; and he made it perfectly clear that he'd

214

no intention of stirring, at all events till he'd seen the doctor.

'Going the rounds now, ain't he?'

'Dr. Martin is a very busy man . . .'

'Much too busy to have to attend inquests, especially when they ain't necessary,' Crook agreed. 'All right, Sister, you can stop worrying over me. I shan't make a pass at any of your nurses, might find myself in one of your wards myself if I did, and if anyone notices me they'll think I'm part of the decorations.'

She couldn't budge him, and really the Crisp affair was very odd, but she murmured a word to Dr. Martin on her way back through the ward.

'Crook?' said Martin, with a grin. 'Well, that'll make a nice change. Try and keep him amused till I get through this lot.'

It was enough to make a conscientious Ward Sister wonder why she hadn't opted for private nursing.

When Martin emerged he was pleased to see Crook still in his place. He went across.

'How goes the enemy?' Crook demanded.

'She's holding her own. She's tough and fit in the stringy way that type of woman often is, and she's got the will to live. That's the great thing.'

'Trouble here is someone else has an equally strong will that she shan't. This one of your visiting days?'

The doctor shook his head. 'To-morrow.'

'That's a comfort. I don't want the attacker smuggled to the bedside disguised as a bunch of roses.' He was frowning. 'My hand's being forced,' he admitted, 'and I don't like it.'

Martin thought it would require something pretty

hefty—forty h.p. say—to force that leg-of-mutton hand.

Crook went on, 'Still, even the best of criminals can't be in two places at once, though it's surprising how many of them have tried. And if I have my little bunch of rosebuds round my office table, they can't be here, can they?'

Martin said, 'You're sure this is a murder attempt? Not just coincidence? I mean, some bagsnatcher . . . ?'

And Crook replied, 'If it was a bagsnatcher why wait till she got inside the booth? There was quite a nice empty stretch, and I think—I think she wasn't altogether unprepared. I don't think she took more chances than she had to—being the sort of dame she is, I mean. My guess 'ud be that X was the other side of the booth, waiting for her.'

'Strike me!' exclaimed the doctor. 'That 'ud mean he knew she was coming and why.'

'That's how I add it up, too,' said Crook and dived back into the Scourge.

'Doing anything this afternoon?' he asked Con. 'If you are, rub it out. I'm givin' a stag party in Brandon Street. Fact is, I've spent time enough on this case. To-night we're going to win the Ashes or bust.'

6

The mid-day editions carried a new story. Two young people, Bessie Trevor and John Lamb, had come forward to say that they'd been in the Mews shortly before 7.30 the previous night, and had seen a man telephoning. They couldn't identify him even if they met him face to face, because he'd had his back to them and all they could see was a dark coat and a dark hat crammed over his eyes.

'Don't it go to show?' said Crook. 'Meanness of Fate, I mean. Round about 7.20, say, and Emmy Crisp left the Hat about 7. Wonder how *he* felt when he heard them coming down the garden path.'

It was a busy day. He hadn't been back long before another visitor was announced—Daisy Price, a haggard rather faded blonde in a state of considerable agitation.

'It's about Miss Crisp,' she began. 'I don't know what I ought to do. She was over at our place last night.'

'Told the police?' asked Crook.

'Not yet. I thought I'd better get some advice.'

'And you couldn't come to a better place.' But he looked no more welcoming than a hammer-headed shark as he offered her a chair and a cigarette out of the box he kept for visitors.

'Why did she come?'

'I don't know.'

'Meaning she didn't tell you?'

'Well, you could say she didn't have a chance. Don and me were having a few words, we didn't even see her come in.'

'But it could be she overheard something she thought would interest me.'

'That's just it.' Daisy twisted her hands in their elaborately embroidered gloves. She waited, but Crook didn't help her. 'All right. Here it is. You know, Don had no money on him—well, five bob—when I left him that Friday night Toby Graves was killed?'

'That's what he told me.'

'It's true, too. Husbands can't hide money from their wives in the same house.'

She looked so much like a spider about to devour her no-longer-required mate that it was Crook's turn to shiver.

'The things bachelors don't know,' he murmured.

'But he went out that night with a tart, all dressed up to the nines.'

She looked as if she expected him to burst out of his tight brown suit, but Crook only said, 'So I understand.'

'You mean, he told you?' Daisy's dismay was somehow shocking.

'I didn't have much of an education, but they did teach us to add one and one,' said Crook. 'And when I heard about the five bob he had and the other five bob Miss—no, Mrs. Benyon—gave him, well, it did occur to me there was something a bit fishy. How come you knew, by the way?'

'I came back,' said Daisy, desperately. 'I'd left something behind, something I didn't want Don to find. I knew he was going up to No. 15 at half-past-six, so I waited by the back entrance till I saw the kitchen light go off. Then I went in, he was gone all right. I went into the bedroom and you could have knocked me down with a feather when I saw his best suit laid out, button-hole, silk handkerchief. Men don't dress up like that to go round to the Wheatsheaf for a pint, and he couldn't afford the dogs—not on ten bob. That's another thing,' she added suddenly. 'I never thought of it till now. He was saying on the Monday something about Pride of Avon—that's a greyhound—can't lose, they said, but it had lost three quid for him. But, Mr. Crook, if he only had ten bob . . .'

'Oh, we know he had more than that,' said Crook, encouragingly, 'He gave Mrs. B. change for a quid.'

'I didn't know. Mr. Crook, where did he get that money?'

'I give you three guesses,' said Crook, 'and you can hand *me* back two with parsley round the dish. How long did you stay, incidentally?'

'Till about a quarter to. The house phone rung twice . . .'

'That 'ud be Mrs. Benyon. She says your husband didn't arrive till a quarter to seven.'

Daisy said slowly, 'His cap was hanging up, both his caps. He has a shabby one for everyday and for going out with me,' her voice was incredibly bitter, 'and a new one for his tarts. And he never went out without a cap, he was funny that way. So . . .'

'Yes,' said Crook, 'it all adds up, don't it? Well, thanks a million. You over at the flats now?'

'Not likely. I'm with my Mum. I don't want to be the third corpse.'

'Prepared to give information against your husband?' asked Crook.

'I—I only want to do what's right,' said Daisy.

Crook nodded, 'Pity you were so friendly with Toby Graves, ain't it?' he said. 'Kind of balls up your evidence.' He shouted to Bill. 'Lady wants a taxi,' he said. 'I'll get in touch, Mrs. Price, if I think you can help.'

'I'm not a toad,' exclaimed Daisy in sudden rage.

Crook said nothing. Toads, according to legend, had jewels in their heads. He couldn't see anything less meretricious than coloured glass about Daisy Price.

CHAPTER ELEVEN

Crook had arranged his stag party for four o'clock; he had secured all his intended guests by a mixture of blarney and blackmail, and just before the hour he went round arranging the chairs—one office desk chair, one handsome library chair, three with polished seats, one from the bedroom (a bit battered) and one from the kitchen with a broken back. It didn't occur to him that the visitors might not be impressed by the set-out. To Crook a chair was something to sit on; if you wanted comfort there was the bar, and if you wanted to go to sleep there was bed. The first guests to arrive were the two young men, Con Gardiner and Henry Smith. They met on the pavement and came up together, as pretty a contrast as you could want, thought Crook smugly. Con was very correctly dressed in black morning coat and striped trousers (only wants a crape arm-band to complete the picture, he decided), Henry was bare-headed and wore a turtle-neck sweater over flannels.

'Joined the Civil Service?' Crook twitted Con, watching him hang his hat in the hall. 'Anything wrong?'

Con looked round. 'Looks different from this morning. My imagination, I suppose.'

Don came next, slinking, venomous, alert. A scorpion in some other existence, reflected Crook. He had no smiles for anyone, was even inclined to keep his cap on till he realised it wouldn't be well looked on in present company. Then he stowed it in his pocket, but he didn't allow either it or the shabby raincoat he was wearing to pass out of his own keeping. He didn't trust anyone an inch—and how right he was!

Joe Bates came next, a big fellow with dark hair flapping in his eyes, thanks to the breeze that had got up since lunch, a duffle coat round his shoulders and his arms full of a carrier bag of beer.

'Thought I might bring something for the party,' he suggested, setting the bottles down on Crook's little sideboard.

'Thanks a million. A very kind thought,' Crook beamed. They had to wait two or three minutes for Lessing, who came hurrying up with a murmured apology—a telephone call, he said—and paused to smooth his fair hair where his hat had flattened it and touch up his tie. In the glass he caught Crook's grinning glance and turned so abruptly he nearly upset the telephone from its little stool.

'Meet Henry Smith,' said Crook. 'You weren't there last night, were you? He's come along to represent the Man in the Street, the chap who sits on juries—no, don't tell me you ain't eligible, you will be one of these days. And anyway juries ain't picked for their I.Q. but for their economic standing. You know everyone else? Right. Then what are we waiting for?'

'What I want to know,' said Don sulkily, 'is what are we here for?'

He stared round. All the men were looking at each other like strange dogs meeting for the first time. All quiet at present, all on guard, but you never knew when one of them wouldn't growl and leap. It was for the leap and the growl that Crook was waiting.

'First over coming up,' he said briskly. 'Now we've got a new witness,' he indicated Henry, 'and

221

we've got a new statement from a lady who begs to be excused, to wit, Mrs. Price.'

Don leaned forward sharply. 'What's that? Where is she?'

'She's gone to Mum.'

'Daise's Mum's a wonder. Ought to be on the halls the way she can be in about four places at once.'

'And she asked me to say if you were thinking of calling you'll find the shutters up.'

'What did she want to come to you for?'

'Maybe she felt a mite responsible for Miss Crisp being where she is now.'

'Daise? What did she know about it?'

'She came to tell me that Miss C. was visiting with you last night.'

'Not by invitation,' declared Don.

'That wouldn't worry her. Anyway, she was there and she picked up two bits of information that she thought I ought to know.'

Don stared. 'You making all this up? Miss Crisp's in hospital, ain't she?'

'*En route* for the mortuary if some as I could mention had their way.'

Lessing interrupted, 'What were those facts, Crook? Do they get us any farther?'

'Well.' Crook stroked his big pugnacious chin. 'Let's say they call for a bit of explanation from Don here.'

'Why me?'

'Because your trouble and strife let on that she was in your flat at 6.30 the night Toby Graves passed in his dinner-pail—*and you weren't there.*'

'Of course I wasn't there,' said Don. 'I was up fixing Mrs. Benyon's curtains.'

'You reached Mrs. Benyon's flat at 6.45. She rang

down to your place twice—at 6.35 and 6.40—Mrs.
P. corroborates that, though, of course, she didn't
answer the phone. Now, it don't take a chap of your
build fifteen minutes to climb five flights of stairs.
You weren't out, because both your caps were in
the flat, you weren't talkin' to a buddy on the stairs,
you weren't sweepin' the hall, you weren't obliging
elsewhere—so where were you between 6.31, say,
and 6.44?'

The tension in the room changed. Joe Bates softly
unclenched his fist beneath the table-rim and looked
hard at Don.

'I was on my way up.'

'Stoppin' at No. 8 on the way?'

'Who says so?'

'I do for one, but these gentlemen don't have to
take my word for it. And while you're about it,
there's another little point we'd like cleared up.
You told your wife—and me—that she cleaned
you out when she left round about six p.m. All
you had left was five bob and whatever you could
coax out of Mrs. B.—so how come you could take
a dame out to dinner, and lose three quid on Pride
of Avon afterwards?'

Don scowled. 'It wasn't straight—that dog, I
mean. I swear it wasn't straight.'

'Don't know how you'd expect to know the
difference,' said Crook. 'Well? What's the answer,
Price?'

Don said, 'I met a chap who owed me a
fiver . . .'

'Met him on the stairs between the basement and
the fifth floor. Because you had the money on you
when you reached Mrs. B's flat. She gave you a
quid—remember?—and you gave her the change,

ANTHONY GILBERT

peeled a ten-bob note off your roll. And according to Mrs. B. it was quite a roll. If you know how to turn five bob into a packet of smackers while walking up five flights of stairs, you can put off your uniform right away. You're the answer to the prayers of all the greedyguts who want to live soft without working, like flukes in a pig's liver.'

Don had turned a dirty drab yellow. 'What are you trying to say? That I killed Toby Graves?'

'Interesting to note that just when he's a hundred pounds short you turn into a capitalist. But maybe you've got a story for us, Price. Spill it,' he added encouragingly. 'We're all listenin'.'

'I didn't kill Toby Graves,' insisted Don.

'I don't care if the Man in the Moon killed him,' explained Crook, patiently. 'All I have to show is that my client's innocent, and if I can prove someone was with him after six-thirty, when she bounced out, then she's in the clear.'

'She could have bounced back, couldn't she?'

'Without keys?'

'There's a bell.'

'To be answered by a corpse?'

'He wasn't a corpse at 7.15. I heard him talking as I went by, and if you think I stopped then you're wrong. I couldn't have done it in the time. I had to change and be out of the place by 7.30 and it was just 7.30 when I left. Suppose Mrs. Graves did go out at half-past six, she might have come in again. Anyway, how can you be sure she ever went out?'

'Because someone visited Toby Graves and brought him a packet of drugs and collected payment. If she'd been on the premises at the time she'd have said, "Someone called to see him . . ." but she didn't—because she didn't know. And she

224

didn't know because she wasn't there. And not being there she couldn't have killed him.'

Price put his hands to his head. 'You could hang a judge the way you run on,' he said in the same sullen voice.

'Hanging ain't my job. I just want to do right by my client. Now, when you left at 7.30 did you see dear Toby in the hall?'

'Of course not. He wasn't there.'

'Not in the telephone box?'

'No. There wasn't anyone in the box.'

'Then how the blazes could he be ringing up anyone at 7.30? His line was cut, remember. If he'd been going to telephone he'd have done it from the hall box. And in any case if you can explain to me or anyone else how he put through the call to the police at 7.55 you ought to be on the Board of the Society of Psychical Research.'

'Why shouldn't it have been Mrs. Graves?' demanded Don.

'What did she use for money? It costs threepence to make a telephone call. And don't tell me she came back to the flat before she telephoned because if so she'd have collected her purse and she wouldn't have needed to borrow a pound from Mr. Gardiner here. You can't have it all ways, Price. By the way, I'll give you a hint. If you should find yourself in the dock, don't forget to mention the gun.'

'The gun?'

'Yes, man, the gun. Toby threatened you with it, remember; you picked up the cosh . . .'

'I never saw the cosh. I was never inside the lounge, and there was no sign of a gun anywhere.'

'Ho! Ho!' said Crook. 'So you were there that

night. Well, we've taken long enough to get the wicket.'

'If you're saying I killed him, how about him talking at 7.15?'

'How about it?' asked Crook pleasantly.

'I tell you I heard him.'

'I know you did. Bad luck for you no one else heard him. Y'see, I've said till I'm tired that a fact ain't a fact till it's proved. You can't prove you heard Toby talking. On the other hand, you could have proved that someone—yourself—saw him after Mrs. G. swep' out, which really makes you accessory after the fact, if nothing worse,' wound up Crook, inaccurately. 'That would have let my client out and that's all I care about.'

Don leaned back, breathing hard. 'Goin' to try and chalk Miss Perishing Crisp up against me, too, I suppose? I tell you, I didn't know she was comin' to ring you up. I was down by the door . . .'

'Couldn't be a better place, if you were going to follow her,' said Crook cordially.

'And if you're going to ask if I can *prove*,' he brought out the word with an exaggerated sneer, 'that I was there all the evening, I can't, because I wasn't.'

'You were there with the rest when young Smith dropped in at closing time?'

'Just having one for the road,' asserted Don.

'And, of course, there might have been some news about Miss Crisp by that time.'

Young Smith leaned forward. 'Question?'

'The floor's yours,' said Crook, graciously.

'Say Price was guilty, why did he leave any of the money in Graves's pocket? Why not trouser the lot?'

'A good point,' said Crook. 'All right, Price, you can put your wattles down. That's the best argument I've heard to date against it being you.'

'Point Two,' continued Smith. 'Would he have told the police he was ringing up from the flat below when he knew the flat was empty?'

'You don't miss much,' Crook approved. 'Ought to be in my racket. Well, he might, of course, arguing that the police would say a chap who knew the flat was empty wouldn't have sent that message. But I doubt if he's as subtle as that. It 'ud be a cosh for him rather than one of those classy murder-methods that come off in books but hardly ever in real life.'

'There's another thing you haven't explained,' said Don, breathing hard. 'What good did it do me for Toby Graves to be dead?'

'Oh, I never thought this was a planned murder. Chaps who go out with that idea in mind take their own weapons along with 'em. But say Toby had said, "It ain't very convenient for me to pay you to-night. Come back on Monday." It wasn't very convenient for you not to have the cash, not with your dame waiting.'

'Mightn't have been very convenient to Mr. Toby Graves not to have his goods. And if you think I'm fool enough to hand over without the cash—why, on Monday he might have said he didn't know anything about it.'

'That's three points in your favour,' Crook allowed.

'I can see how it is,' Don added. 'You think I'm the working man, the chap that can't hit back. Why don't you ask these two,' he waved a strong, not very clean hand in the direction of Lessing and Joe Bates, 'what they had against Toby?'

'Yes,' agreed Lessing. 'I was going to ask that. What conceivable advantage would it be to me to have a dead partner instead of a living one?'

'Living partners can have a nuisance value, too,' Crook reminded him. 'Say you went round that evening . . .'

'Went round? I was in the Hat and Feather.'

'You were in the Hat and Feather at seven o'clock and you were there round about seven-thirty, but can anyone prove—prove, mark you—you were there all the time between?'

'I don't get you,' said Lessing, looking bewildered.

'It might have occurred to you that Toby didn't mean to show up. Well, he was half an hour behind schedule as it was. And the flats were only a couple of minutes away. You could have beetled out, no one was hanging around in Morris House, up you went—and, you know, Toby really had you on a string. He couldn't pay over the money—by the way, what currency did you really expect . . . ?'

'I don't admit there was anything unethical in my arrangement with Graves,' exclaimed Lessing.

'Ethics be blowed,' said Crook. 'It's law the police are interested in. Smugglers are only tryin' to make life easier for the mugs, at a margin of profit, of course, but that don't stop them being fined or even going to quod. Well, say Toby asked you what you were going to do about it, were you goin' to the police? Of course not. He had you on toast and he knew it. Chaps like Toby are always in a strong position, because they've nothing to lose, no reputation, no job, in this case not even a wife. Not like you, Lessing.'

'You can leave my wife out of it.'

'Can I? That's just the point. All you married men have given hostages to fortune, all your wives come into the picture. I don't for a minute suppose Toby was goin' near the police, but—Mrs. Lessing in your confidence about this little business arrangement of yours? I thought not. And I daresay she might have taken the same view as the police. And Mrs. L. holds the purse-strings, don't she, Lessing? All right, all right, take it easy. Another murder at this stage won't help. But you do see how it could have been rigged, don't you?'

Lessing controlled himself with an effort. 'And then I rang up the Hat and Feather from a disconnected phone?'

'No need for that. There was a box just opposite. Is still, ain't there, Joe? You could have popped into that—your luck was holding that evening—and by the time Mrs. Joe found time to pass the message on you'd have been back in the bar. Friday night's a crowded night—Darts Match night, ain't it, Joe?'

'It's very ingenious,' Lessing allowed. 'But, if I may say so, you could use precisely the same arguments for Bates here.'

'So I could,' Crook agreed. 'How about it, Joe? You've got one of those convenient bars, where, when you're in the Public, you can't be seen from the Saloon and vice-versa. Nice when you're looking for an alibi.'

'What motive had I for putting Toby Graves underground?' Joe's face was dangerous. Henry Smith leaned forward, absorbed.

'Well, you hated his guts, didn't you?'

'I'd only seen him half a dozen times, well, perhaps eight or nine, in my bar.'

'That's what makes it so curious,' allowed Crook. 'With all the custom you get you'd hardly have time—didn't know him outside the Hat and Feather, I take it?'

'I never set eyes on him till the first time he came into my bar,' said Joe, emphatically.

'Well, then, maybe Mrs. Joe . . .'

Joe put out his uninjured hand and caught Crook's wrist.

'Careful,' Crook warned him. 'You'll break it.'

'That was the idea.'

Young Smith moved. It was as quick as a lizard flashing in sunlight, but a moment later Crook was free, and Joe was staring at the young man.

'That's a commando trick,' he exclaimed. 'Where did you learn it?'

'My eldest brother was one. He showed me a few things before he went over with the Liberation forces.' There was no need for Henry to add that he hadn't come back.

Con joined in suddenly. 'Look here, if Bates was a commando he wouldn't need to use a cosh. He . . .'

'Be your age,' advised Crook mildly. 'If he was going to use commando methods he might as well have left a signed confession. All the same, we can't put him out of the picture, as Lessing says.'

'If you can tell me how a man takes time off on his busiest evening to commit a murder,' Joe began, but Crook broke in, 'There was that beer delivery, remember. Rosa said you were away a heck of a time. And Lessing had made you a present of the fact that he was expecting Toby over, inference bein' he was on his own premises at the time.'

'I take it,' said Lessing, 'you're suggesting blackmail.'

'Toby wasn't any stranger to that kind of thing,' Crook murmured. 'Bill's been doin' a bit of diggin' with a sexton's spade, and you'd be surprised what he's turned up. And you admit yourself Toby was a wrong 'un. How about those books in his flat? Police don't care for that sort of thing much.'

'I can only assure you he never tried to blackmail me.'

'Well, we've just your word for that. Still, burden of proof lies with the prosecution. By the way, those ear-rings? Did he show them to you that night?'

'I didn't see him that night.'

'Oh yes, you told us. Well, then, when did you see them? I mean to say, you told me they weren't worth more than fifty quid at most, though he was trying to pass them for a hundred.'

'If you'd known Toby as well as I did you'd automatically halve anything he told you.'

'I'd have said a tenth was more likely. Quite sure he didn't suggest your taking them in lieu of the hundred pounds?'

'I've told you, I wasn't there.'

'You do seem to know your own mind. Right. We come to last night. Miss Crisp dashes into the Hat and Feather and announces to all and sundry she's going to ring me up? Right?'

'She told me,' admitted Joe, 'and Lessing was sitting near by.'

'Yes,' said Lessing frankly, 'I heard her. So did about a dozen other people. Why should I mind?

She couldn't tell you anything against me, because there wasn't anything to tell.'

'Sez you,' commented Crook, as doubting as St. Thomas.

'But—half an hour later someone trailed her to the telephone box and it's no thanks to X that we ain't passing the hat round for a wreath this very minute. Well, she didn't do that herself.'

'A cosh-boy,' said Lessing. 'Elderly woman swinging a handbag, I don't doubt, going down a cul-de-sac, not much light, street above crowded, Thursday night, see, no one particularly likely to notice what's going on—didn't I see that the police had found the bag?'

'Chucked over the wall,' Crook approved. 'But cosh-boys generally strip a bag before they let it go.'

'And this one wasn't?'

'Purse had been removed, but there was a pocket inside the bag fastening with a zip—I'm told that's the latest thing . . .'

Lessing shook his head. 'I wouldn't know. My wife . . .' He let the sentence trail off.

'And then why wait till she got inside the box? A good biff, a snatch and—there you are. Besides, there was the fellow these young people saw, telephoning just before 7.30.'

'And you think you know who he was?'

'I could make a good guess. It's all here.' He slapped the newspaper lying on the table. 'Mind you, I couldn't care less about Toby Graves, but Miss Crisp's my client, see.'

'I can only repeat,' said Lessing in patient tones, 'she had nothing on me. Admittedly she'd picked up some information about Price which he naturally wouldn't want made public. I don't, of course, know what she might have had on Bates.'

Crook's glance came back to the big figure of the ex-commando.

'Nothing to tell us, Joe? Well, can't say I blame you. Most chaps prefer to wash their dirty linen in private. And if anyone tells me he hasn't got any, I know he's a liar—or a nudist.'

Joe leaned back. 'All right. Say Toby Graves had got something on me that might have cost me my job, how do I improve matters by getting myself gaoled for murder?'

'No murderer believes he's going to be picked up,' Crook assured him.

Once again Henry Smith leaned forward. 'With great respect, Mr. Crook, I don't see how Bates could have attacked Miss Crisp. I found the body and I'm by way of being a doctor, as you know. I saw the marks on her throat; no chap with only one hand could have done that.'

'Who says he's got anything wrong with the other?' demanded Don, shrilly.

'Well, that'll be easy to prove,' said Crook. 'We've got a medicine man here, as Smith's just reminded us.'

Joe pushed forward the bandaged hand; his face was like granite. As though this were all in the day's work Henry Smith unwound the bandage.

'Well, well,' he said a moment later. 'What did you do that with? A hatchet? If you want to prove your innocence you've only got to go down to the station and show them that hand.'

He proceeded to replace the bandage. 'As a matter of fact,' said Crook sunnily, 'Joe wasn't in the running. Y'see, the chap in the telephone box was wearing a dark hat crammed over his eyes. Don wears a cap, so it couldn't have been him. Joe don't wear a hat, so it couldn't have been him.'

'And I do?' Lessing laughed scornfully. 'There can't be more than about a million dark hats in London.'

'But only one in the box that night.'

'There's nothing to tie that chap up with the attack on Miss Crisp.'

'You forget. The lad looked over his shoulder as they reached the mouth of the Mews and noticed that the light had gone out. Well, it hadn't gone out so much as been taken out. That was the mistake X made. If he'd left the light where it was he'd have noticed the shoe—and most likely the button as well.'

'The button?' All three men looked up in a surprise.

'Yes. Henry Smith stepped on a blue button and put it in his pocket. Wearing a blue suit last night by any chance, Mr. Lessing?'

'I was not,' said Lessing in a deadly voice.

'Sure?' Crook tossed the button on the table. All three men craned forward for a sight of it.

Lessing laughed again. 'You're slipping this time, Crook. That never came off a man's suit. That came off the blue mackintosh she was wearing.'

He threw himself back in his chair. Joe slewed round his head. Crook drew a deep breath.

'Might open that window, Gardiner,' he said. 'It's a mite stuffy in here.'

Joe was still watching Lessing. 'Blue mackintosh?' he repeated. 'She wasn't wearing any mackintosh when she came into my bar last night.'

'Then she must have been carrying it,' said

Lessing, carelessly. 'A blue mackintosh with a hood.'

Don shoved his oar in. 'She wasn't wearing or carrying one when she came round to our place,' he announced. 'And she didn't stop and pick it up, because she was under my eye all the way to the Hat and Feather. Fact, she was wearing a red straw hat; it got blown off—or she chucked it away—after she left the flats; I saw some old guy pick it up. And as she went out of the pub there was a remark passed about Belisha beacons. Well, that hair of hers . . .'

'I wasn't there last night,' put in Con. It was like a round game with everyone having a turn. 'But she was certainly wearing one of these transparent affairs in the afternoon when I saw her. Only it wasn't blue—it was bright red to match the hat.' He stopped. 'I don't remember if it had a hood.'

Lessing shrugged. 'Well, I don't suppose it's particularly important . . .'

Crook nearly shot through the ceiling. 'Not important? Why, it's the crux of the situation. Because Smith here will tell you that when he found Miss Crisp in the alley she was wearing a blue mackintosh with a hood. Right?'

Young Smith nodded. 'That's right. I remember thinking it was lucky for her she *was* wearing it. It was on the big side and the mackintosh was fastened at the throat, which made it more difficult for her attacker to get a good grip. In fact, without the mackintosh I don't think she'd have stood a chance.'

'And—get this, Lessing—Emmy Crisp bought that mac *after she left the Hat and Feather last night*. The girl in the shop remembers her—well, who wouldn't?—and in any case the receipted bill was found in her pocket, with not only the date but also the time on it. Some firms are fussy that way. So you see no one could have known she was wearing a blue mac except someone *who saw her after she left the Hat and Feather.*'

He pushed his hands into his coat pockets. Lessing looked paralysed. Everyone else looked at Lessing. Suddenly the electric bell shrilled and Crook jumped up, saying, 'I'll take it. Watch him, fellers.'

They saw him plunge into the hall and fling open the door of the flat. An instant later the room seemed full of strangers, headed by a tall dark man who walked with a slight limp. Henry Smith was standing on one side of Lessing and Joe Bates on the other. Each had a wrist and held him in a grip even a fellow-commando might have found it hard to break.

'I think if you open the hand I'm holding,' said Henry Smith, 'you'll find something of interest.'

Lessing wrenched ineffectually for his freedom, but he didn't stand a chance. One of the policemen forced the fingers apart and took possession of the little capsule they concealed.

'Came prepared,' he said.

'Oh, I fancy that was meant for me,' said Crook. 'He couldn't be certain if Emmy was going to come round or not, and if she didn't, and I let him see I'd rumbled him, I was to get my quietus before I could spill the beans. And if I couldn't have got him any other way,' he added, 'I'd have given him his chance. I could have faked a telephone call the same way as I faked that bell just now . . .' he drew his hand out of his pocket and showed them a bit of board fitted with an electric battery and a bell-push.

'Never done any amateur theatricals? It's what they use for sound effects. While I was answerin' my mythical correspondent in the hall—I borrowed an instrument, not connected, of course, but who was to tell? I suppose that's what you noticed without knowin' you noticed it,' he added to Con, 'well, while I was doing my act I'd have suggested to Bates he might distribute the beer, and I rather fancy Lessing would have offered to take it round.'

'How would you have been sure?' began Joe, and Crook jerking his thumb over his shoulder said, 'That's a mighty useful glass in the hall. You can see everything that's going on, and, of course, I'd have left the door ajar. Wouldn't have looked too healthy for Joe, either, seeing he brought the beer along and would have poured it out.'

'And of course the window was part of the game?' exclaimed Con.

'It was the signal to Bill to collect his bluebottles and beetle up the stairs. Well, in the words of the old song—Take it away, take it away, take it away. But I'll tell you this, Lessing, if you'd copied Brer Rabbit, laid low and said nuffin I'd never have got you. Oh, you gave it away that you'd been in Toby's flat—how else did you know about the pornographic library?—but a smart lawyer 'ud have got you out of that. And you knew the ear-rings weren't worth more than half Toby said. That proved to me you must have seen 'em sometime (and admittedly not on Mrs. G.) because otherwise you'd have thought they were probably worth about a tenner, knowing Toby the way you did. But no, you had to go and stick your head in a noose trying to play it safe. I hate a bungler, I always did. I'd put the whole lot of 'em on a bonfire if I had my way.'

* ★ *

Con and Henry Smith exchanged horrified glances. The malignity of Crook's voice shocked them. He saw it and when the police had departed with their man he said in what was meant to be an apologetic tone, 'Emmy Crisp's sort of a pal of mine. No, don't shut the window. Place wants fumigating. You saw her,' he butted his head in Smith's direction. 'No sense pitying a swine who could do a thing like that. Toby was different, Toby had it coming to him anyway, but that little *champion* . . .' He stopped, half-choked. Then, 'What the hell did you bring that beer for, Joe, if it's going to stop in the bottle?' he demanded.

Joe stayed after the rest had gone. 'You knew?' he said.

'About Ben Fisk and your tie-up with him in the early days of the war? Yes, that's one of the things Bill uncovered. I'd seen a picture of you—smart of you to use another name.'

'I'd no idea Fisk was armed,' said Joe. 'I was going on eighteen, trying to get into uniform, my only brother killed in the Battle of Britain, no people; and with the world going to pieces, Poland gone, Finland gone, there didn't seem any special harm having a crack at easy money.'

'Cigarettes, wasn't it?' murmured Crook.

'Yes. As I say, I didn't know Fisk was armed, and when I heard the shot that killed the night watchman I just stood like a gaby waiting to be picked up. They gave me a year—and when I came out they were getting pressed for men, no difficulty getting a job even for a jailbird. Later I joined the commandos and when I came back all that was like another life.'

'And Toby unearthed it. That explains where the money went. Rosa said you never seemed able to keep it in your pocket.'

'Mind you,' said Joe, 'if I could have found a way of putting that little squirt underground without Rosa having to suffer for it—all right, all right. She's expecting a kid in the autumn,' he went on. 'I wouldn't want her to know . . .'

'No reason why she should. Toby's gone, Don 'ull be enjoying Her Majesty's hospitality for quite a while—the police are so damned unreasonable, they don't like dope-peddlers—you don't have to worry about those two youngsters, they're wrapped up in their own affairs . . .'

'And Miss Crisp?' asked Joe. 'Does she stand a chance?'

'Emmy Crisp? My dear chap, she'll be watering the flowers on our graves while we're trying to put one past St. Peter. And all I hope,' he added piously, 'is that when her turn comes to storm the Pearly Gates, I may be there to see.'

CHAPTER TWELVE

Con had been dining at the Live and Let Live. It hadn't changed a bit, same bar, same dining-room, same waitresses, Nora telling him, 'Take the lamb to-night, Mr. Gardiner,' and Belotti ambling up with the wine-list. A lot of the regulars were there; they looked at him incuriously. He couldn't believe it. The whole world had turned topsy-turvy and they hadn't noticed a thing.

Oh well, to-morrow he was going to see Caro. He'd wanted to camp outside the prison, until she came out, but Crook and Emmy between them had dissuaded him.

'Poor girl's had enough publicity as it is,' Crook urged.

To-morrow seemed as far away as the end of the world. He paid his bill, collected his hat, came out into Redman Street.

The girl was standing under the second lamp-post, and as incredulous, unsteady as a sick man, he advanced, she moved and came to meet him. She had a red bag swinging from her shoulder.

'Hullo!' she said, and she sounded just like the girl who had accosted him—oh, a lifetime ago—'I've come to pay you back your pound.'

She held it out to him; it fluttered in the evening breeze. Still scarcely able to believe that this was true, he took it, trembling, and in exchange he put all his life into her hands.

THE END

>>> If you've enjoyed this book and would like to discover more great vintage crime and thriller titles, as well as the most exciting crime and thriller authors writing today, visit: >>>

The Murder Room
Where Criminal Minds Meet

themurderroom.com